CELESTIAL ASHES

THE CELESTIAL MARKED SERIES: BOOK THREE

EMMA L. ADAMS

I crept through the corridor, my gravity-defying, super-stealth shoes cushioning my steps. Despite the daylight hour, darkness permeated the landing of the so-called 'safe house'. Aside from the boots, I wore dark colours, and my dark brown hair was tied back out of the way. Long sleeves hid my wrists, and the twin marks on them which marked me as belonging to both heaven and hell. Or neither. *I can't believe I'm actually saving vampires from the celestials.*

Vampires were determined to be the bane of my existence lately. Normal vamps slept in coffins but wandered around at night. That meant anyone who hadn't taken the cure would be passed out right now—an easy way to make the distinction between regular vampires and the ones who'd knowingly or unknowingly drank an infusion of demon venom.

After the celestials' elite soldiers had massacred three groups of innocent vampires on their own territory, I'd snapped. It was one thing to take down the vamps intentionally spreading the demonic venom by biting people, and quite another to kill innocents. The celestial guild of Haven

City, once the arbiters of justice chosen by the angelic Divinities themselves, had restyled themselves thanks to their new leader, Inspector Deacon. His Grade Four celestial soldiers were once given the job of executioner in absolutely dire situations only, but now the merest hint of the presence of demon venom would lead them to shoot first, ask questions later.

I reached the door, made of reinforced steel to keep the prisoners caged in, since vampires were much stronger than humans. Then I pressed the demon mark on my right hand—which I'd charged up with Nikolas's lightning power earlier—into the lock. A jolt of demonic energy rippled up the door, and as I'd suspected, it wasn't demigod-proof. I could only borrow so much power at a time, and it turned out I had a limit. But zapping a door open was a pretty neat trick.

Inside the room, the shapes of bodies draped on the floor came into view in the dim light. The smell of blood was faint, so presumably they were all alive. Relatively speaking.

"Rise and shine, sleepyheads," I whispered.

Vamps slept like the dead. Or undead. I grabbed one of them and shook him. He mumbled something unintelligible and started snoring again. I gave him another shake.

"Wake up!" I snapped.

"Bugger off," he grumbled. Like a lot of vamps I met, he was probably in his late teens. I figured the large proportion of vampires in that demographic was due to the alarming number of students who thought it amusing to wander drunkenly into vampire territory in the middle of the night, and then woke up with immortality to go with their hangovers.

I jabbed my fingernail into his cheek. He yelped, abruptly cut off when I covered his mouth with my hand. "Quiet. I'm doing you a favour. Help me wake up the others."

"Wait till morning," he mumbled.

"It *is* morning. That's why I'm here. Unless you want to still be here when I burn this house down and kill the morons who captured you."

He groaned. I rolled my eyes. "Sorry I interrupted your kidnapping," I said.

"Who are you?" asked a female vampire in a slurred voice.

"I'm Devi," I said. "And I've come to rescue you."

"I'm Kelly," she said, blinking. "Wait—aren't you a celestial?"

"I was," I said. "But trust me, if they showed up before I did, they wouldn't stop to ask whether any of you had been bitten or not before bringing the lights out. Come with me."

"Where?" asked Kelly.

I flashed them a smile. "What do you think? Somewhere safe."

"How do we know you're not one of them?" demanded the first vampire I'd woken.

I shone the light underneath my face. Seeing my eyes were dark brown—no hint of vampire bloodlust, nor the pupil-like darkness of someone who'd taken in the demon's venom—his expression relaxed.

"I knocked out the guards, but they'll wake soon," I whispered. "Wake the others. Let's move."

Normally, I'd have taken out the guards in a more permanent manner, but the annoying thing about leaving corpses around vampires is that they tend to get a little distracted by the presence of fresh blood. Besides, I needed to leave as little trace of my presence as possible. Aside from the missing vamps, obviously.

They shuffled after me. From their red-tinted eyes, they'd been starved and were on the verge of a blood craze—which meant if one of them flew into a frenzy, they could cause a bloodbath I'd prefer to avoid. I hadn't expected any less, given the conditions they'd been kept in. The whole building had not only been locked, it'd also been warded against demons using the celestials' own technology. Damian Greenwood, former celestial and traitor, had apparently passed on his knowledge before he'd challenged me and got himself killed. He'd also been the one to give the demons the idea to spread the virus through fake bloodstones. After switching out the energy sources the vamps used as a substitute for drinking blood with demon eggs containing a demonic parasite, they'd changed the landscape of all things preternatural in this city forever.

When we reached the door leading outside, I checked the nearby guard was still unconscious then pulled a mass of fabric from my bag. "We're going outside. Cover your faces, but try to look where you're going. We don't have much time."

Vampires burned in sunlight, often turning to ash in seconds. Most bright lights were painful for them, but it was the light of the day that signalled their demise. Yet another way to tell the difference between the fake vamps and the real ones—the vamps who'd taken the demon-tainted 'cure' could walk in the day just fine. Which meant there was a high chance of running into one of them before we reached safety, but I'd take the vamps over the celestials at the moment.

The vampires looked at the hooded coats with confused expressions.

"Put the coats on," I told them. "Honestly. It's that or catch on fire."

There was a flurry of movement. I waited, listening out for signs that someone had discovered the empty room, but none came.

"How'd they get so many of you?" I asked the female

vampire.

"They brought us in a few at a time," Kelly mumbled. "They feed us the cure, then pit us against one another to see what happens. Some volunteered… they wanted out."

I suppressed a shudder. The vampires who chose to take the so-called cure had signed their own death warrants. The celestials saw no distinction between villains and victims, and unless the difference was obvious—like the vamps locked in the cage—I couldn't afford to, either. I'd got a tip off that the celestials intended to target this place in less than two hours. So I had that long to sneak the innocent vamps out of here and if anyone went bad, kill them.

"You're all definitely not infected, right? No bites, and no blood?"

"None. I haven't seen any blood for days," she said.

"Don't worry. They'll get what's coming to them. Everyone set? C'mon."

I beckoned them to follow me, easing the door open into the daylight.

Javos—my warlock boss—disapproved of my new hobby, but *I* disapproved of the city turning into a battlefield. If the celestials crossed a line and murdered someone close to Madame White, the vampires' leader, I'd get to find out the hard way if the warlocks would stand with the vamps against the guild—or if the whole city would be torn apart in warfare without the netherworld needing to lift a finger. My agreement with the local warlocks only covered my employment, plus training to use my newly acquired demonic powers. When you added in vampire rescue missions, my schedule was pretty full. But it was my contribution towards preventing the end of the world as we knew it.

"Okay," I whispered. "Go over there. See the big security guard? It's one of my allies in disguise."

Rachel was a chameleon demon who could take on the

form of anyone—a useful ability for someone whose natural demon form had three sets of serrated teeth and a taste for flesh. She'd taken on the shape of a burly male human, standing next to the minibus I'd hired for easy transportation. It even had window drapes.

One of the vampires whimpered, cringing away from the light.

"Keep the coat on," I told him. "I'll take care of the rest."

Once I'd checked they were on their way to the minibus, I turned back to the dark corridor. The guard hadn't been alone. And when he woke up—

A hand grabbed my throat and spun me around, slamming me into the wall.

"Stealing my vampires, are you?" whispered a voice.

You are *a vampire,* I thought dizzily. No human was that strong. When they took the demon venom, vamps lost their sensitivity to daylight. I wished they lost their super-speed and strength along with it, but instead, they kept their advantages and lost the drawbacks. Considering a lot of them ended up losing their minds and murdering anyone nearby, some might have considered it a fair trade-off. And there'd be vamps out there who'd taken the cure by accident.

The vamp who'd grabbed me, however, definitely wasn't an innocent bystander. His pale skin glowed, but judging by the way he didn't shrink away from the sunlight, he'd been through the full transformation and was now a day-walking vampire.

"They're not your property," I said. "Clearly, you aren't their sire, otherwise they'd be like you."

"You say that like it's a bad thing." His eyes shone, luminescent black—a side effect of the parasite living in his head. I doubted he'd be as cocky if he knew precisely what the cure had done to him. But they didn't. They hadn't even asked.

"Give them over," he purred.

"Let me think about that one." The demonic power I'd taken from the arch-demon Themedes still resided in my hand. I used it sparingly, but now was as good a time as any. A flame leaped into my hand. The vampire hissed and sprang back—too late. I raised my right hand and threw the flame at him, igniting him in demonic fire.

He yelled, the skin melting off his bones. My demon mark tingled, pleased that I was using its power, and it took everything I had to tone it down. As much as I wanted to burn this place to cinders, it'd be a dead giveaway that I was no longer the same as the other celestials.

Instead, I used my left hand. White light, the flames of divine fire, leaped to life in my other palm. The light burned out evil and sin, and all vampires fell into that category. Demonic vamps, several times over.

I turned to face the two vamps who'd come out behind him. They had the same dark eyes, the same confident manner—though they looked warily at my right hand.

"What kind of celestial are you?" they asked.

"Oh, you know the celestials? Even better." I strode casually towards them, kicking the ashes of their fallen companion aside. "I don't suppose you'd like to tell me who put you up to this? What's the point in this whole operation?"

He stepped back, fear flashing across his face. "They just told us to bite as many people as possible. The ones who don't react badly to the venom—"

"They get to live, right?" I asked. "And on whose orders are you acting?"

"Why should I tell you? You'll only kill me anyway."

I smiled sweetly. "It's death at my hands, or death via the Grade Four celestial soldiers. And I'm the easy option. At least I'll make it quick. Tell me who your boss is."

"Ryman..."

One of the sires. Vamps in this city tended to answer to

the one who'd given them their blood, who'd turned them. I should have known a sire was behind it. The venom had spread so fast, the demons must have sent it in via someone whose designated role in vampire society involved biting people. A lot of people. The last week had been a crash course in all things vampire.

"And you thought it was funny to watch them fight to the death as sport," I said. "I should have let the celestials burn you. Too bad… you get me instead."

Celestial light blazed from my left hand, and the vampires screamed. Even the demonic virus didn't prevent them from burning alive, as the divine fire scorched out their souls.

I ran to the bus. The curtains were closed, giving no clues that we were about to smuggle a bunch of vampires across the city. Thanks to Nikolas's mind-altering abilities, nobody stopped to ask questions. While he drove, I joined Rachel in the front row of seats. The vampires huddled in behind, giving me wary looks. They'd probably seen the light's glare imprinted on the outside of the curtains. Doubtless some of them would have heard the rumours I was no normal celestial soldier.

I pulled my sleeves down. My demon mark itched constantly these days. A side effect of absorbing so much contradictory magic, maybe.

Or maybe because I was actively working against the person who'd marked me.

The Divinity—fallen, turned into an arch-demon—hadn't only marked me, but had gifted the vampires' original leader with the same mark as me. Sure, he was dead, but it was a glaring reminder that the magic I used was on loan from a dangerous, impossibly powerful being which might easily turn against me. The divine forces doing battle for dominance cared nothing for our lives. They'd mow us down in their battle—a fight I barely knew anything about. Souls were currency, and mine was marked by the demons.

The world believed I was a fugitive, on the side of the netherworld. And maybe I was. Maybe we were all puppets in this war. But I had no intention whatsoever of being anyone's pawn.

"Two sires, now," I said to Nikolas and Rachel, who sat on the sofa in the office in the warlocks' headquarters. "I got his address, though. I can go in person, or Javos can send a visitor or two to deal with the problem. It's a bad sign, that the sires are willing to sacrifice their own people with no care for the fact that the celestials are hunting them all."

"It's to be expected," Nikolas said. "Everyone looks out for their own interests. Like we all do."

For two warlocks—adopted siblings, even—Nikolas and Rachel didn't look anything alike. Rachel had bright pink hair—not dyed, since she could change her appearance at will—and resembled a nineteen-year-old human girl when she wasn't running around in her true demon form. As for Nikolas, he was typical of a warlock in some ways, but not in others. For one, he appeared to actually have a conscience, unlike the demons which formed one side of his heritage. For another, his appearance was closer to human… at least, for now it was. Golden eyes, tanned skin, tousled brown hair tinged with dark red, and a broad-shouldered physique that drew the attention of warlocks and humans alike. Vampires didn't tend to be interested in other preternaturals, but I swore I'd seen some of them eyeing him with interest when we'd coaxed them out of the minibus and into the block of flats we'd used as a temporary shelter for the vampires we'd rescued.

Nikolas had taken care of that. Apparently he had the cash lying around, supposedly for his services to the warlocks. I got the impression his mind-controlling power had played into it somehow, because the building had been closed for maintenance before he'd moved in. But it worked. The vampires were rehoused where nobody would find them, until this all blew over.

Or so I told them. I had the sinking feeling this wasn't a storm which would depart easily, and the celestials' newfound anti-vampire measures were only the beginning.

I swivelled on the desk chair, the one place in the office that wasn't covered in bottles, jars, and books. I'd turned the place into a lab, and Rachel had backed me up, so we were perpetually surrounded by the various demonic ingredients I used to make simple charms and spells. Rachel was more skilled than I was—I still didn't know how she'd made my super-stealth boots—but it was always good to have a few surprises up our sleeves.

"I doubt we'll find many more sires involved, considering recent events," Nikolas said. "From the way the virus spread, there weren't more than a handful of higher vampires involved at the start, otherwise word would have made it to Madame White. And now they know just how deadly that virus is—and that the celestials are hunting them—nobody will decide to try the cure on a whim. Not with the source cut off."

"For now," I added.

We'd managed to stop the vamps from using demonglass

to make a portal into the demonic realm, the source of the virus, but we'd only stalled them. But since their leader was dead, I was far less concerned with their ill-advised attempts to contact the netherworld than I was with the celestials' new habit of murdering every vampire they came across.

My own name hadn't yet come up in the announcements from the celestial guild, but it would. The inspector wanted me locked up because I'd committed the unforgiveable crime of insulting him, not to mention told him his former hunting partner had gone rogue in one of the nether realms. I still couldn't wrap my head around that one. Inspector Deacon might have betrayed his friend and kicked him out of the guild to further his own ambitions, but there was a significant leap between that and turning dark, especially as a highly ranked celestial. Inspector Angler, aka the vampires' king, had been marked the same way I was, and whatever he'd heard from the demons had been reason enough to turn his back on a lifetime as a devoted celestial soldier.

Nikolas glanced at me. "You think they have a communication line with Pandemonium."

"That's where all this started," I said. "With Azurial. And Themedes."

"The demonglass is out of commission," Nikolas said. "Three venos demons materialised the last time Javos tried to use it."

I grimaced. The demonglass was my one means of travelling into the demon dimensions via my own ability. "It seems like whenever we turn our backs on that place, a new demon takes over."

"You're not seriously thinking of going back?" My friend Fiona entered the room, bearing a plate of sandwiches. Javos had adapted surprisingly well to having a human living here, albeit one who was possessed by a demonic parasite none of us had been able to get rid of. She'd been bitten by a vampire carrying the virus, but because she hadn't drank the blood of an infected vampire—otherwise known as the 'cure'—she hadn't fully turned into one of them. So she was in limbo, helping us look for a solution to the problem.

I picked up a sandwich and took a bite. "Cheers," I said to Fiona.

"I have to be good for something, right?" She rested her hands anxiously on the desk, which was scattered with my various attempts at manufacturing a solution to the virus. Even knowing which demon it came from didn't help me work out how to counter it. The demon was inside her head, and the one sure-fire way to rid her of it would be to use my celestial power to burn it out. And I wasn't convinced she'd survive the process. Whenever I'd come close, she'd screamed, her skin burning, and I'd lost my nerve. I wouldn't lose another friend to the netherworld, especially one who'd been drawn in because of me in the first place.

"You found more vampires?" she asked me.

I took another bite of the sandwich, passing the plate to the others. "Yep. They were captured on a sire's orders, but I don't know if *he* was taking orders from elsewhere. Whoever it was, they wanted an army of the new vamps. If the celestials had got there first, they'd have killed the prisoners as well."

Fiona winced. She wasn't actively on their hit list, as she hadn't been a vampire to begin with. Other humans might be carrying the virus without knowing it yet, too. So far, the celestials hadn't targeted humans like they had the vampires carrying the virus, but I wouldn't put anything past Inspector Deacon. He wouldn't easily give up the power he'd gained.

"What the celestials need is a proper cure," I said. "Ideally, we need to raid the palace in Pandemonium and find more of those saphor demon eggs. There must be a store, for them to have infiltrated Haven City so quickly." Demon eggs didn't fall out of the sky, but we hadn't found a secret stash in the time we'd been there. "Hasn't Javos fixed the glass yet? He's had enough time."

By 'fixed', I meant 'found a way to stop demons randomly spawning out of it'.

"No," Nikolas said. "I don't think it *can* be fixed. The netherworld is in chaos because of the link you formed between that realm and Babylon. It even affects me when I use my shadow-walking ability. And Babylon's inhabitants are restless. That ability of yours, Devi—it's drawn attention, and not in a good way."

"Wait, Babylon too?" asked Fiona. "Are you sure going back is a good idea? Because the vampires are making enough trouble here, let alone on other worlds. Divinity-Watch said the more people go into other realms, the more likely it is that this one will break."

"You're still on there?" DivinityWatch was a human-run site for people obsessed with uploading pictures of celestials, preternaturals, and occasionally Divinities. Not that anyone had actually seen one for real. The photos were generally fake.

She nodded. "They're a decent source of rumours. If you know where to look. People have been speculating on where the virus actually came from. Some have actually come close to guessing."

"That's not a good thing, Fi. We can't afford word to spread. The celestials' new kill-them-all approach isn't helping either. Because once people realise that they're over-reacting because they're afraid of being wiped out…"

"Then they reap what they sow," Rachel said, with a shrug. "I never liked their self-righteous bullshit. I know you used to work with them, Devi, but if they come after the warlocks…" She trailed off, and I could fill in the blanks pretty easily. We'd had this argument before. Rachel might generally be mild-mannered for a warlock, but she was hard-wired to defend herself and her fellow warlocks, and if it were up to her, we'd have gone directly up against the celestials in person.

"The inspector and his lackeys will burn before this is over," I said. "But I don't need to mention how bad it'll be for the rest of us."

"You know what to do. Kill their leader," said Rachel.

My jaw dropped, as did Fiona's. "Er… not that I haven't been tempted, but that'll open up a whole other can of worms," I said. "There's no backup leader in the city, and the inspector isn't one of a kind. Not to mention the power gap will mean the celestials are doubly vulnerable to an attack from the netherworld. And there will be one."

The arch-demons were moving. As much as the demon mark was a necessary evil in doing my job, I didn't forget for an instant that the primary goal of the arch-demons was to bring all the realms down to their level, and flood them with the hellions of the nether realms. And I'd bet the vampires, somehow, were involved in their plan.

My phone rang, breaking the tense silence.

I rose to my feet. "I'd better answer that." I knew the number. I'd been wondering when I'd hear from her again.

Closing the office door behind me, I walked down the corridor and tapped my phone screen. "Clover?"

"Devi," she said. "I thought I told you to lie low. There was a raid on a vampire's property today and the scorched remains of several vampires were found inside. You wouldn't happen to know anything about that, would you?"

Clover was a retired celestial soldier who'd given me a lot of help, but only seemed to call me whenever it was convenient for her. There wasn't a lot she could do to stop the celestials' rampage, but she must know I wouldn't take it lying down.

"The guild's practically inciting a war," I said. "Once they kill the wrong person, the vamps will retaliate. I don't know what the inspector feels like he's going to achieve by starting a war with the preternaturals, but it's the demons who are supposed to be the enemy."

"He thinks the vampires and demons are in alignment. That's how he's justifying it. If he finds out I'm talking to you, then I'll be jailed."

"Then why did you call me?"

"Because I found Damian Greenwood's files. There are no signs he was working with demons. Either he turned recently, or he covered his tracks. And there's no record of his history before he joined the guild at all."

"I think it took him a while to let himself get bitten," I said. "Because he knew having a partially demonic aura would risk one of the Grade Fours seeing him and working it out. But it's possible he messed with his own records."

"Perhaps," she said. "The guild does have a history of deleting information whenever convenient. Or the inspector does, anyway. Things haven't been right for weeks now."

"He seemed convinced the guild was hiding information on curing vampirism," I told her. "Not sure why he'd have a specific interest in that..."

"I do," she said. "Seems his sister was bitten by a vamp. She died a couple of years ago... sentenced to death by the Grade Four celestials for accidentally killing a human."

"*Oh.*" I swallowed. I didn't want to feel sympathy for someone who'd wrecked so many lives, but it was a reminder that the Grade Fours' bloodthirsty rampage wasn't a recent development.

"Meanwhile, I did some research of my own," she added. "It seems some demon venoms *do* counter vampirism, but with terrible consequences. That young man didn't see the potential harm of his actions."

"He was a fanatic," I said. "Did nobody realise when they spoke to him? Because he's been listening to the demons for a long time. And he stole the report from Rory's death—the whole case file. Just how much info access did he have?"

"I can't say for certain. Even I didn't know. I was too late. I'd retired from the field long before the incident at the old guild, and after that, Gav didn't contact me with any suspicions until a few weeks ago."

"But you do know something."

She paused. "There's a chance someone might be listening to me. It's not too risky to talk about the venom—after all, everyone is. But there are some things which aren't meant to be discussed where we might be overheard."

"What do you mean? Someone's… tapping the phone lines?"

Clover cleared her throat. "I have to leave. But I'd advise you to keep your head down until we know what exactly is happening at the guild."

And she hung up. Dammit, Clover. Cryptic to the end.

Damian Greenwood… what the hell, maybe he *had* been a spy. But you couldn't fake being a celestial soldier, not when any celestial at Grade Four or higher could see auras. A demonic influence was impossible to miss, and besides, the headquarters had been entirely warded against demons until a couple of weeks ago. Damian had got away with hiding his demonic influence by pretending to have been bitten by a vampire carrying the virus.

Really, it all started four years ago when the old guild burned down. The reports said a celestial called Faye Carruthers had been the one to summon a demon, in an attack which had claimed many lives including Inspector Angler's. But not only had he turned out to be alive, he'd insinuated the whole thing had been a setup. By the demons. I didn't trust anyone at the guild. And I didn't blame Clover for not trusting them either. But from the lack of background noise, she hadn't called me from the guild itself. The way she'd paused, in fear… like she thought there was something not human listening in.

Arch-demons couldn't tap phone lines. Right? They worked in mysterious ways, that was for sure, but that—no. Absolutely not. My life was my own business, nobody else's. Arch-demons and gods included.

3

"Devi?" Nikolas emerged from the lab as I slipped my phone back into my pocket. "There's something else I should tell you."

"Oh, boy," I said. "You're using your 'major understatement' voice."

His brow furrowed. "I have one of those?"

I'd struggled to accept that it was in his nature to be secretive about the warlocks. After all, their survival depended on keeping secrets from demons and humans alike, including the celestials. *Especially* the celestials. And then I'd come along and shaken everything up. But it wasn't unreasonable to expect a little warning before he dropped a bombshell on me.

"Go on, get on with it."

"Zadok," he said. "Apparently he's told everyone in Babylon about your mark."

I opened my mouth and closed it again. "Oh. Shit."

Nikolas's demigod brother Zadok had, for some bizarre reason, elected to help us during the battle. He'd saved my life, and I'd borrowed his magic to win. But unlike his brother, he didn't give anything without asking for a price.

"Exactly."

"It's not like we were subtle during the battle, anyway," I said. "Anyone who was watching the fight would have seen me use both celestial and demon magic at once."

"Yes, but this isn't something I can ignore." His brows drew together, and the golden hint to his eyes gleamed underneath the ceiling lights. "I feared word would spread after the battle. The fact is—they saw the divine fire of your battle on the bridge. And after that, there's no chance they will let the situation slide. Unless I bring you to them myself, they'll find a way to contact you."

"Contact me. Wait. We're talking warlocks… or demons?"

"Both," he said. "Mostly warlocks. The castle essentially belongs to the surviving half demons who elected to stay in Babylon rather than relocating after my father left that realm. And while they don't answer directly to an arch-demon, they do answer to the Castor family. That is, my brother and I."

"So the castle is full of warlocks who do… what, exactly? Function like an army?"

"More or less. The castle is under constant siege from outside forces—the other inhabitants of Babylon. But it's fairly stable as far as the nether realms go. You are in no danger there, as long as you watch your back."

"Hmm. You know your brother tried to kill me the first time I went there, right? There's no way they'll trust a celestial. We're extinct there, right?"

"Yes," he said. "And I did anticipate that slight issue."

"Understatement again."

"You're more than capable of defending yourself against them," he said. "Few are higher than Grade Three, and there are no demigods aside from my brother and myself."

"But I'm marked by a rival arch-demon, right? Doesn't that make me their enemy even if you ignore the celestial part?"

He shook his head. "It's complicated. More so because whoever marked you fell fairly recently. That makes the arch-demon a new player, and an unknown one. Not unlike yourself. They won't strike you until they've got your measure, and you might make a valuable ally."

"But that's—" I cut off. "Look, I appreciate that this is bigger than me, but *this* is my home. I didn't choose this. And I'm not picking a side until I know what I'm getting myself into. The celestial guild operates on blind faith, and look what happened to them."

Even I'd fallen victim to it. I'd believed the gods were punishing me when Rory died. And while I trusted Nikolas, he was an exception to the rule. Most shadow demons were manipulative and considered humans tools at best.

"I'm not asking you to pick a side," he said slowly, as though choosing his words carefully. "I'd rather you present yourself to them as a show of good faith, to prove you aren't their enemy. Unlike the warlocks in this realm, they're not under Javos's jurisdiction. They're open to persuasion."

"Hmm."

"Relax." He moved closer to me, taking my hand—the right, demon-marked one. "I won't allow you to come to harm."

His thumb stroked my palm, sending a pleasant tingle up my spine. Okay, my demon mark wanted to steal his magic— I couldn't deny that—but the warmth that flooded me at his touch was a different kind entirely. His heated gaze swept my body, carrying promises as yet unfulfilled, and he leaned over and kissed me. His strong hands gripped my waist, pulling me against him.

"Nikolas Castor," Javos said irritably, "It just so happens I set up the demonglass again this afternoon, and so far, nothing's come through it. If you aren't too busy to use it."

Dammit. The master warlock had the worst sense of timing. I let go of Nikolas and gave him a fake smile. "We're good."

Javos shook his horned head. It was a testament to my level of distraction that I hadn't heard him coming, because he was huge, muscular and seven feet tall, with a pair of iron-like horns stooped under the low ceiling. Like Nikolas, he was a demigod, but I didn't know either the nature of his magic *or* his demigod parent. Unlike Nikolas, he was a bad-tempered brute with a penchant for terrifying every non-warlock he met. At least he didn't look pissed off at having seen the two of us making out with one another, because I had no intention of stopping. It was thanks to Javos that we'd hardly had a moment alone together in weeks.

"The demonglass is open for use?" Nikolas asked. "We planned to request—"

"Rachel asked me herself, while you two were occupied."

"We've been here two seconds. I was on the phone," I said. "So you said yes?"

"With conditions," Javos said. "I'm allowing this only because your ability lets you use the glass even in its dormant state, reducing the risk of any demons breaking through. See to it that you don't bring any trouble back with you."

He turned and stalked away.

"Huh," I muttered. "Can't make any promises there, but at least he said yes. Guess we get to spend this afternoon raiding a demon nest. Did you expect him to say no?"

"I did." Nikolas's mouth twitched into a smile. "Now, that's a pity. I can think of several other things I'd much rather be doing."

"Nikolas." I pressed a firm hand to his chest. "Same here, but if we find out we could have stopped the apocalypse sooner but we didn't because we were too busy making out, I'll be pissed."

He grinned. "Then I'd better make the wait worthwhile."

"You'd better." I stepped back. "I'm going to find my weapons."

Firstly, I ducked back into the lab to fetch the potion which enabled me to see auras, even when it wasn't easy at first glance to tell if demonic influence was present. Unfortunately, it didn't do too much to distinguish the demon-infected vampires, but it did help me identify different species of demons. Then I loaded up on weapons. Stakes and knives were a safe bet. Anything heavier was liable to slow me down.

I met Nikolas in the warlocks' spare room, which contained little except a few boxes and a sheet of clear, shimmering glass. My blurred reflection showed my aura—half light, half dark. To warlocks, celestials' auras looked blue. According to Nikolas, most warlocks couldn't see auras, like most celestials couldn't. His own aura, to me at least, was dark and shadowy, and when he was using his magic to its full extent, it extended like a pair of wings. A shiver traced down my spine, intensifying when he took hold of my right hand. My demon mark reached towards him, insistent.

"Nikolas…"

Shadowy power burned into the mark on my wrist, flooding my body. I gasped, gripping his wrist, his power feeding into my demon mark. The dizzying sensation must be close to what humans felt when they were bitten by a vampire. Power sizzled between us, and if he held onto me a moment longer, I might well orgasm on the spot.

He dropped his hand. Energy coursed through me, and from the way his chest heaved, you'd think I was the one who'd transferred my power over to him, not the other way around.

"You didn't have to do that," I said, when I'd caught my breath. "You won't be able to recharge if we aren't in your realm. Or does it work anywhere?"

"All of the nether realms boost my power to some degree," he said. "I only gave you a small amount."

"Damn." I shook my head. "Better wait until we're alone together before you try it again."

Nikolas grinned. "That good?"

"Who needs a lure when you have a partner who gets high on demonic magic?"

He stilled, jerking his head towards the glass. "Come on. Rachel, I know you're there."

"Didn't want to interrupt." She sauntered into view, knives strapped to her arms and legs, and her bright pink hair tied back.

Huh. Was he bothered by my allusion to my demon mark having a mind of its own, or the word 'partner'? Maybe I'd been too forward, but I doubted it. If not for the constant interruptions, we'd have consummated our relationship sooner.

"Bye, Devi." Fiona joined Rachel in the doorway. "Don't die."

"I'll try not to."

With Rachel and Nikolas directly behind me, I pressed my right palm to the glass. Then I thought clearly—*take me to the place where the demon eggs came from.*

Babylon's corridor floated before my eyes. Wrong world. At least it wasn't projecting Zadok's tower at me. I pictured Pandemonium's palace as clearly as possible, but no matter how intently I focused on the image, it refused to appear in the glass.

"I can't find them," I said.

"I thought not," said Nikolas. "There are chambers underneath the palace which aren't made of demonglass. I think that's where the remaining vampires must be hiding, and it makes sense that they kept their store of demon eggs there, too. Saphor demons like tunnels and caves."

"And it explains how they got in without using the gate," I said, recalling when we'd followed them once. "But obviously, they used a regular portal to do that. And we can't, because we don't have contacts on the other side. I mean, aside from that little prick Dienes."

I'd only left the horned demon alive because he was a source of information. Not a reliable one, but demons in general weren't given to confiding netherworld secrets.

"Okay, we'll go into the main palace," I said. "Ready?"

I pressed my right hand to the demonglass again. My demon mark hummed, and the glass reflected a wide hall. Empty, thank the Divinities. Nikolas rested a hand on my shoulder, Rachel grabbed my other arm, and we passed through the glass surface like stepping through a door.

Pillars supported a high ceiling, all made of demonglass. The reflections made the hall seem twice the size it actually was, while balconies in the back looked out over the rolling rooftops of the city below. A slate grey sky topped the undulating sand-coloured houses, as far as the eye could see.

Rachel hesitated behind me. "You know, maybe this isn't a good plan. We don't know what might have moved in here since they left."

"Maybe not," I said. "But the vampires' leader and Azurial are both dead. And it's been a while since the battle. If there's anyone new in their place, they won't have the vamps' loyalty. The survivors, that is."

"Hmm." She hung back, biting her lip in an uncharacteristically nervous manner.

Rachel came from this dimension originally, but had never been forthcoming with information about her history, and how she'd ended up coming to Earth. Much less how

Nikolas had ended up in contact with Themedes in the first place. Maybe I'd get answers today... assuming nothing waited to kill us here.

In the hall's centre sat an empty golden throne, made for an arch-demon. Gleaming demonglass pillars flanked it, and faint traces of blood on the floor were the sole indication of the battles which had ravaged this city. Endless reflections pursued us, my aura following me like a second shadow. For some reason, demonglass reflected what regular glass couldn't—an aura half light, half dark. A split soul—according to Zadok, anyway. In the demon realms, souls were currency. And mine was divided between heaven and hell. I'd planted myself on hell's side out of necessity, and because there was no place for me amongst the celestials any longer. Didn't mean I'd forgotten demons were as conniving with each other as they were with everyone else, and their cut-throat world might easily take my life.

"It's all empty," Nikolas said. "I'd be able to sense any demonic presence."

"Let's head downstairs," I said. "Damn place is a maze... it's not like I was observant when we were here last. Since, you know, we were either fighting or running for our lives."

"The palace is confusing even to those who lived here," said Nikolas. "But most of it is uninhabited."

We stepped through one pillar and out of another, into another wide hall decorated opulently. Golden chandeliers dominated the ceiling, while elaborately carved chairs surrounded a table set for a king. Dust covered every surface, and the smell of decay permeated the air.

"How pretentious," I said. "This place really belonged to one person?"

"His family," said Nikolas. "There were no other demigods, however. Themedes knew he was dying and had no interest in expending energy seeking out his other offspring."

"There are others? Might they come here?" I asked warily. It'd solve the leadership issue, but the person who took over would also have to deal with the aftermath of the palace's previous inhabitants opening a gigantic portal in the courtyard. Not to mention the vampires.

"No more than any other demigod," he said. "Demons don't always see ownership in the same way we do. This palace might have belonged to Themedes, but he'd have cast it aside in a heartbeat if a better opportunity presented itself. It also wasn't originally his, nor was he from this dimension. The hellish dimensions intermingle. Some of them do, anyway."

But not Babylon. From Nikolas's own admission, it didn't used to be possible to summon anything in that realm. Whether that would change after I'd used Zadok's pentagram to draw the vampire king there remained to be seen.

"So you just stride from one dimension to another? How? Not all demons have your ability."

"Most lesser demons stay put," he said. "The more adventurous will leap through any available portal. Your own realm proves that."

"True." I continued to walk, my footsteps echoing against the polished floor. "Where'd they get the demonglass to build this, anyway?"

"I never thought to ask," Nikolas said. "As I said— Themedes wasn't originally from this dimension. It's possible the palace was constructed before his time. Demigods might possess some of the powers of our demon parents, but not their longevity. Much of history remains shrouded to us, as it does to other mortals. The arch-demons don't make a habit of telling us their history unless it comes to boasting about their victories in battle."

"He knew your name, though," I said. "When he used to summon you. Right? What was the deal with that?"

"My father settled here, for a time, before I was born. For whatever reason, Themedes once felt it amusing to summon him. He used the name—my family's true name—and somehow, I was summoned in his place. He never would tell me why."

"Did you say, *true* name? You mean Nikolas Castor—"

"It is my name. Demigods have another, one we don't tell to anyone. Trust has nothing to do with it. It gives one absolute power over the person they summoned."

"I summoned you," I pointed out.

"You did," he acknowledged, "but part of me is tied to my own dimension, and you used an extremely powerful summoning device."

"Hmm." I'd also summoned Zadok, but his magic had been bound at the time. "Are you sure you aren't making excuses to disguise the fact that I might be more powerful than you?"

"I wouldn't assume anything."

I suppressed a grin. Okay, I didn't have the regenerative powers most demigods seemed to have... but who knew, maybe I could steal them, too. Sure, I was borrowing my magic from an arch-demon who didn't care for my well-being, but I might as well use it to my advantage.

Several empty corridors later and the novelty of the demon realm had thoroughly worn off.

"I suppose being able to fly helped when Themedes or Azurial wanted to go from one side of the palace to the other without taking a car," I said. "Honestly. We'll be here all day at this rate. Would you object if I summoned someone from this dimension to ask for directions?"

"Your demon contact?" asked Nikolas, arching a brow.

I shrugged. "He's a dick, but he also knows stuff and can't

keep his mouth shut. Plus, he was their messenger. He must have had some access to wherever they concocted their plans."

"Which messenger?" asked Rachel. Her hair had turned dark brown and she'd lost some of the shine she normally wore. The vast corridors made her look smaller than usual, and younger.

"Dienes," I said. "Lesser demon… he knows all the lower fiends, but also acted as a messenger for the vamps here. If anyone might know where they hid their stash of demon eggs, it's him."

"Go on," Nikolas said. "Summoning a lesser demon won't cause any harm."

I searched for a blank spot of wall, and used my celestial light to sketch out a pentagram. Using demonglass as the base made the spell ten times as potent, but the pentagram would keep the little demon caged.

"I summon you, Dienes."

He appeared with a yelp, jerking away from the pentagram's edges. Horns topped his small pointed face, while his goblin-like body crouched within the confines of the summoning device I'd conjured.

"Devi," he said in lower Chthonic, the language most inhabitants of the city spoke. "It's an honour to serve—"

"Spare me the bullshit. I'd like you to tell me whereabouts Azurial kept his store of pet vampires. It wasn't inside the palace."

He shook his head. "I wasn't allowed to hear."

"You were their messenger. You mean to say they didn't summon you directly here?"

I turned up the light.

"Ahh!" he yelled. "I—they summoned me into a tunnel. A big one."

"Told you," I said to the others. "So it's underground, huh."

"Maybe."

I looked at the others, than back at Dienes. "I doubt anyone would come to clean up if we left you for dead here. It'll be an unpleasant few hours unless you answer my question. Tell me where the entrance to the underground is."

He winced. "It's on the west side of the courtyard."

"Good enough."

I snapped my fingers and the pentagram and demon vanished. "He's probably right," I told the others. "The portal was set up right there."

Neither of them argued. This time when I led them through the demonglass, I pictured the palace's exterior where the courtyard began. I'd entered from the air last time and nearly fallen to my death, so I made sure to clearly imagine walking out of the palace on ground level, not up on the balconies.

No signs of the whirling portal remained. Scorched earth marked the place where the five-pointed pentagram had been. And beyond it, a set of stone stairs led right into the earth. That explained where their army had come from, too. My demon mark tingled. *Here we go.*

"I know it looks like a trap," I said. "I think we can expect to find full-grown saphor demons down there at the very least, but they're oversized maggots. It's who was in charge of breeding them we want to watch out for."

Not to mention some vampires would have survived, since the main part of the battle hadn't taken place in this realm. And they would have gone knowingly along with their master's plan. This realm's vampires weren't innocent, and would be out for blood.

Then I'd spill theirs in turn.

"Let's get this done," Nikolas said, and we walked down into the dark.

4

My demon mark glowed faintly red in the darkness. *That's new.* Was it reacting to a demonic presence, the same way my celestial mark lit up when I was near a powerful demon? Nikolas seemed to know where the demons were, using a similar sort of compass.

Step by step, I was turning into a warlock, or demigod. The one thing that separated me from the others was that my power was on loan, and I had my celestial magic to contend with as well. When it came down to it, I didn't understand the mechanics of either of them—but then again, neither did the celestials. And the Grade Fours, the ones who were supposedly closest to the divine, were the least careful about the magic they wielded in their hands.

Dark steps descended, seemingly into the depths of the earth. My celestial blade worked as a handy torch, as well as a beacon that pointed me in the likely direction of any nearby demons. I paused, realising Rachel had fallen behind. She shrank away into the darkness, having shapeshifted into a little girl of around four years old.

"Rachel," I said. "You can stay outside if you like."

She shuddered. "I was hoping one of you would come to your senses. This is a *terrible* idea."

"We knew that when we came here," I said. "We take out the maggots, we stop any more false bloodstones being planted on Earth."

She shook her head. "Or we die down here in the dark. Like they did."

A cold feeling took root inside me, but I squashed it down. "It'll be fine," I said. My voice echoed back at me, and my heart began to race faster. This was the first time I'd been in a cave since Rory's death.

"Wait outside," Nikolas said to her, in the closest to a comforting tone I'd ever heard from him. "We won't be long."

"Damn right we won't be." My heart continued to thump against my ribs. "Give us half an hour, tops."

I took the lead before I changed my mind. The ceiling scraped the top of my head, indicating the tunnel had narrowed. My throat dried, my pulse pounding in my wrist. I clenched my hands to stop them shaking and carried on walking, trying to shut out the images.

Rory had picked up those demon eggs without knowing what they did. If I'd known… but even the guild hadn't. Lesser demons wouldn't have registered on their radar. He never should have died. Didn't mean it was in any way my fault, but hindsight—

Nikolas put a hand on my shoulder, and I jumped, my head colliding with the ceiling. Ow.

"Are you okay?" asked Nikolas. Even in the pitch dark, he'd picked up that something wasn't quite right. But anyone would feel edgy in a place like this.

"Yeah," I croaked. "I—"

A deafening boom shook the wall, and pieces of dirt fell onto my head. "Tell me it isn't caving in."

"It isn't," he said, "but there's something moving ahead."

"Something like a giant worm?"

"I would guess so."

More bits of earth fell, and I moved out of range, as a huge shadow passed along the tunnel in front of us. If I hadn't known what was coming, I wouldn't have had a clue what the giant pinkish shape was. But when its head came into view—all mouth, with sharp teeth bared—I unfroze, summoning my celestial blade.

Its shimmering white edges glowed bright in the dim cave, angelic runes etched along its edge. The beast hissed and shrank away, while Nikolas wielded palms of demonic lightning. This was a full-grown saphor demon—bigger than I'd thought they grew. The ancestor of the parasite that lived in the vampires' heads.

The beast's teeth snapped, and I danced out of reach, using every inch of space. My blade sliced through its jaw like paper, and then through its thick body, severing it in two. The two halves fell... and began to move again. Twin mouths appeared, one on either end, baring sharp teeth.

"Oh, lovely."

Nikolas moved forwards, lightning sparking from his hands. Blades of dark-edged demonic energy pierced through the worms, which emitted a high-pitched shrieking noise. This time when they fell, they didn't get up.

Casting a dark look behind, he turned the corner. I climbed over the demon's ashes and followed.

Beyond lay a wider cave containing a pile of saphor demon eggs. False bloodstones... but the resemblance really was uncanny. If I hadn't seen both together, I'd have thought them identical. Whoever had come up with the whole scheme was a genius. *Or an arch-demon.*

My hand lit up in white, but Nikolas got there first, picking one of them up.

"They're certainly tough," he said.

"They would be," I said. "If they broke easily, it'd give away that they have maggots living in them." I let the light die. "We have to bring them back if we want to make a cure. If it's possible."

I shoved the eggs into my pockets before I succumbed to the instinct to blast the lot into ashes. If the worms were common to this realm, and lived all under the city, killing all of them was a futile prospect. So how to stop them from continuing to infect people in Haven City—and from eradicating the celestials?

Footsteps sounded. I tensed, my celestial hand lighting up. *Vampires.*

I was right. Two of them entered the cave through the opening in front, pale skin glowing, teeth gleaming, eyes flat black. Both were male and dressed in dark colours.

"Nice to meet you," I said. "Want to tell me who runs this place and spare yourselves?"

They lunged forwards, fangs bared. *Figures.*

Dark-edged lightning shot from Nikolas's palms, striking one of them down. I met the other with celestial fire at my fingertips, the glow enveloping him until he was ashes. They might no longer have reason to fear the light, but I'd give them a damn good reason to fear me.

"All right," I said, eyeing the tunnel entrance. "Time to flush them out."

I raised a hand, and light blazed, scorching a path down the tunnel. A scream came from ahead, followed by the crackle of flames. *Bye, bye, vampires.*

Ashes and dust were all that remained, but shuffling footsteps came from inside an alcove. I approached casually, and at the last second, dove into the gap, grabbing a vampire by the scruff of his neck.

"Tell me what's going on down here," I demanded. "I've

killed enough of you. Who's running the show now your king is dead?"

"The king," he gasped. "He—"

"Is dead," I said. "Unless there's someone else?"

He shook his head.

"Tell me," I said. "Some of you were originally from Haven City. You were brought here by your king to bring the vampires' virus into our dimension. Right? Tell me where the saphor demons are. I'm intending to kill every last one of them."

"That's pointless, celestial," growled a second vampire. He lay sprawled inside the alcove, and the foul smell of tainted blood surrounded him. "The saphor demons breed like maggots. We are the instruments of your demise, and we cannot be beaten."

"Like hell," I said. "I can kill a thousand of you in my sleep. Tell me: are you still in contact with Haven City?"

The vampire in my grip gave a coughing growl. "We follow the Great One, the one who sees all."

"Which demon?"

The vampire leapt in answer, right onto my blade. His body dissolved mid-jump, and I cursed.

The second vampire laughed. "A new stage in this game we play has evolved, celestial. I hope I'm here to see the end of it."

Nikolas blasted him with lightning and he fell to the ground, dead.

"He wasn't going to tell us anything useful," he said. "He's serving whoever is convenient at any one time. They all are."

"They're serving an arch-demon," I said. "Maybe the one who was guiding Azurial... and the former inspector. But I don't know if it's the same arch-demon who marked me."

"It wouldn't have been in Azurial's nature to take the orders of another arch-demon," he said. "Remember... this is a game they play. The arch-demons don't see individual lives as significant."

"Yeah, but maybe he *thought* he was acting on his own. Inspector Angler did, too. But what was that about a new stage in the game?"

I had a horrible suspicion I already knew. The virus had already crept into the city. If there really wasn't a cure—and there wasn't one, not for regular vampirism—then the celestials would have to deal with it for the rest of their lives. Those who were bitten would die, or would turn like Damian Greenwood—into a celestial vampire.

Then we'll find another way to destroy them.

The tunnel trembled, the ground rocking under our feet. More pieces of earth fell from the ceiling. Nikolas shouted my name, and the world lit up in a flash of golden light as a blast of energy took me off my feet. My back hit the wall, a curtain of soil flooding my vision.

Spitting out earth, I rolled onto my side. *That was a magical attack.*

"Rachel? Nikolas?" I spat out more dirt, grimacing. The demon eggs in my pockets had survived intact, judging by the way they poked me in the side. I crawled forwards under the newly collapsed ceiling, trying to pinpoint where the hell I was. It'd felt like I'd flown for several metres, but the cave was entirely buried, leaving unfamiliar tunnels behind.

Using my celestial light as a torch, I continued to crawl. A foul smell came from ahead, like a rotting corpse left in the sun.

The tunnel widened, allowing me to lift my head. A row of spikes blocked the way. Spiky armour. A demon.

Oh crap.

It must be massive, because I couldn't see its head, only its body. Like the worm demon, but with bristling spines forming a barrier between me and the way forward. The tunnel was too narrow to properly wield a weapon, and the creature ahead looked a hell of a lot sturdier than the last demon. And it stank like a drain. Or maybe the collapsing caves had unearthed another nest.

Trying not to inhale too deeply, I pressed my hand to the wall, scraping my fingernails along it. Ideally I'd dig my way through without running into the giant spiky thing, except digging might cause another cave-in.

"I can hear you, celestial," purred a female voice. She spoke Higher Chthonic—the language usually reserved for demigods and other higher demons on this realm.

Please say that wasn't the worm. I ignored it, continuing to scrape away at the tunnel wall. The soil cleared a little, with no cave-ins. Encouraged, I used both hands to dig at the packed earth, freeing a space big enough to fit my head through.

And then wished I'd stayed put. The worm demon was easily twice the size as the last one, covered in dark red spiked armour, and a pale hand that looked like it'd belonged to a vampire dangled from her serrated jaws. A pair of malevolent dark eyes fixed on me. Her aura was a revolting greenish haze, like poisonous fog.

"I am the Mother of demons," she whispered. "And you're the first celestial I've ever had the pleasure to meet."

"Pleasure's all mine, whatever the hell *you* are."

Crap. How the hell was I supposed to get out? I couldn't fight while pressed flat to the ground with packed soil over my head, let alone grip my sword properly. And the only way back led to a dead end. Cold fear grew in my chest. I had no shield to defend myself if she lunged at me. Those spines looked dagger-sharp. Not to mention the teeth.

A flash of lightning shattered the earthen wall at her side, and she turned her head, hissing.

Thanks, Nikolas. I couldn't see him, but his power shivered through my demon mark. When she turned on me, I blasted her in the face with it, conjuring celestial light in my other hand. Taking advantage of her hesitation, I shoved at the wall with my elbow, trying to get to where Nikolas must be buried. She whipped her head around, lashing down, but lightning speared her again. I crawled further, using my light as a shield. It didn't appear to burn her at all. *She can't be immune to my sword, at least.* But my celestial training had made it clear that there were some times to fight, and others where the smarter idea was to run—or crawl—as far away as possible.

She turned back to me, baring her fangs.

Okay then. Fight it is.

My blade appeared in my outstretched hand, blocking her from biting my face. I propped onto one elbow, stabbing awkwardly. The blade bounced off her teeth, but allowed me to crawl a little further.

Lightning burst from the soil once more, colliding with her armour. I lunged at her again. Her teeth closed on the blade, forcing me to let go. Her body writhed and the movement shook the ground beneath me, sending me tumbling downhill. Right towards her spiked body. My fingertips grasped soil, which fell away between my fingers. Agony exploded up my arm and chest as I crashed into her. Her teeth sank into my arm, and I screamed.

The sword had gone. Light flared before me—familiar light, close enough to touch. My vision swam, that tantalising light closing in. All sensation disappeared. *I'm dying.*

Energy surged up my demon mark. I gasped, my eyes flying open. Nikolas's hand gripped mine. The pain faded with each breath. From the looks of things, we'd landed in another cave. Or he'd brought me here. "Where—is she?"

"Gone," he said, his voice low.

That light… it'd looked the same as the light I'd seen when I'd died in the car crash ten years ago.

I didn't mention that to Nikolas. The fury brimming in his golden eyes was a clear enough warning.

"She's a Grade Four," I croaked. "I've never met one of those."

She killed me. If Nikolas hadn't transferred over his regenerative power, she would have. My demon mark tingled with the sensation of his magical transfer, not as concerned with the near-miss as I was. It'd been so fast—too fast to respond with my divine fire.

"She's also supposed to be dead. We need to find Rachel." He climbed to his feet. "The Mother is buried for now, but she'll be back."

"The *Mother?* Why's she called that?"

"Because she's the origin of the saphor demons," he said grimly. "And she's the beast behind the demon virus."

"Not an arch-demon."

He took off at a fast pace through the cave opening, presumably using his demonic sixth sense to track Rachel, because there were no other recognisable signs of life.

"No," he said. "There might well be one calling the shots, considering there's only one Mother, and I killed her myself."

"Wait—what?"

"We'll talk later. We need to find Rachel."

I hurried after him. "Are you saying she came back from the dead?"

But… people couldn't be raised from the dead. Demons included.

The one person I'd met who could mess with life and death… was the Divinity who'd saved me.

5

It took at least half an hour to find an alternate route to the surface, and I spent every second tense as a wire, thinking the Mother would erupt from the ground to strike us again. We found Rachel huddled at the cave entrance, refusing to speak.

Javos glowered at us when we emerged from the demon-glass into the storeroom. "About time," he said. "What happened?"

"Trouble, as usual." I glanced at Rachel. She'd turned back into her pink-haired self, but I'd seen genuine fear in her eyes when we'd found her outside the tunnel. She'd never been this rattled before. Meanwhile, Nikolas and I were covered in mud, blood, demonic ichor and heaven knew what else.

"The demon known as the Mother is apparently alive and kicking," Nikolas said to Javos. "That, or another demon is imitating her."

"Seemed pretty damn real to me. I'd really like an explanation." I looked pointedly at Nikolas.

"There isn't one," he said. "She died. I killed her. I've killed a lot of demons. I'd happily have killed her again."

"I think I get the picture, thanks." I'd ask more later, because from the fuzziness around Javos's torch-like aura, we were in danger of a warlock temper tantrum any second now. I pulled the demon eggs from my pocket. "Mission accomplished."

Javos's gaze flickered to the eggs. "Those were worth risking life and limb for? I do hope you find the answers you seek."

"The vamps implied this is all pointless," I said. "The virus is already in this realm. Whoever started this knew what they were doing. They tipped the playing field in the demons' favour. If there's no cure, then… that's it. The more people know, the more people can wipe out the celestials."

"Some of us wouldn't mind," said Javos. His aura had somewhat calmed, but I clenched my fist to avoid punching him on the nose.

"If not for the virus, they wouldn't have turned into murdering despots," I said. "The demons *wanted* the inspector in charge, for that reason."

"I'm not denying that the arch-demons are manipulative," Javos said, in positively bright tones. "Or intelligent. But if your people weren't predisposed towards overreacting anyway…"

"It's not an overreaction when the world is being invaded by demons." *Prick.* Living in close proximity with Javos had begun to slowly erode what remained of my patience, and I'd bet my fixation on helping innocent vampires escape was the reason he was trying to get a rise out of me. At least he didn't know where I'd hidden them.

"I seem to remember this all started with a single murder," he said. "This is what happens when the celestials prize the lives of their own above the safety of others."

"Javos," I said, "can you please kindly shut the fuck up and get back on topic? The virus. Do *you* think there's a cure?"

"Perhaps. But it's not my area of expertise, and if human history is anything to go by, it might take a few centuries to work it out."

Dammit. "Not if I have anything to do with it."

"Guys!" said Rachel. "You're giving me a headache. The Mother is alive. Somehow. Nobody aside from arch-demons and their offspring can regenerate, and she's been in the earth for years."

"What, you're saying she's a zombie?"

"I'm saying it wasn't her." She looked down. "It *can't* be."

"She's a giant armoured worm," I said. "I don't know. Maybe she… got infected by the vampire virus? Vampires can't die."

"Demons are immune to venom," said Rachel. "Vampire or otherwise."

Of course. Way to overlook the obvious.

I scrubbed a hand over my forehead. "I'm going to shower. I'm tired and pissed off, and I don't want to 'accidentally' hit someone for making annoying comments—"

A knocking sound came from the front door. Then the doorbell rang.

"Expecting someone?" I asked Javos.

"No." He turned and sloped down the corridor. I put the demon eggs back in my coat pockets, and followed.

A blond vampire of around twenty stood on the doorstep. Because today couldn't get any worse.

"Hey, Alec," I said.

His eyes widened at my appearance. "What have you been doing?"

Like I needed those other vamps to know about our jaunt into Pandemonium. Some of them were addicted to the cure, and knowing my luck, they'd try to follow me.

Nikolas scowled at him. "You're not supposed to be here."

You're telling me. Javos wants to hand you in. Madame

White, the actual leader of the city's vampires, didn't give a crap that the celestials had put some of her people on their kill list. Unlike the warlocks, who took care of their own, the vampires were divided along a hierarchy that I didn't fully understand. Because Madame White and her cohorts belonged to an older generation of vampires who kept human blood slaves rather than biting random people, they had no reason to depend on bloodstones for an energy source. The result was that none of her people carried the virus, but none wanted to give the rest of us a helping hand dealing with the fallout amongst the newer vampires who didn't have the same advantages. I doubted she'd stand up even if war broke out with the celestials—unless, of course, they directly threatened her. And then we'd be in trouble.

"The others are turning," he admitted. "And—and I heard from one of them that you're helping us. That means a cure, right?"

Great. "Don't get ahead of yourself." I might have got hold of the demon eggs, but that didn't mean we'd be able to manufacture a cure out of them. The original 'cure' had turned out to be something else entirely. "We're working on it, but more than half my experiments end in disaster. And in order to fully test it out—"

"You need someone to test it on," he finished.

I sighed. "I'm not taking responsibility for the side effects if this goes wrong. If you want to volunteer and end up growing an extra head, then it's on you."

"Anything's better than wondering when I'm going to turn," he said. "I have no supplies of blood, and the cure's in short supply."

"You're saying you still have the stuff?" I asked sharply.

"No. Just the blood of one of the others. It's the same, so..."

Of course. The cure *was* infected blood, and as much as I

wanted rid of it, we couldn't kill off all the other vampires—that was exactly the celestials' plan, and it hadn't proved effective so far. There was no easy solution.

"I should tell you I've no idea of the mechanics of vampire venom," I said. "You get bitten, you become addicted to the sensation, and when you drink their blood… you turn. You're attached to your sire for a few weeks, then you start drinking others' blood. Or use bloodstones. So how does the virus fit in with that?"

Alec shuffled his feet. "The virus… it doesn't work the same way. We need to drink the blood more than once to be able to walk in the day, and then it fades within twenty-four hours. So we need to keep drinking it. And if we don't, it increases the likelihood of side effects. Two people attacked us after trying to go more than a day without drinking it."

"If that's the case," I said, "you can't stay here while we develop it. I can't trust you not to drink everything that resembles the cure, or spread it to anyone else. Lucky for all of us that warlocks are immune." More than a few had been bitten in their clashes with the vamps and hadn't turned yet. Of course, warlocks were immune to most kinds of demon venom, too.

Alec shook his head. "I can't go back either. The others, too. They're driving us into a corner."

"Absolutely not." Javos scowled at me as though the vampires weren't there. "We're not a shelter for vampires. Your friend's only allowed to stay here because she isn't one."

"But we'll have our lab rat right here." Trying to appeal to compassion didn't generally work with Javos. He was the definition of a demon—self-centred and pragmatic to the point of downright brutality. "Put him in the shed again."

"No deal. He's on the celestials' wanted list."

"Then we'll make a deal," I said, ignoring a warning look

from Nikolas. "Let the vamps stay here, and I'll develop the cure. Isn't that enough of an exchange?"

"Not good enough," he said. "You said yourself that there's no guarantee you'll actually be able to develop a real cure, and until then, we're a potential target for those celestial bastards. Not to mention, I don't like vampires. At all."

Power radiated from his huge, formidable form. *Oh boy.* I dug my hand in my pocket for my phone, readied to blast him with classical music if needed.

"Then what?" I asked. "What would you accept in trade?"

There was a heartbeat's pause. "Since you can't seem to refrain from using your magical powers anyway," Javos said, "I want access to those abilities on my command, for my own personal use."

I blinked. "What—you *want* me to use them? After all this time telling me I can't?"

Alec was watching with interest, but I kept my eyes on Javos.

"You're not allowed to use it alone," he said. "But there are a number of reasons your ability might come in very handy for my purposes, amongst the demonic dimensions. You'll be my assistant, and I'll allow your pet vampires to stay here. Deal?"

"Javos," Nikolas said warningly.

"Yes," I said. "I accept." I didn't doubt there was a sting in the tail, but using my ability to help him out would give *me* access to the demon dimensions in a way I never had before. It might even allow me to find the arch-demon who'd marked me. I knew better than to think his primary purpose was to help me out, but I'd take any deal.

Anything to save Fiona before she turned, too.

Javos turned to Alec. "Bring your friends here. You have until noon, otherwise my doors will be closed to you."

The vampire all but fled from the doorstep. I closed the

door behind him. "Now he's gone, let's have a look at those demon eggs."

————

After showering and cleaning the residue of Pandemonium' tunnels off my clothes, I joined the others in the lab. Nikolas was uncharacteristically quiet, probably because I'd annoyed him with my decision. But I flat-out refused to test anything on Fiona, and Alec was a willing guinea pig. An annoying one, but a potential asset all the same.

We already had several samples of the venom, so now we needed to figure out what would neutralise it. Aside from celestial fire. One touch of my celestial hand made the eggs instantly disintegrate. Unfortunately, it'd also cause the person infected to disintegrate, too, which wasn't exactly the desired outcome.

"Demon venom outdoes anything, vampire venom included," I muttered, picking up one ingredient jar after another. "So humans who turn effectively skip the vampire stage and go straight to demonic vamp. What we need is a way to remove the virus altogether, to stop the transformation before it starts."

"Because you think it's already too late for those who've turned," said Nikolas.

My throat closed up. "The most we can do is maybe figure out how to stop the side effects, and to be honest, I don't even know where to start with that. What flips the switch to turn them into killers?"

"I suppose that was a rhetorical question." His gaze travelled along the ingredient jars I'd collected. Rachel had provided most of them, but Nikolas had a collection of his own at his house. I knew how to whip up antidotes to some mild demon venoms, but nothing quite this toxic. Sighing, I tipped some brimstone into the mixing bowl, giving it a stir. A noxious-smelling green liquid was my latest concoction. Gritting my teeth, I dropped the demon egg into it.

The egg exploded, green gunk splattering me all over my face. Rachel dived behind the sofa, too late. Spitting out a mouthful of slime, I thanked the Divinities that celestials were immune to dubious lab concoctions, too.

Nikolas, traitor that he was, had disappeared. A moment later, a human-shaped shadow appeared, and he stepped casually out of it without so much as a smudge on him.

Rachel picked bits of egg out of her hair. "Nice one," she said.

"That wasn't supposed to happen." I looked down at the egg's remains, which contained a skeletal worm-shaped lump. It seemed to have drowned.

"Ugh. Maggots." I shuddered, remembering the worm in the tunnel all too clearly. The essence of this creature had infected my friend. I'd read all the files on saphor demons, but nothing explained how exactly they took over their victims' minds. Whether Fiona was turning into a demon, or —what.

And it wasn't like there was anyone who might know. Not in this realm, anyway.

"See anything interesting in the shadow dimension?" I asked Nikolas, remembering I was supposed to be going with him to meet the other warlocks at some point. Assuming I didn't drown us all in liquefied demon egg.

"No," he said. "How did you manage that? Xeren demon ichor isn't an explosive."

"I have an aptitude for blowing shit up. The inspector said so, anyway, though not in those words."

I'd driven my tutors loopy with my experiments. But they usually worked. I hadn't run into a problem that had me this perplexed. Nor with so much pressure attached to it.

Rachel snorted. "We've discovered another way to destroy those eggs. I think you should shine your light into the vampire's ear."

"I'm not killing our lab rat."

"Yet," Nikolas said.

"Don't be mean," I told him. "Come on, there's got to be a way to at least make someone immune to the virus. It doesn't seem right that it can infect anyone, celestials and vampires included."

"Not demons or warlocks," Rachel said. "I always wondered why the celestials can be made, but not demons." She looked at me with interest. "Except you, Devi."

"Not just me," I reminded her. "Damian Greenwood was, too. He got bitten but survived the virus. But it was only him, as far as I know. Not like I can get a blood sample to see how the virus didn't destroy the celestial part of him."

Thanks to me, he'd burned to ashes all the same. But other celestials might survive the virus and wake up changed, no longer human. Damian had willingly given himself to the demons, unlike the other celestials, but if they survived the virus, would it switch off the killer instinct that had turned Alyson into a murderer—or would it make them worse?

Rachel bounded to the door. "I'm going to clean this crap off me. You should probably scrub down this room before Javos gets back."

As she left, I looked at Nikolas. "I'm glad she's recovered. She was really freaked out down in those tunnels."

"Rachel had a less than pleasant experience with the Mother." He paused. "That demon claimed the title because she saw herself as the foster mother of all orphaned warlocks underneath the palace in Pandemonium, who were usually the slaves of the arch-demon."

"Shit, really?" I'd had the impression Rachel's life in her home realm hadn't been a pleasant one, though demon realms in general weren't a nice place for warlocks to live. The thought of going anywhere near that giant armoured worm demon again made me shudder.

"And you killed her?" I asked. "Did Themedes mind?"

"He never knew." He shrugged. "I saw that foul monster devour anyone who disrespected Themedes or his son. Azurial was particularly fond of feeding servants to her."

I grimaced. "I'm not surprised. So you saved Rachel from her? And she came here?"

"This realm suits her better. Whatever's happening in Pandemonium… it's a direct consequence of our actions there."

"Figures. What a mess." I looked at the goo-splattered wall. "This realm's in enough trouble as it is."

Nikolas's arm circled my waist, avoiding the demon slime. "I know you're frustrated," he said gently.

"Damn right I am," I said. "We're trying to outrace the celestials *and* the vampires. It just seems so… hopeless. I mean, nobody's ever come up with a cure for vampirism. Not in centuries."

"They say vampirism itself was originally a demonic virus," he said. "As for the new one… the only adverse side effect is the unpredictable violence, correct?"

"That we know of," I said. "Otherwise, the infected vamps can walk in the day, and are determined to spread the virus amongst as many people as possible."

"Not all of them are," he said. "Don't forget regular vampires do exactly the same thing. They've learnt control. And those who don't are put to the death. I think we're making a mistake in seeing the virus as any different to regular vampirism, in practical terms at least. Suppose we catch all the perpetrators and find a way to combat the side effects. Isn't that enough?"

"Not for Fiona." My eyes stung. "I get what you're saying.

And it isn't all that different on the surface. Except for what it does to celestials. And you know, after everything they've done—I don't want the vampires, or whichever demon is driving them, to win this. If the celestials fall, we die."

"You don't know that," he said softly. "But the effect on celestials... don't you find it suspicious that it's never happened before the last few years?"

"You mean, Rory's death. Yeah, maybe. Everything the demons do is designed to wipe us out. Look how many times they succeeded. For all I know, the same virus is what destroyed us in other realms."

A chill raced down my back. The virus might seem a natural extension of demonic magic, but its cause might well be beyond one world, beyond all of us. Just like the cause of the mark on my wrist. Maybe Clover was right to fear that we were being controlled by invisible forces outside of our awareness.

"Perhaps," he said. "But the war is fair to neither side. Think what your celestial light does to demons. One touch and they die. Maybe this is the gods' attempt to even the playing field."

"You didn't just say that." I looked at him in shock. "You— look, it's not an even playing field when the demons won every realm except this one. That we know of, anyway."

"I don't deny that, but think about it. The Divinities are capable of doing things that arch-demons aren't. They choose their warriors, mark them and give them a piece of their own power to use. Those who wield that power can kill demons with a touch."

My heart sank. "Now you put it like that... an arch-demon *did* mark someone. Aside from me, that is. I never got Inspector Angler's full story. So you're saying the arch-demons can do the same as the Divinities now? And the virus is like their celestial power?"

Come to think of it, vampires often described the transformation as being reborn…

Nikolas said, "I wouldn't go that far, but there are definite similarities."

"Oh… shit," I said. "Vamps are immortal. Are the demon-infected ones? Because if they are, they're a step up from celestials. Sure, they can die in battle, but they live forever otherwise. We don't."

"Perhaps that's the trade-off," he said. "It's not like there's any way to check."

I smiled grimly and shook my head. "Because we might not live long enough to see if they survive to old age."

I hadn't thought it was possible to feel *more* hopeless about the situation, but you'd think we were set up to fail. Damian Greenwood had certainly believed that. And the former inspector. Looking at the evidence, it was easy to believe. To give up on the faith the celestials instilled in us and turn ourselves over to the side most likely to win.

No. No victory where the arch-demons took this realm was any victory at all.

I took in a calming breath. Nikolas didn't understand—or at least, he didn't care about the celestials. He *did* care about me.

"If this realm falls," I said, "then I either die or become a pawn for whoever marked me. To be honest, I'm not particularly keen on either of those options, so you'd better believe I'm going to do everything I can to counter this demon virus. And if not, then I'll kill the vamps who want to spread the virus and defend the rest from the celestials with my life."

And if necessary, take down the one responsible. But there were others who'd step up to take his place. The guild needed a hell of a wakeup call. And I was starting to think I was the only person who could give it to them.

Demon and celestial. Two marks, two worlds, and nobody willing to listen to reason on either side.

"Don't forget about the bargains you've made yourself," he said. "Javos won't let you off easily with the demonglass. And as for me…"

"You want me to come to Babylon."

Despite my lingering reservations… damn it all. Zadok knew demon magic. He'd told me how to use mine. And while he didn't have outright experience with the virus, he *did* know the name of the demon which was responsible.

But… I also owed him for saving my life. Going back there was giving him free rein to rope me in again.

"I'm not clear on why this is in any way relevant to what's happening now," I said. "I get that you have ties there, but I have to help Fiona. Not to mention the vampires, and stopping the celestials from starting a war."

Even though our progress had led us in circles, and my curiosity about the demon realms burned brighter by the day. Because to beat them, I needed to understand them.

"You've done more than enough here," he said. "Rachel can take over from you in the lab. I only agreed to introduce you to them, no more commitment than that."

"Hmm. You said they'd haul me in anyway, right?"

"I gave them a false name to prevent that from happening before you were ready to choose."

I blinked. "You—what? Does that have to do with that *true name* business you mentioned before? Do I have one of those?"

"If you have one or not, I can't say," he said. "We're usually born with them."

When the demons want you, they'll call your name, and you'll be unable to resist. That is what it means to be marked by us.

"What about Zadok?" I asked. "He thinks I owe him for saving my neck in the fight. He helped me, twice, and let me borrow his power. I doubt he'll let me set foot in the castle without trying to claim my soul."

"I'm keeping an eye on him, and he doesn't seem to have left his tower," Nikolas said. "We can't avoid that realm forever. Thanks to the imprint left on it by the link with Pandemonium, other demons will target it eventually. We need to be ready."

"This is… a really reckless idea. I mean, if I die on that realm, I can't help this one."

"You won't die," he said. "I won't let you. And the power in your hand is worth ten times theirs."

"You said something similar when you dumped me in Themedes's palace."

"That was different," he said. "You were different. Now you're a warrior to be reckoned with, and more than a match for anyone in that castle. Besides," he added, "I thought you wanted to see my room."

Damn him. He just had to play that card.

Fastening a glare on my face, I folded my demon-goo-soaked arms. "You'd better keep your word."

6

Before leaving for Babylon, I thoroughly cleaned the demon gunk off me, then restocked my weapons supply. I had no illusions about getting through without a fight, if not a fatal one.

All I knew about Babylon was that the celestials had lost the war with hell and most demons had perished, too, leaving nothing but wasteland. The arch-demon ruler, who'd fathered Nikolas and Zadok, had left them to rule in his place. Hopefully my connection to Nikolas meant nobody would attack me on sight, but I still brought as many daggers and stakes as I could physically strap to my body, plus my trusty anti-warlock trap. If anyone grabbed me without warning, they'd get a full-body blister attack like the one I'd unleashed on Zadok the first time we'd met.

Lastly, I took another dose of the aura vision potion—luckily, it'd survived the lab explosion intact—and went to find Nikolas. He stood in the hallway, clad in dark-coloured clothes almost like army fatigues, though with no visible weapons. He didn't need them, with the ability to shoot lightning from his fingertips and affect his enemy's minds using either mind control or his lure ability. Most warlocks and humans had reason to fear him. Cloaked in darkness, Nikolas's aura was as dense as the shadows he used to move between dimensions. If I didn't know him, I'd think the shadowy outlines of wings extending from his shoulder blades marked him as a fallen angel, one of hell's minions.

"So," he said, "which way do you want to go? The quickest route into the shadow realm is through the demonglass, but Javos is hanging about in the storeroom waiting to send you on errands. Alternatively, we could drive up to the celestial guild and cross over there."

The guild overlapped with Nikolas's castle almost exactly, and I couldn't deny I was curious to see how the celestials had recovered from the devastating attack on their head-quarters. Besides, I'd rather go into a dangerous realm with Nikolas than with Javos.

"The guild," I said. "I can always shortcut out through the demonglass if necessary."

His piercing gaze hinted that he'd guessed my real motives, but he nodded.

"Good luck," Rachel said, waving us out the doors. "Try not to get thrown out of any windows this time!"

I opted to let Nikolas drive, since I'd taken my own car close to the celestial guild one too many times, and it wouldn't do to forget my name was on their list.

Settling into the passenger seat, I looked at Nikolas. "So I assume they're expecting me. What exactly do I have to do?"

"We'll get to that later," he said. "You have questions about the nature of my arrangement with that realm, right?"

"Obviously," I said. Where to even start? "You were born on Earth, right? To a human mother? What...?"

"She died," he said. "Then Javos took me in, as he used to do with many warlock orphans at the time. This was before he became leader of the local warlock community."

I frowned. I saw Javos as many things. Kind parent to orphaned warlock children was definitely not one of them. "So… how did Zadok wind up living in the tower on Babylon?"

"Because they claimed him first," he said. "My mother couldn't take care of both of us. So she chose to keep me, and let the demons take him."

"That's why he hates you?"

He gave a nod. "Perhaps it's jealousy, in a way. I got to experience what it might be like to be human, and he didn't. But the demon in him has always been… dominant. He never learnt the discipline that those of us who live in your realm must practise to keep our natures under control."

"No kidding," I said. "Okay, so Zadok got given the tower, you got the rest of the castle."

"Technically, it's on loan from my father," he said. "And I never said I had absolute control. They respect and fear me, so they allow me to act as though I own the place. That is all."

"They let you lock an arch-demon up…"

"They didn't know. It's not unheard of for demons to wander in. Zadok makes frequent attempts at coups."

"And he wants me on his side to take the castle," I said. "That's where this is going. Right?"

"In his mind, yes," he said. "However, we're going directly into the castle itself without him realising we're there. In that time, you and I are going to convince the others that supporting the pair of us over Zadok is essential to their survival."

"Hang on," I said. "What do you mean, convince them? I thought they wanted to see my magic. Nobody there has any claim on me, and they sure as hell didn't put this mark on me."

"No, but if you're assumed to be an enemy, they may try to take you off the playing field themselves. I'd prefer not to cause a disturbance that might draw other demons into that realm, so our task is to convince them that you're on their side. Otherwise, one way or another, they'll find some way to contact you themselves, and it's likely to be unpleasant."

I didn't like the sound of that one bit. "I thought Zadok was the one who wanted to call me in. He managed to summon me once already. What did you do with that pentagram of his?"

"I have it secured in a place it cannot be used, least of all by him. However, I must warn you that the other warlocks are not disposed to trust outsiders. I'd advise you to keep that celestial mark of yours under wraps."

I blinked. "You didn't tell them I'm a celestial?"

"If I had, they'd attack you on sight."

"And they might do that anyway, right?"

"If they do, I'll personally see to it that they never live to do so again."

A chill raced down my back, a tingle that went straight to my demon mark. There never wasn't a risk where demons were involved. It wasn't like this was the first time I'd been to a demon dimension. Part of me was drawn to the shadows... to him. Why else would the demonglass tower keep appearing whenever I looked in the glass?

The truth about the war is in that realm somewhere. I know it.

"It's not that I don't trust you," I said. "Just you know, every time we go into that realm, things have a tendency to spin out of control."

"Precisely why I'm not going to promise it won't be dangerous," he said. "You've seen what lives there—and that's only the open part. Demons come into the castle on a whim, and even I can't prevent them from doing that."

"Any demigods?"

"For the most part, no. Zadok is the only other demigod who lives in the castle."

Hmm. "So the warlocks chose that dimension? Or were born into it?"

"Many reasons. I'd advise you not to ask. They have a tendency not to react well to personal questions. And there's a reason I've never brought any of them into this dimension. However, once you've won their respect, they'll follow you."

"You said respect, not trust," I said. "They're on the demons' side, right? So that means they might stab me in the back."

"Correct," he said. "Your power, however, far outranks theirs."

"Right," I said, doubly glad I wore my anti-warlock trap and carried weapons. "So you introduce me, I demonstrate my magic, and that's it?"

"Precisely."

We pulled to a halt in a street parallel to the guild, where we'd crossed over before.

"I'll make it up to you later," Nikolas said, leaning over to me, his lips inches from my ear. Just far enough away to avoid my demon trap. "Ready?"

I nodded, opening the car door. *He'd better be right.* I'd gathered he'd removed Zadok's pentagram following the battle on Babylon's bridge, but the images were all too clear in my mind. Where the gods were involved, was any victory permanent?

Shadows folded over Nikolas and me, and the next second, we stood on earthy ground outside a pair of wide oak doors. The castle behind it was a fearsome sight, silhouetted against the perpetually violet-coloured sky. Stars studded it like tiny gems, stark beauty in a realm as cold and merciless as any of the demon realms. Zadok's tower stood apart from the main castle, separated by a bridge, with a river surging beneath. The sun never seemed to rise here. The realm existed in darkness, beneath a giant luminous moon that appeared much larger than Earth's sun. Cool night air wrapped around me, chilling my blood, calling to the magic within my demon mark.

Nikolas unlocked the main doors with a key, pushing them open. The entrance hall had nothing on Pandemonium's palace, but the dark flagstones seemed to go on forever. Shadowy corners and staircases, with a long balcony overlooking the hall. And warlocks… everywhere. At least fifty of them, ranging from fork-tailed succubi to horned roak demons. Or half demons, anyway. They'd been expecting us, all right. And they were covered in shadowy auras to match Nikolas's, talking amongst themselves in Malthric, the demonic language of this realm. Though I might not be able to make out every word, I got the gist—they were eager to get the measure of their unexpected visitor.

A large muscular man, his bare, tanned chest covered in swirling tattoos, strode up to Nikolas. He wielded a long spear in one hand, and his forked tail lashed the flagstones.

"Why did you bring a celestial in here?" he demanded.

So much for keeping my identity a secret.

"Not exactly," I said, but my words were drowned in outraged shouts from behind him.

"No celestials here," one of them roared. "Crush her bones and boil her blood!"

"Don't be too hasty," I said, taking an alarmed step back. I couldn't watch all of them at once. And even knowing what a formidable force Nikolas and I were didn't take away from the fear of being faced with so many powerful warlocks at once.

"This is Devi," said Nikolas loudly. "She's an ally."

"Prove it," growled the large demon.

I'd expected the demand. Pushing my right sleeve up, I held the demon mark high. "No celestial bears this mark," I said loudly in their own language. "Nor this magic."

I didn't want them all to know I could steal magic—yet. I highly doubted it'd improve the situation for them to know I had the ability to rob them of their demonic power. But Nikolas had said *respect* and not *trust* for good reason.

Lightning danced over my palm, the echo of his own. Dark-edged sparks spiralled up to the ceiling. "This is no celestial power," I told the warlocks. "I'm marked as a demon."

"You aren't one of us," growled the fork-tailed demon. "You're an interloper. A thief, and an impostor. If Castor has really chosen to ally with our natural enemies, then we will have no choice but to turn to someone else."

Crap. Guess that means Zadok.

"That won't be necessary," I said loudly. "As you can see, I'm not a celestial. The arch-demons chose to mark me, and they have authority over all of you."

"You dare to claim to work for the arch-demons?" growled the demon. Power pulsed from his aura, shadowy and dark. My demon mark itched, demanding I take it in.

Fine, then.

Power surged through my hand as I called his magic into me. My whole body trembled with the force of it, but I kept my hand steady. At the last second, I aimed the torrent of power at the wall. It trembled but didn't break, but the message was clear.

Fury surged around the warlock's aura.

"You *stole* my power?" he roared. "You human scum."

"That's *my* ability." No need to mention the demonglass. "I can use anyone's power by proxy. Anyone. Arch-demons included."

I doubted I'd be able to steal an arch-demon's power if they were at full strength the way I'd done to Themedes, but you never knew. Some of the warlocks took a not-so-subtle step back.

"Liar," hissed a female warlock with horns and a forked tail.

"Want to volunteer?" I held the mark and willed her power to flood into it, the way Nikolas and I had practised. Once again, the warlock's magic flooded my mark. I didn't have a clue *what* new powers I'd just taken in, but at that, all the warlocks lowered their weapons.

"Anyone else want a go?" I asked. "Once I take the power, I can't give it back. It becomes mine."

"Scum," growled the female warlock. "Human scum. You drained my power."

"Too bad," I said. "I don't make the rules. Now if you don't mind—"

A third warlock threw a spear at me. I raised my hand, and the mark activated. A rippling curtain of light appeared in front of me, deflecting his weapon.

A shield. I can make a shield. From the aura around my hand, it was the power I'd stolen from the first warlock. Damn, that was useful. I'd see what I could do with it later.

"You might wield our magic, but you will *never* be one of us," snarled the warlock whose power I'd used. His companion nodded in agreement.

"Then let me prove it," I said. "Let me duel any one of you. You've seen what I can do."

The warlock spat at my feet. "Deal. We'll send our best. You send yours."

He sloped into the crowd, who dissolved into arguments. I wasn't fluent enough in Malthric to understand every word. But I got the gist: a fair number of them weren't at all keen on the notion of having their own powers used against them.

"That went well," I whispered to Nikolas. "You knew they'd do this, didn't you?"

"I hoped that seeing your mark would be enough for them," he said.

"I knew I'd get attacked at least once," I said. "Because that's what always seems to happen here. I'm allowed to use magic, right?"

"Yes, you are. The downside is that they know now, though anyone might have guessed during the battle a few weeks ago."

"Yeah, I figured," I muttered. "Doesn't mean I can tell what their magic is by sight." My gaze travelled across horned heads and dark auras, even a few with wings. The warlocks cleared a space in the middle of the hall, leaving one of their own behind. A warlock the height of a man, built like a tank, with curling horns entirely too similar to Javos's. I'd never seen Javos use his power and it still terrified me. This guy looked to be made from the same mould.

Nikolas swore under his breath. Then he reached for my wrist. Power jolted up my arm, a shiver of electricity. Lightning magic… and a rejuvenating power that shivered in my very bones.

Did he just—?

He nodded sharply. "Good luck, Devi."

The other warlock bared his teeth in a challenge as I stepped forwards, the crowd clearing a space on the flagstones.

Bring it. I raised my demon mark.

7

The warlock and I faced one another. As much as I wanted to blast him with the power of heaven and hell combined, this wasn't a fight to the death, and I might well bring the castle crashing down around us if I used the same power I'd used in the battle on the bridge.

The ground shifted beneath my feet. *Aha. He's an earth elemental power, then.*

Luckily, I wore Rachel's specially doctored boots, which could stick to anything. As the ground split in two, causing the other warlocks to back further away against the wide staircase at the hall's end, I jumped aside, aiming for the nearest stone pillar.

My boots stuck to the pillar, giving me leverage to push myself higher. Kicking off from the pillar, I shot lightning from my fingertips. At the last second, he raised his hands and the earth rose to form a shield in front of him. *Dammit.*

I landed at a crouch in front of the earthen barrier, which parted, revealing spears in both of his hands.

"Deadly weapons aren't permitted in a simple brawl," Nikolas warned him.

"This is no simple brawl," he said. "When the girl challenged me, she accepted my terms."

"No," snarled Nikolas. "I forbid it."

"I am no longer loyal to you," growled the warlock. "As you should know well, traitor to the shadows that you are."

"Oh, I knew you were treacherous vermin," he said calmly. "If you'd like to raise the stakes of this bout, then the consequences are on you."

What the hell is he playing at? Maybe it was an invitation to unleash my magic to its full extent. If I was allowed to kill my opponent, I no longer had to keep my divine power under wraps. But using it would make me into a target for the others.

I fired lightning at the warlock instead, but a torrent of earth smacked into my chest with the force of a train. Gasping, winded, I stumbled backwards, my eyes watering with pain. *Bloody warlocks.* Another wall of soil rose, hitting me side-on. I stumbled onto my right leg, pain shooting up my left side. *Ow.* I was pretty sure he'd broken a rib or two.

The spear arced through the air, aiming at my chest. I dodged, but not fast enough, and the spear ripped up my already wounded side. *Damn, that stings.*

The warlock grinned at me. "Bye, celestial."

Coolness sang through my right wrist, and the pain faded. The wound was already healing. *Damn.* I'd been right. Nikolas had intentionally given me some of his own regenerative power, knowing this fight would end in death.

The warlock's eyes widened. "You—"

I grabbed the spear and hurled it at the warlock, propelled by Nikolas's lightning power. Yet another shield of dirt rose, but the spear pierced through it. *It's a magical artefact.* His own creation had been his undoing.

The spear sank into the warlock's neck, and he fell back with a gurgling cry. Shock rippled through the crowd, murmurs that brushed over me. I grimaced and ran a hand down my side to check the damage. The healing power Nikolas had given me had sealed the wound almost the instant the spear had struck.

All around, I saw coins exchange hands. *Some of them bet on me?* It looked as though the huge fork-tailed warlock who'd started this whole bout in the first place had collected the lion's share of the earnings. Seeing my incredulous expression, he shrugged. "I always bet on the underdog."

"None of you are to challenge her again," Nikolas said. The shadows of a pair of wings extended from his shoulder blades, and power rippled through the room, forked lightning dancing between his fingertips. They didn't know he'd weakened himself to give the power to me, but he was still a force to be reckoned with.

And so was I.

"She wins," roared the muscular warlock who'd greeted us, and chaos erupted.

I stood rigid, unsure for a moment whether I was witnessing a celebration or a riot. The warlocks rampaged around, some of them dancing, others trampling on one another, mosh pit style.

Nikolas moved smoothly to my side. "It's over," he said. "You won."

"I get a spontaneous warlock party?" I raised an eyebrow.

"Be flattered. They accept you."

"I should bloody hope so." I eyed some of the dancers, who were wrapped around one another in the corner. "Please tell me I don't have to watch an incubus orgy."

"You don't have to watch."

"Great." I fixed my eyes on his face instead. "That's what you wanted me to do. Steal their magic. It was a setup, wasn't it? Divinities above, Nikolas. I thought you were better than that."

His jaw tightened. "There's no 'better than' when it comes to demigods, Devi. Would you have done the same thing?"

"No, because I'm not a demon. I don't manipulate people."

He spoke softly, his words almost lost beneath the pounding of warlock feet. "I suppose that time you summoned my brother was an accident, then."

Crap. I'd forgotten all about that—and hadn't realised he knew.

"That's not the same thing, Nikolas. No lives were at risk."

"Just a little white lie?" He smiled, but there was no warmth in his eyes. "It's so very simple to the celestials. Black and white—except when convenient."

"Don't be a prick," I said. "I lied because I knew you'd start an unnecessary argument and Javos would flip out at me again. You lied because you wanted to use me to make a point to your fellow warlocks."

"That's not why I misled you," he said. "You're human, essentially. That means they were always going to try to break you. I intended to demonstrate that it wouldn't be wise."

"Well, you succeeded. I hope you're happy."

"Not in the slightest," he said. "I'd have preferred to keep you away from here at all, but we don't always get to choose these things."

"Maybe I'll choose my own path instead," I said.

"That's what I'm afraid of."

I glanced at him. He was serious. He was actually frightened of what was coming—for both of us. Maybe not in this realm, but the netherworld in general had its eyes on me. And for all his power, demigods didn't hold any cards in the battle between the Divinities and the arch-demons.

"The angel who blessed you was in the midst of a fall. It echoes your own dilemma, Devi," whispered a voice from the shadows beside my ear.

I jumped back into Nikolas, my heart pounding. He reached out to steady me. "What is it?"

"Did you hear that?" I asked.

"Hear what?"

The resounding crash of a wooden door slamming echoed through the hall, and someone screamed.

"Fallen!" screeched a voice.

The sounds of celebrating turned to outraged shrieks. What with the warlocks trampling around, treading on one another's tails, it was impossible to see what might be attacking.

Nikolas shot me an alarmed look. "Sometimes things escape the catacombs. There's a reason we never went that route into the celestials' morgue."

"It's not Zadok?" I asked.

"No," he said grimly. "It's not Zadok. It's best for us to leave."

"But—"

He was already moving, beckoning me to follow. Not keen on getting trampled, I made my way after him into the corridor. From what I remembered, we were still on top of the celestial guild, so Nikolas couldn't cross over here without materialising in the middle of their headquarters.

At the corridor's end, Nikolas halted as a bald, naked man-shaped figure crawled across the stone floor in front of us. His face was pale as bone and just as skeletal, like he'd been left in the dark for a very long time. Except his hands were clawed, and his aura... I nearly threw up at the sight of it. Pus yellow and oozing, like an infected wound.

Lightning shot from Nikolas's hands. The person-shaped... thing recoiled, hissing like a snake, and shrank away into shadows.

"What the hell was that?" I gasped.

"Fallen," he said grimly.

"Not fallen angels?"

"No. We need to cross back to Earth." He ran, and I hurried to catch up, trying to push that awful image out of my mind. As we veered around a corner, the shadows split. Dust blew in, scented of decay and brimstone. Damian Greenwood had opened a portal on top of the guild's west tower, and it looked like we were right beside it. Far too close to the enemy. But I'd rather risk the guild than see another of those awful, broken creatures.

"It's safe."

Shadows folded over us. The cold air of the castle was replaced by the milder temperature of Haven City, though the scent of brimstone remained in the ruins of the collapsed tower. Though there was too much debris in the way for anyone to spot us, I felt exposed. Vulnerable. And I couldn't get the image of that creature out of my head.

I didn't stop running until I reached Nikolas's car, where I threw up at the road's side, my whole body shaking. My demon mark itched, insistently, and the fallen's aura swam before my eyes.

"Devi!" Nikolas held my hair back, though it was a little late for that.

"What was up with that thing's aura?" I coughed. "I've never seen anything like it before, and that includes those infected vampires."

"If you're okay to drive back, I'll tell you. We shouldn't stay too close to the guild."

I climbed into the car, my hands shaking so much, it took several attempts to fasten my seat belt. Nikolas didn't touch me. After all, I still wore the anti-warlock trap... though come to think of it, it hadn't reacted when he'd touched my wrist to transfer me his magic. Maybe because the demon mark wasn't exactly part of me. *Oh, who the fuck cares.* I wrenched off the anti-warlock trap with my left hand, glancing behind me at the guild as Nikolas put the car in reverse. Auras. Why did it look so familiar—?

Cold horror racked my body. If I'd been driving, I'd have crashed.

"No," I said. "Celestials. They weren't—they can't be."

Nikolas took in a breath, his hands gripping the steering wheel. "I didn't want to tell you back then, but the fallen… they weren't human in the usual sense."

"Not—not celestials?"

"Close enough," he said, taking a sharp turn. Apparently I wasn't the only one whose focus was scattered. "They were once the offspring of humans and angels—the children of Divinities."

My jaw hit the floor. "What?"

He veered down a side road, heading away from the celestial guild. "They're sad, dangerous creatures. What magic they inherited keeps them alive, but their power became corrupted when their divine parents fell. They can't be reasoned with, and they attempt to kill anyone who goes near them. Babylon is their home because it's a dead end. A realm where, until recently, nothing could be summoned, and nothing could leave."

"Except you," I said quietly. "And now Zadok. Does *he* know? He hinted—he said something about the celestials' fate on your realm. Was that it?"

"They're the closest to celestials in our realm, inasmuch as they once bore the powers of the gods. Perhaps they fell as their parents did, perhaps of their own accord. Nobody knows. They're powerful, and can't die—not that easily, anyway. The warlocks have a superstition about killing them. Because they're all that remains of the angels in that realm."

"And you keep them underground?"

"Demons inhabit the rest of the realm. Besides—it was my

father's single request of me when he left. Keep them contained."

"Zadok set them loose," I said. "It was his voice I heard from the shadows right before the attack. He—I think he wanted me to see them."

"I suspected as much," he said. "He's not bound the way he was before. Now he's won support from amongst my own people… and worse, he knows how to weaken the boundaries of that realm to other nether dimensions."

"But you—you're not surprised at what he did. You knew he had free rein to come after me? What does that mean?"

His jaw set. "It means the next time I see my brother, I have to kill him."

8

Despite the upheaval of the day before, I crashed hard that night. Roused from muddled dreams by a knock on my bedroom door, I rolled to the side and grimaced with pain. My whole body ached. I tugged a hand through my tangled hair and glanced at my reflection in the mirror opposite the bed to check I didn't look as bad as I felt. Nope, I looked even worse. Bruises had formed in places I couldn't remember being hit. Apparently Nikolas's regenerative power only worked on life-threatening injuries.

"Devi," Nikolas said from behind the door. "Javos is asking for you."

"Oh, *shit.* Tell me it's not about the demonglass." I opened the door to find Nikolas standing outside, arms crossed over his chest.

"I did warn you," he said, with barely a hint of an apology in his tone.

I groaned. "Tell me I'm at least allowed to eat and shower first."

He gave me a once-over. "Better make it quick. He's not in a good mood."

"In other words, a day ending in 'y'," I said to his retreating back.

Nikolas was apparently in a mood, too, though I didn't blame him considering what'd happened yesterday. I trudged to the en-suite shower, deliberately taking my time. *You made a promise.* Javos had let me stay here on sufferance, and while I hadn't moved most of my possessions into this room from my flat, it'd slowly taken on the appearance of 'home'. My clothes filled the drawers, my weapons were strewn about the floor, and Nikolas had moved the Northern Lights poster to the wall, the one he knew I liked. Before it'd turned out he knew I'd summoned his brother behind his back. And to top it all, I hadn't got to see his room yesterday. What a let-down.

Unfortunately, it wasn't Nikolas who waited for me at the foot of the stairs, but Javos. He wore an oversized check shirt that barely fitted his huge body, and even without my aura-vision potion, his whole being exuded menace.

"I wondered where you were," Javos said. "Devi, I need your demonglass ability. Come and meet me in the store-room in twenty minutes."

Bloody Javos. I had literally asked for it, though. Rolling my eyes after him, I went into the kitchen to scrounge for some food. I'd planned on spending the day working on potential vampire cures. Sure, I'd wanted to test the limits of my powers for weeks, but not as Javos's lapdog.

"You really offered to help him?" asked Rachel, who sat at the table eating cereal.

"Yep," I said, helping myself to a bowl. "In exchange for letting the vamps stay here. Can you take over at the lab while I'm gone? I wanted to make some headway today."

"Sure. The vamps are dead to the world, upstairs. Totally out cold. I'm surprised they didn't bring coffins in."

"I'm surprised Javos didn't toss them out the window." I munched on my cereal.

"Nikolas managed to distract him by explaining what went down on Babylon. Nice going beating that warlock, by the way."

"Thanks. Where *is* Nikolas?"

"Probably trying to talk Javos out of this."

"They're both pissed off this morning. To be honest, I'm not thrilled with either of them either." I put my cereal bowl aside, hearing the thud of Javos's footsteps in the hall, returning to the storeroom. Glancing at the clock on the oven, I sighed. "Best get this over with."

Sure enough, I found Javos waiting expectantly beside the demonglass.

"Devi," he said. "Since you claim to be an expert in travelling via demonglass, I took the liberty of placing some of our remaining demonglass fragments throughout the city. I want you to find them."

I stared at him. "What? You want me to... you do realise those are demon summoning ingredients, don't you? You left them lying around town?"

"In strategic locations. Go on." He jerked his horned head towards the glass. My heart dropped as its surface shimmered, showing me the side of Zadok's tower again. *Nope. Not now. Definitely not now.* If Javos found out... oh, who cared. He'd actually left bits of demonglass lying around town as part of some twisted test for me? Had he lost his mind?

One glance at his serious expression told me there was no point in arguing. *You asked for this.* Holding up my demon-marked hand, I thought as carefully as possible about the demonglass fragments I'd seen Nikolas use in a spell. Then I touched the glass.

And fell. My legs flailed without a surface to land on, my hands grabbing for anything to slow my fall. I managed to grip the edge of a rooftop, digging my fingernails into the gutter. *Holy shit. He put it on a roof?*

Cursing Javos, I pulled myself over the gutter and onto the solidness of the roof tiles. My body felt like all my cells had been rearranged backwards. I crawled towards the scattered pieces of demonglass, pictured the store room, and pressed my hands to them.

Once again, I fell, this time landing on the carpet of the storeroom besides an impassive-looking Javos.

"You *bastard,*" I said. "Did you just try to have me killed?"

"You're wearing Rachel's shoes, aren't you? They'd have stopped you injuring yourself."

He was right. I'd totally forgotten in the shock of falling out of the air. Glaring at him, I brushed dirt from my knees. "I'm supposed to thank you for that?"

"I suspected you'd be able to travel through small fragments of the glass," he said. "Think about what it means."

Oh. I can carry it in my pockets. That's... really handy, actually.

"If you can find all the demonglass I left around the city, you can keep it."

Seriously? There was bound to be a catch, but getting my own demonglass was too good an opportunity to miss. Gritting my teeth, I pressed my hand to the glass.

By the time I crashed back into the office for the fifth time, my head rung with pain and I wanted to wrap my hands around Javos's neck and strangle him.

"There," I said. "Happy?"

"One more stop," Javos said, with an amused undercurrent to his voice. I'd never seen him in such a good mood. *You complete arsehole.* "This time, I'd like you to visit a fellow warlock of mine. I've entrusted him with one of the few other samples of demonglass in the city, so I'd like to ensure that he isn't using it to summon anything. Picture a room covered in landscape paintings."

"And if he's there?" I rubbed the back of my neck, grimacing.

"You can deal with him. No warlock in this city is more powerful than the ones you've faced already."

That's promising. "I swear, if this isn't the last mission—"

"The missions will end when I say so. Unless you'd prefer to hand over your vampire friends to the celestial guild."

"I'd prefer to kick your teeth in."

Javos's aura flared bright orange, and he took a step towards me. Okay, maybe I'd pushed too far this time. I pressed my hands to the demonglass once more, visualising a room of paintings.

I melted out of the wall, into what appeared to be an artist's studio. A fur-covered man dropped a paintbrush on the floor, rising to his feet. "Get back, demon," he growled.

He looked like he'd stepped out of an illustration of the word 'werewolf', except for the paint all over the edges of his grey fur. A were-warlock who painted landscapes? That was new.

I raised my hands. "I'm not here to harm you—"

He threw the paintbrush. Immediately, it transformed into a sharp instrument. *Because of course. Warlocks.*

I sidestepped, and the paintbrush hit the wall instead. "What are you?" he roared.

"Nobody of your concern." *I'm going to kill you, Javos.*

I grabbed a knife, but he tackled me. The back of my head slammed into the wall, narrowly missing the paintbrush. My demon mark itched insistently, drawing his power into it. He grabbed the scruff of my neck in his furred hand, and I freed my hand, hitting out wildly. My fist connected with his jaw, but there was probably too much fur in the way for him to feel my punch.

I kicked him in the groin instead. He snarled but didn't collapse like I'd hoped. Twisting my knife hand, he slammed my head against the wall. I saw stars—and the brief control on my demon mark snapped.

The warlock's power rushed out of the mark, flooding my body. His grip slackened and he stepped back, confusion flashing across his features. Struggling for breath, I looked down. My body had vanished.

He can turn invisible? Apparently so.

Raising my hand, I struck him on the temple with my knife hilt. He went down, hard. Then I ran back to the demonglass. Or rather, tripped over my own invisible shoelace and fell through the glass. The warlocks' storeroom and Javos appeared. My body didn't. Oh hell. How much power had I accidentally borrowed?

Javos looked in my direction, no surprise evident on his face. "Just draw the power back into your mark. You'll need it later."

I did as he said, willing the demonic power to leave my body and withdraw into the mark. My body flickered back into view. "You did that on purpose."

"It worked. You pass."

I bit down furious words, running a hand over the back of my head where I'd hit the wall. I'd have a hell of a bruise, but I didn't think I had a concussion. Demons above and below. He couldn't let me take the warlock's power in an honest and fair way. Nope, he'd had to make a song and dance of it.

"What exactly would you have done if I'd had to kill the guy?" I asked. "This isn't Babylon. I might get arrested here."

"I assumed you'd handle it in the appropriate way. Now for our errand."

"What?" I paused, inches from the demonglass. "That wasn't it?"

"No, it wasn't." He gave me an assessing look. "I think you're ready. I want you to spy on someone for me."

"Who?" I asked warily.

"The celestial guild." He gave me a truly demonic grin. "I took the liberty of setting up a link while they were preoccupied with the aftermath of the attack."

"You have *got* to be kidding me."

His eyes gleamed like lava. Oh hell. He was very definitely not kidding. I'd get worse than a were-warlock with a deadly paintbrush on my tail if I sneaked in there.

"Just how did you get it into the guild without being detected?"

"Because the guild is distracted," he said. "Their inspector is, anyway. You've been close to him before, correct?"

"If you're asking me to assassinate him, just say it. And remember the celestials will trace it right back to you."

Sure, I wanted him gone, but Inspector Deacon was merely a symptom of the madness infecting the celestial guild. Their crusade against vampires wouldn't end with his death.

"No," he said. "I heard a rumour I'd like confirmed."

"You know they'll kill me on sight," I said. "And if I use my demon power, I'm contributing towards the arch-demons winning the war."

"It looks like events are heading that way regardless." He moved to the sheet of glass and tapped it with his hand. "Take a look and see if you change your mind."

"No," I said. "I won't. I didn't bargain with you to put my life, and the safety of everyone into this city at risk. I don't care if you think you'll survive the fallout if they declare war —I won't."

"Devina, you stubborn human, I'm not asking you to risk anything more than a few minutes of your time. You forget which power you now wield."

"Invisibility," I said. "You know it's not permanent, right? I can't accurately measure how much I took." I closed my mouth as the demonglass flickered, showing a desk… a very familiar desk. "You booby-trapped the inspector's office?"

"It took a significant amount of work to disguise the demonglass, not to mention arrange it in such a way that it's harmless to the people around it."

"You did that while they were picking up the bodies of their dead soldiers?" I might hate the inspector, but there were decent people trapped under his control who'd died that day.

He gave me a withering look. "You wanted to spy on the inspector. Don't deny it. Now you have an easy way."

"You sent in Rachel." And she hadn't told me. Bloody warlocks. "It'll serve you right if they did the same to you. You do know normal people use security cameras, right? *Demonglass?* Seriously?"

"Tiny particles of it," he said. "Harmless, and contained."

"I'll give you harmless," I muttered. Despite myself, I reached for the magic I'd absorbed into my demon mark, and my body flickered out of existence again. Beyond the glass was the inspector's office. He wasn't there, but his desk lay directly in front of me. And on top of a pile of documents lay a mobile phone. *Gav's* mobile phone.

I stared in total confusion. The phone in question had once been in the possession of Damian Greenwood, and I'd thought he still had it when he'd died. But maybe he'd left it behind when he'd blown up the west tower. The evidence which had once been stored on that phone was obsolete, since the demonglass had been taken in by the warlocks after the portal in the warehouse had exploded. But why was it in the office in the first place?

Curiosity gripped me, and before I'd quite thought my plan through, I pressed my hand to the glass.

The world spun around me, and I tumbled onto the office floor, my head ringing. I sat up dizzily, then climbed to my feet to get a closer look at the desk. Gav's phone lay on top of a piece of paper which contained a list of names. *Is it the vampires? Or the celestials who got bitten?*

I scanned for a familiar name, and my blood chilled. Javos's name was on the list. Warlocks. And beside his name… a list of weaknesses.

The inspector was compiling a list of every warlock's weak spot.

I have to do something. I darted to the door and peered through the glass. Novices talked in hushed whispers, sticking together in close groups. There were very few Grade Threes in the city, since they were out on missions, and Grade Twos and novices couldn't fight most of the demons alone. Nor the warlocks. So why the list of names?

I pulled back from the door, returning to the desk. I'd learnt to forge handwriting to get myself out of detention, and the inspector's was no exception. Leaning over the papers, I 'corrected' every warlock's weakness, switching some of them around. I lifted the page to see the one underneath—and froze.

The document was titled: VAMPIRE CURE.

What?

My hand flickered and appeared again, holding the page. *Oh crap.* My store of magic was low.

Panicking, I grabbed another document at random and copied the title onto it. Then, paper clutched in my hand, I ran back to the pile of demonglass fragments.

My right hand barely brushed it before the glass sucked me through, and I tumbled into a heap on the storeroom floor.

"Ow." I lifted my head to glare at Javos. "It's bad. They were assembling lists of the weaknesses of the city's warlocks. Don't worry, I 'fixed' it for them."

Javos's aura surged into being, a burning orange shield

like looking directly into the sun. "That's tantamount to a declaration of war. I'll see to it that the warlocks will not lie down and accept this treason."

"Javos, hang on." I held up the paper—which disintegrated in my hand, turning to ashes. "Did you just—?"

No. He hadn't used magic. The paper had fallen apart on its own. A defence mechanism, maybe. *Dammit.*

Another aura appeared on the edge of my vision. Nikolas appeared in the doorway, shadows radiating from his body. "Calm, Javos. The vampire queen has requested to speak to Devi immediately."

"What?" I said. "Why?"

"The words *on pain of death* were involved."

Because it was apparently that sort of day.

9

"What did I do to piss her off?" I asked Nikolas, ignoring Javos's warning look and joining him in the corridor. "I've already screwed with the celestials, Babylon's warlocks, and the invisible man."

"The what?" asked Nikolas.

"Javos sent me through the glass to tangle with a were-warlock with a stabby paintbrush."

"He did?" Nikolas scowled over his shoulder at the store-room, but I shook my head and walked to the lab. I'd rather talk where Javos couldn't listen in. Rachel wasn't in here, so I assumed Javos had sent her on some pointless errand, too. One would think he didn't give a shit whether I found a cure for the virus or not.

"He had good reason, supposedly," I said. "So I could borrow his power to sneak into the celestial guild."

Nikolas closed the door behind us. "I hate to say this, Devi, but that's only a taste of what working for Javos is like. He does it to the rest of us, too. Luckily, whenever he threw me into undesirable situations, I used my shadow magic to escape. He stopped trying after that."

"Unfortunately, he has total control over where I use the demonglass power, so that option's out," I said. "Unless—can I borrow your shadow power? I've never tried, but I'd have thought it'd happen automatically."

"I suspect not. The nature of my ability to move between realms isn't the same as my other powers. It's woven into the fabric of the realm itself. What did you see at the guild?"

"They have—I think they have a cure for the venom. I had the paper in my hand and the damn thing fell to pieces." Damn it all. The guild was ten steps ahead of us—but they *shouldn't* have been able to move so quickly, especially after the recent attacks. They should be subdued. Devastated. The inspector… I'd underestimated him, all right.

Nikolas's gaze slid over me, and I wondered if he was thinking the same. "We'll discuss the guild later. Are you ready to go and see Madame White?"

"Everyone wants a piece of me today, don't they? It's not even noon yet."

My weapons had survived the ordeal intact, so I went with Nikolas to the car, after picking up my anti-warlock trap. It'd work on vampires, infected or not, but wouldn't endear me to their queen. *Don't tell me she found out about our guests sleeping upstairs.* What a mess. I hadn't even been able to *start* looking for the cure.

"Fair warning," I said, climbing into the front seat. "I've had a day and a half of it already, and if this vampire lady wants to dismember me, then I can't say I won't 'accidentally' activate the blister spell on her. And to top it off, it was Rachel who put the demonglass in the inspector's office in the first place. If you didn't know that."

"I didn't," he said. "I would guess that Javos volunteered her for the job."

"Right." I rolled my eyes. "I'm trying to give people the benefit of the doubt, but I can count the number of people who haven't screwed me over lately on one hand. Meaning, Fiona. And I've screwed *her* over by not helping with the cure, and losing that document. If the celestials get the solution before we do, I doubt they'll distribute it willingly. They want those vampires dead."

"True," he acknowledged, "but if they find a way to stop the venom, they won't need to punish the vampires."

"Inspector Deacon still seems to be expecting a war with Javos." My throat closed up. "He knew—the document had all your weaknesses listed. I switched them around and tampered with the list."

"*My* weaknesses?"

I shook my head. "You weren't listed. But they definitely know about your powers at the very least. They knew Javos's weakness. And others."

"Then they must have broken into our archives," he growled. "Unlike the celestials, we don't store things like that electronically. It's too easy to hack."

"The celestials aren't exactly tech-savvy," I said. "Not the older generation, anyway. So I don't know how they got that information. Unless there's an insider—"

"There isn't," he said.

"They had a spy from the vampires amongst them," I said. "From the demons' side, anyway. I didn't see enough to be certain. I hope I slowed them down at least, but if they're compiling that data, they must expect to use it."

"Precisely," he said tightly. "As for the vampires…"

"What does she want? I can't think what I've done this time. Except take in Alec and the other vamps, and I thought she didn't care about them."

"She doesn't." A worried note tinged his voice. "Or so I thought. She wouldn't say why she needed you."

"I have too many employers already. She'll have to get in line behind the invisible man."

Nikolas parked the car across the road from the manor house that was home to the city's elite vampires. Music drifted over the rooftops, a promising sign that things were normal with the vampires. Which was more than I could say for the celestials.

The gates had been left open, the path up the gravel drive clear. Hedges lined the path, while a male human waited on the doorstep, holding open the oak door. Human blood slave. I was surprised they'd stuck around, considering. Of course, the blood slaves here were a lot happier and cleaner-looking than the ones I'd seen in vampire night clubs.

"Not him," he said to Nikolas. "She wishes to see the girl only."

Oh, does she? I gave Nikolas a nod to say *I'll handle this,* and went through the door alone.

In the dark hallway, the only source of light came from dim candles, presumably lit by the human blood slaves. Considering vamps could see in the dark, it couldn't be much fun to live here as a human, luxurious though the conditions might be.

Inside the hall, I found the queen waiting... alone. No other vampires surrounded her as they had before. Not even a single human blood slave. The queen sat alone on her cushioned chair. Her pale skin was underscored by a glowing undercurrent that made her skin look like diamonds shone beneath the surface. She wore the same black-and-white-and-crimson shades as before, and a waterfall of dark hair cascaded over her shoulders.

"Madame White," I said, in my politest voice.

"Devina Lawson," she said. "I'm told you're hiding some illegal vampires."

So it *was* about them. Should have guessed. Maybe she

was finally taking the virus threat seriously. Hell, maybe *that* was why she was alone. She'd kicked out of all the other vamps in case they infected her. It seemed the sort of callous thing she'd do. But it didn't explain why she wanted to speak to me alone. The rumours about my abilities must have reached her by now.

"Last time I came here, you said you weren't responsible for every vampire, and refused an alliance to help stop the virus," I said. "There's no rule saying I can't help those who are left behind."

"Actually, as of today, there is," she said. "We're compiling a register of anyone infected by the virus so as to prevent it from corrupting my people further. Anyone not listed within the next forty-eight hours is liable to be put to death."

"What do you mean by 'we'?"

Crap. Why would she hand in her own people? Reject them, sure. But willingly hand them over to the celestials? No way.

A dark-haired, pale guy stepped up behind her. Damian Greenwood.

I'd always thought he looked more like a vampire than a celestial. Under the candle lights, he bared vampire-sharp teeth in a smile. He was dressed in dark clothes, not unlike the long dark coat his boss on Pandemonium had worn. And his eyes were dark as any infected vampire's.

"You have *got* to be joking," I said. "He's—you do realise he's the one who set up the portal to summon those demons in the middle of town?"

He was also supposed to be dead. I'd pushed him into the fire… into the portal. Had he survived? It seemed impossible, and yet I'd seen more impossible things in the past twenty-four hours than I'd ever expected.

Like the vampire queen working with the celestials. No—with a traitor to the celestials who wanted to burn the world down.

"Damian here assisted with compiling the register," said Madame White. "He brought me the names of many vampires who are infected, out of concern for my people. It seems the issue is on a scale greater than I anticipated. Luckily, the celestials are working on developing a cure, and will be sharing their findings with me."

Was there truth in that document after all? More to the point… nothing explained why the inspector appeared to be working with someone who'd tried to kill him. With Damian. *It's impossible. Unless…*

"I'm the emissary," Damian said, with a smile. "Hoping to reach an agreement between Madame White and Inspector Deacon. We'd rather settle our differences without the celestials acting against the vampires, and I'm happy to say the negotiations so far have been successful."

I blinked. My mind had helpfully decided to wipe itself clean of any suitable responses. Did that demonglass scramble things up and spit me out into the wrong dimension entirely? If I hadn't known there were no dimensions even close to this one, I'd have suspected it. The level of *what the fuck* had flown up to the ceiling.

"But—you're on *their* side," I said. "The demons. Technically, you're the enemy of both the vamps *and* the celestials. Doesn't the inspector know you tried to kill him?"

What the hell was he playing at? And Madame White? Surely she didn't seriously believe his crap. He *wanted* the demon virus to infect everyone.

He held up his left hand, bearing the arrowhead mark. "My loyalty is to my Divinity. Unlike yours, apparently."

"You're so full of shit," I said quietly. "There's no cure. The whole thing was a lie. You're screwing with people on purpose. You can't seriously expect me to believe the inspector accepted your story. You worked with the guy he tried to bump off to bring down the guild from the inside."

"If I may interject," Madame White said coldly, "whatever history the two of you have doesn't interest me in the slightest."

"I thought you were level-headed," I said. "I thought you were smart enough not to be fooled by an obvious traitor. For crying out loud, have you not even talked to the guild? His reports say it all. He killed people, blew up their tower, and was responsible for the portal. Not to mention the virus itself."

"Are you done?" she asked. "Mr Greenwood here has offered to help form an agreement between us and the celestials so that the town doesn't suffer further bloodshed."

"He wants worse than that," I said. "He wants war."

She'd never met him, but she didn't strike me as the sort of person who'd accept the word of anyone without question, let alone someone whose people had been threatening genocide against her people. No… he must have shown her proof, however false it might have been.

When she didn't respond, I said, "So he's the one who told you to make a register? How many centuries have you lived through that told you that's ever been a good idea?"

"How many people have died as a result of that virus?" she said, her nostrils flaring. "My people and I will survive, make no mistake. But we will not let our blood be tainted by traitors. And if you hide enemies from us, then your blood will stain our floors."

"Wow." I raised an eyebrow. "Now we've got the death threats out the way, let's assume I don't give a shit if you threaten me. What else have you got?"

"We have the cure," said Damian. "The real one."

My heart gave a sickening lurch. Even knowing Damian was a devious bastard, the possibility gripped me. After all, Madame White was clearly fooled. What if he'd developed something that seemed to be a cure in the pretence of helping her—but then planned to infect her people? Without bloodstones, it was the obvious conclusion. I had to get through to her before that happened.

"Why trust him?" I asked her. "Why take his word for it?"

"Why?" She laughed. "Because he took the cure himself. Damian is a vampire-celestial, the first of his kind."

More like demon-celestial. Seven hells. Damian had been through the full transformation and survived it without turning to madness. A celestial vampire who hadn't died yet. And now he held the cure as a beacon above all vampires, all the celestials... and me.

"Bullshit," I said. "There is no cure, and if there was, you sure as hell wouldn't be the one in charge of it. Quit screwing with the vampires and we'll finish what we started."

"I did take the cure," he said. "What's so difficult to believe about it? The celestial guild and the vampires might have had our differences, but cooperation is essential to survival. Thanks to Madame White, the guild's been able to develop a solution which will enable us to wipe out the virus in any humans who've been bitten. Of course, it's too late for the vampires, but they're not innocents. They did this to themselves."

"*You* did it to yourself, you lying piece of shit." I looked at her. "He's hiding it, but he got bitten forever ago, before this even started. He's the perpetrator—a spy in the guild for the demon realms."

"What absolute nonsense," she said. "Tell the guild your grievances, not me. I only care for my people, and if you continue to harbour dangerous fugitives, your life will be forfeit."

"It's not worth it, Devi," Damian put in. "Cooperate. We can achieve the peace you want so badly."

"Nice speech," I said. Turning to Madame White, I added, "Have you ever heard of Inspector Angler? He's the one this guy used to work for. He tried to take over the demon realms using the same venom his little friend here is claiming to be able to cure. If it looks like a duck and quacks like a duck…"

"Cease your human babbling," she said. "I've also spoken to Inspector Deacon in person. I retain the hope that we, at least, will resolve our issues without bloodshed. You, on the other hand… if you don't hand over those vampires, we'll see it as a declaration of war on behalf of the warlocks."

I took a step back. "I'm willing to listen when you come to your senses and beg me for help."

"Two days," she said. "You have two days, precisely. That is all I'll give you."

Her blood slave stepped up to me. I elbowed him aside, and stalked from the room before I activated my celestial hand and set the place on fire.

This will come to war before the week's over. Whether I handed over the vampires or not, someone would snap. The celestials and the vampires, all fooled by a madman who was supposed to be dead.

Forty-eight hours until the celestials killed every infected vampire in the city.

No pressure, Devi.

10

"What is it?" Nikolas asked when I joined him at the car. He had his phone out, probably messaging Rachel.

"She asked me to hand over every vampire I've helped. They're onto us."

He pocketed his phone, his expression tightening. "Why? To deal with the virus herself?"

"Worse." I climbed into the car and ran through what she'd told me, finishing up with my suspicions that Damian Greenwood had not only apparently risen from the dead, he'd managed to fool both Madame White *and* Inspector Deacon. Which should have been impossible, given his history with the guild.

Nikolas didn't respond for a moment. Then he turned to the house, his aura pulsing with darkness. The message was clear.

I grabbed his arm. "Nikolas. Don't start a war before we have to. Of course I'm not going to hand anyone in. We'll find somewhere else for the vamps to go. If anything, I think she just wants an excuse to start a war between the vamps and the warlocks. Or Damian does."

He turned back to me, his golden eyes burning with fury. "Yes, I suspect he does. That's why I thought I'd get there first."

"Don't you find this whole setup suspicious as hell? I *have* a shortcut to the guild. I can get in there and find out how deep Damian's influence goes. Or even if it's there at all. You know he worked for the inspector's enemy."

"Did the inspector know that?"

"I have *no* idea. I don't even know what the guild is doing. If I didn't know better, *they're* in on this. But I don't know who, and for how long." My arms dropped to my sides. "And if they have a cure, I can steal it. If Damian's not there in person…"

His jaw clenched. "We're no closer to finding a cure. You didn't see anything the last time you were at the guild?"

"No," I said. "But I didn't search the whole building. They've moved things around since the tower blew up. Their defences are probably back up so we can't get in from the outside, but I can use the demonglass… wait. Can I borrow Rachel's power?"

His brows rose. "Haven't you tried?"

"No. I didn't think… but Damian can't teleport—or hell, maybe he can. I don't even know *what* he is—if he's actually a celestial-vampire or a demon masquerading as one. I didn't check he actually died. But I have to try."

He nodded. "Then we'll go."

We drove back in silence. My mind spun in circles. I took it for granted the guild was demon-proofed, but I hadn't actually checked while I'd been snooping around the inspector's office. If Damian wasn't human—if anyone else there wasn't—then it meant the inspector hadn't reset the wards after the attacks. Which seemed impossible. Someone surely would have noticed. But if Damian really did have an arch-demon helping him, the whole world was set against us.

Rachel waited in the hall with her hair sticking up all over—judging by the state of her eyebrows, there'd been another explosion.

"I was in the lab," she said unnecessarily. "Your friend… she volunteered to help. What happened?"

"Trouble," I said. "A metric crap-ton of it."

I gave her a run-down. She bit her lip, looking uncharacteristically grim. "You want to try taking my magic? I have no issue with you borrowing my power, but you've only stolen from higher demons before. Dunno if I'm high level enough. I'm more of a Grade Two than a Three."

"You're powerful," I said. "I don't know anyone else who can do what you can."

"If you're sure," she said dubiously.

I raised my right hand. Immediately, my demon mark snapped on, power tingling up my arm. I stepped back, looking at the glowing arrowhead symbol. "Er… when you use your power, do you just picture who you want to turn into?"

Rachel's eyes gleamed with interest. "More or less."

I thought. Then my body thickened and I shot several inches up into the air. *Whoa.*

"Ugh," she said. "Who's that guy? He has terrible hair."

"Bad Haircut Sammy," I said, in his voice. "Wow. That's weird as hell. Wonder if I can try…"

I shrank, turning into Rachel herself. Then I tried Javos. Rachel lost it at that point, collapsing into shrieking giggles. "I'm Javos and I have a stick jammed up my arse," I said in his rumbling voice. I gave a pirouette and turned into Rachel again. Then the inspector.

"My name is Inspector Deacon," I said in a serious tone. "I'm the biggest dickhead on the planet."

"Devi," said Nikolas in an exasperated voice.

"I wish I could read this guy's thoughts." I turned into me again. "That'd help us work out what the hell's going on."

"I wish," said Rachel. "Even the Divinities can't read minds."

But they can raise the dead. I sobered instantly. "All right. I think Sammy is the least conspicuous, but he spends a lot of time around the inspector anyway. I know most of the senior management, too. What I don't know is how many are in league with Damian. Sammy's a clueless sycophant, so he'll copy what everyone else does. I reckon I can fake that. Even if he's told Sammy something important, he'll probably have forgotten it."

"If you're sure," he said. "You've taken enough risks today already."

"No kidding," I said. "Warlocks, celestials, vampires… want to check into Babylon again so I can piss off your brother, too?"

"I really wouldn't," he said.

Bad joke. After all, Zadok might be planning a coup. As though all the crap in this realm wasn't dire enough on its own, Babylon had its own issues, which Nikolas was neglecting in order to help me. Maybe he'd understood my indecision about which side to help better than I'd thought, after all.

I turned to the corridor, checking my weapons were still in place. The jolt of demonic power had given me an energy high, but my head throbbed and the prospect of jumping through those demonglass fragments into the celestials' place again wasn't appealing in the slightest. Luckily, Javos wasn't in the storeroom, and the main demonglass sheet was free. *Here we go again.*

I stepped through the glass, emerging in a painful heap in the inspector's office. Gritting my teeth, I got to my feet and turned into Sammy. He was so much bigger and clumsier than I was, so I hoped I'd at least retained my skills and reflexes.

Apparently, I'd left my intelligence behind. Because the door was locked from the outside, trapping me in the office. *Great.* In fairness, getting locked in empty rooms was the sort of thing Sammy did. I looked around for something to use as a lockpick—and froze, staring at the cabinet at the back.

The guild's gold-plated pentagram was gone. I hadn't even looked behind last time I'd been here. Who'd moved it? Now I knew Damian had been here… had he taken it elsewhere? Oh *damn.* I'd completely forgotten about it. But given recent events, its absence couldn't mean anything good.

I stopped again at the sound of a key turning in a lock. Putting on my best approximation of Sammy's perpetually clueless expression, I turned around to face the inspector.

"What are you doing?" he asked sharply.

"Got locked in," I said in Sammy's voice.

"Why not tell me you were there?"

"Couldn't do it with the door locked, sir." Maybe I was laying it on a bit too thick, but he gave me an exasperated look and stepped aside to let me out.

"I wondered where you were," Inspector Deacon said. "I need you to watch the patients. Take notes. Better notes, this time. Did you fail *all* your English classes?"

"Yeah," I said, figuring *that* was a safe bet. "Four times."

"For the Great Divinity's Sake," he growled. "This way, and try not to spill anything this time."

Okay. So either Sammy was in on the plan, or did whatever he said anyway.

Divinities above, I'd better not regret this.

I'd bet my demon marked hand that the 'patients' he referred to were either celestials or humans who'd been bitten. Perhaps he was testing the cure on them. Actually—

that didn't seem far out of the realms of possibility. Or they were imprisoned, awaiting execution. Damn. I was already wanted for harbouring supposed criminals. What I needed was a way to permanently sabotage this whole operation.

"When do I get to try it?" I asked, in Sammy's most whiny voice. "Can't I be super-powered like them, too? I've proved I'll do as I'm asked to. I can help."

"You'd certainly loyal," he said. "Unfortunately, you're not ready to take the serum yet. If you die, I'll have to find someone else to assist me. It'd be inconvenient at the least."

So he was distributing the 'cure'... the one that wasn't a cure at all? But he must *know* what it did. The inspector of all people always seemed to have it together, but either recent events had driven him over the edge, or he'd actually been totally batshit the whole time. Not like anyone would have noticed the difference. But there was something... off about him. Not so much the words as the cold way he spoke. He *looked* the same, but...

My gaze drifted downward. His right hand was covered.

Oh fuck.

Looked like Sammy—and even Damian Greenwood— weren't the ones I should be worrying about. The inspector was in the service of an arch-demon. I'd bet he had Damian, too, if it was actually him. They'd taken the guild, all right. And I wasn't powerful enough to go head to head with the gods. I was willing to bet I couldn't steal *their* powers.

Covering my panic behind Sammy's whiny voice, I said. "But can't I at least *see* it?"

"You've seen enough," he said. "If you don't get on with the job, I'll find someone else."

"I haven't seen the vampires yet," he said. "I heard— Madame White, I heard she's beautiful."

He scowled. "That's Damian's job. You're not reliable enough."

I'd got it dead right. He was in on it. She hadn't lied. Damian had got to both of them. Which didn't leave me with a ton of options, to be honest.

Except my own demon magic.

In the medical bay, several celestials lay on hospital beds, unmoving. Either they'd been bitten, or injected with the so-called cure, or both. I couldn't carry unconscious people out of here, and besides, it wouldn't stop the inspector—or the demon. They'd just bring in more.

"Stay," he said. "Watch them. Report any symptoms."

He roughly shoved a clipboard and pen into my hand. I took them without speaking, my mind racing. None of the patients stirred. I scanned the room, taking a mental note of the layout. The actual nurse wasn't in here—hadn't been here in ages, if the smell was any indication. Nobody had cleaned this place in a long time. Dust covered every surface, including the patients. They weren't hooked up to machines, so I assumed they were drugged. Then I looked closer. Straps held each one of them to their respective beds. *In case they wake up and the demon takes over?* Rage surged through me, and my right hand tingled in anticipation of violence on the bastards who'd done this. Two celestials I recognised as the inspector's most trusted novices aside from Sammy stood guard outside the door. *Let's go, then.*

When I was certain the inspector had gone, I stepped back against the wall, and sent a current of Nikolas's lightning magic from the palm of my hand. The ceiling lights flickered and died. In the dark, I approached the female celestial who'd been guarding the room, and zapped her from behind. She gave a startled scream, then fell. I whirled on her partner and zapped him in the same manner.

If I'd had the slightest sliver of doubt that the place was unprotected, I knew it now. Because the demon detectors should have been set off the instant I used my magic. But they hadn't. Someone had dismantled them. This whole building was vulnerable from the outside, even as the worst threat came from within.

In the dim light of my celestial hand, I scanned the clipboard's papers, picked up the most likely ones and stuck them in my pockets. From what I could discern from the notes, these celestials were mid-transformation. Everyone who'd been bitten had been elevated to the next stage of the transformation. They hadn't been executed at all.

They'd been upgraded.

There was nothing to do for them. When they woke, they'd be bloodthirsty killers, stripped of all reason. Those who survived with their sanity intact as Damian apparently had would be forced to serve the enemy anyway. There was no answer, not here. But I needed to figure out how the demon had got into the guild and marked Inspector Deacon in the first place. The inspector hadn't left the guild according to all reports, so the arch-demon must have come here. Possibly through the portal. But how had nobody noticed?

I left the medical bay through the back entrance. Voices came from behind, but I didn't slow. I took the shortcut around to the west tower. As I'd feared, it was no longer locked. After all, it'd been destroyed. Crumbled brick was heaped where it'd once stood tall, the smell of burning lingered... and something else. Brimstone.

I moved in closer, pushing the door inward. It hung from its hinges, and behind came an eerie red glow. The pentagram. *I knew it.*

Damian must have left the portal open, and a demon had slipped out. But what—and how deep did its influence run? What about the Grade Fours? Were the celestial guild's elite demon hunters now demons themselves? And the rest of the world—they were following the orders of an arch-demon, without even knowing it.

I have to tell them.

A voice spoke from the pentagram. "I know it's you, Devi. I'd sense your magic anywhere."

Damian Greenwood stepped out of the pentagram, wreathed in fire and smiling broadly.

11

Damian smiled at me across the ruined tower. I glared back, willing the disguise to recede so I could face him as me. "Get the hell out of here."

"That's not very nice, Devi. Don't you want to know how I survived?"

"I was raised from the dead before you were even a novice," I said, with a shrug. "Reckon I got a better deal too." If he could borrow magic like me, he'd have done so already. So if he bore a demon's mark, it must give him some other power. As though being a celestial vampire who'd come back from the dead wasn't enough.

"A real-life miracle," he said, with a barely-concealed laugh. "That's what the inspector believed, anyway. It wasn't even that hard to convince him in the end. The Divinity who raised me asked for a meeting... and we all know how that goes."

"Wait, the demon who got him pretended to be a *Divinity?*"

"Don't sound so shocked, Devi. You forget arch-demons

were once divine. It takes one misstep to fall. As you should know well."

Damn. The inspector… well, it made sense. Appeal to his ego, make him think an actual Divinity was present… and then get into his head, or mark him. The guy had blinds spots, and after the recent attacks, he'd have been desperate enough to believe anything. Oldest trick in the demons' playbook.

"Of course, I have you to thank for allowing us access to this city in the first place," he added.

"Don't pin this one on me," I snapped. "You've been scheming this for a long time. Before Rory died, even. You were behind the attack on the old guild HQ, right? I wasn't even in the country at the time."

"That doesn't lessen your role," he said. "That Divinity of yours… has he spoken to you about what his intentions are?"

I wish. It would help if he gave me a clue.

"I'm more concerned with what *your* arch-demon wants," I said. "But I guess you weren't important enough to tell, right? You're not that special. You're a pawn. We all are. And if you don't want to end up dead for good, I'd tell me what the arch-demon wants with the celestials. Where is everyone else?"

"Wouldn't you like to know?" He stepped back into the pentagram, and vanished.

Damn him. *Damn him.* He was gone.

"Devi," hissed a voice from the shadows. "Devi. Leave. Now."

The pentagram vibrated, and power rushed over me, shaking the ground under my feet. An alarm sounded from within the building, and I ducked out of sight, around the rubble of the tower.

"This way," whispered a voice. Clover.

"What are you doing?" I moved over to join her, casting a

wary glance at the guild's darkened windows. "Please tell me *you* at least know what's going on in there."

"I know." She moved forward a little, the moonlight painting white stripes on her scarred face. "There's nothing that can be done."

"Is there anyone in there who *isn't* working with the demons?" I spoke more to myself than anything. Part of me still hardly believed it'd happened so fast. The last attack had hit too hard for anyone to notice the demon slip into their midst. Even I hadn't paid enough attention. But I'd thought Damian was dead, and so were the demons he worked with.

"Anyone who wasn't bitten and isn't the inspector or Damian," she said. "The others—there aren't many left, but they're the ones he selected as the most loyal."

I glanced back over my shoulder at the ruins. "But—the defences are out. There's a giant pentagram inside that tower. Have they really not checked?"

"They aren't here, Devi," she said. "The majority of the active soldiers, and novices, relocated to the academy. The story is that the injured are too unstable to move, but you and I know that isn't true."

"He gathered his most loyal people around him," I murmured. "It's the perfect setup. Add in those vampires— the whole thing about him making a register is just an act. He's not planning to kill those infected. It's a cover. They're recruiting an army."

She didn't need to respond for me to know my guess was right on the mark.

"And there's no cure," I added bitterly. "My best friend's turning, and they—they're tricking the vampires into thinking they can help. But they just want them in their army. Against... us? The rest of the celestials, or the warlocks?"

"I can't say I know," she admitted. "But all isn't lost. They might be ahead of us, but not as far ahead as they'd like to be. You weren't supposed to find out any of this. That ability of yours has given you access to information you'd never have found otherwise."

"Everyone wants to use me as a bargaining chip, and I'm not even deep into the war yet," I said heatedly.

"I'm afraid you are."

I frowned at her. "Look. You have an awfully convenient habit of disappearing right up until the convenient moment, Clover. Call me suspicious, but *you're* not supposed to know any of this either. You're supposed to be a retired soldier who doesn't even come to the guild anymore."

"You're right."

"Then…" I paused. "Who *are* you, exactly?"

"A friend."

"I should hope so," I muttered.

"You might need these." I jumped as her cold hands scattered demonglass fragments into my hands.

"Thank you," I said. "I can still reach you by phone, right? Because seriously—shit's going to fly one way or another if I don't meet the vampire queen's deadline."

And even if I did, she'd kill the vampires I'd helped, believing the celestials' orders were the right ones. Damian really had fooled her. Like the celestials.

"You can reach me for now," Clover said, "but I can't promise I'll always be able to help you. This war… it's beyond both of us."

Not if I can help it.

I threw down the demonglass, and stepped through.

The journey back passed in a painful rush, the glass spitting me out onto the storeroom floor. I groaned and rolled over. "Nikolas."

He wasn't there. *Oh no. Did something else happen?* We supposedly had forty-eight hours before the vampire queen came, but then again, the other side had no intention of playing by the rules.

I lurched to my feet and ran from the room, in the direction of the smell of brimstone. *Nikolas. Rachel.* "Hey!" I shouted, running around the corner. "Guys—"

I stopped. The lab was in ruins. Burn marks scorched the walls, half my ingredient jars lay shattered, and Rachel stood amongst the mess, picking up bits of broken glass.

"What the hell is going on here?"

Rachel turned around, her face pale. "Fiona," she said. "She—she turned."

No. Please, no.

"She went vampire?" I stared at the scorch marks on the walls. "But—what did that?"

"She didn't go vamp. I don't know what she did, but fire came out of her hands."

"Shit." I stared at her. "Where—?"

"In her room. We managed to sedate her. Not before she burned us all. Good job Javos isn't here."

"Where in seven hells is he, then? I've had a night of it already. Did she do it before I left?"

She winced. "I didn't have the chance to tell you. You were all set on going to the guild, and considering everything else—it'd only have distracted you. I hoped they did have a cure there."

"Believe me, so did I," I said heatedly. "But they didn't. There isn't one. It's a cover. But Fiona... It wasn't Azurial who bit her, was it? Or his power?"

A human couldn't turn into a fire demon. Right? That was too much, even for today.

"What do you mean by a cover?" Nikolas asked, entering the room.

I sank onto the ruined sofa. And told them.

"Just who is this Clover person?" was the first question

Rachel asked. Not what I'd expected.

"A friend," I said. "Well. I thought she was. She retired from the celestial guild years ago, but considering she always seems to know what's going on… I've no idea. Maybe it doesn't matter. Let's just say she's on our team, for what it's worth."

"But she's not around," Rachel said. "And those vamps—they might not know it, but they're on the enemy team."

"I know." I scrubbed my hands over my face. "It's a mess. I don't know what else to do. The guild's gone off the rails. This arch-demon… he's taken over the city, effectively, and the ordinary humans don't even know it."

"Did you see the inspector's demon mark?" asked Nikolas.

"No," I said. "His hand was covered, and he didn't use magic either. So I'm guessing you don't know which arch-demon it is?"

"Unfortunately not," he said. "Without the mark or a signature, I can't make an educated guess. You said you didn't know which realm was on the other side of the pentagram?"

"Probably Pandemonium. But the demon responsible might have raised Damian from the dead."

"That's not possible." He frowned deeply. "Arch-demons can't raise the dead. Are you certain it was really him?"

"I'm not certain of anything, to be honest."

Whichever arch-demon it was, they were on the side of Azurial and the vampire king… which suggested it might be the same one who'd marked me. But that wasn't necessarily true. From what I knew of arch-demons, though, they disliked one another at best. They didn't work together.

Maybe *I* needed divine assistance to win.

I left the lab and went to Fiona's room. She lay prone on the bed, breathing evenly. No signs of demon marks. But my aura vision potion would have worn off, and the evidence was clear. She was no longer human.

Nikolas placed a hand on my arm. "It'll be okay."

"She's *marked.*"

"So are you, and you've done a remarkable job defying authority anyway."

Not if the arch-demon calls my name. Damn it all. I turned to him, tears of frustration pricking my eyes. Nikolas's arms came around me, and I sobbed, surprised by the force of the emotion. I hadn't cried hard since the night Gav died. Things had happened too quickly to process, and seeing Fiona lying there—knowing I was responsible—unravelled me.

Nikolas's strong arms were my anchor, and I held onto him, wishing the world would stop spinning, wishing I could just *breathe.* Wishing I could undo the damage I'd done and the lives I'd ruined.

When he lifted me off my feet and carried me to my room, I didn't object.

I blinked awake hours later, confused and disorientated. I had vague memories of being carried to my room, but I'd thought I'd been covered in weapons at the time. Someone had removed them, not to mention my jacket. I hadn't been wearing the anti-warlock trap... which was a relief, considering I wasn't alone.

Nikolas lay beside me, and our bodies had moulded together while I'd slept. A shiver traced down my back. I hadn't been this close to someone since Rory. Not for lack of trying, but every relationship I'd pursued in the last two years had felt trivial compared to the bond I'd formed with my partner. Stupid, really. Rory would have wanted me to move on. But every time I tried to connect with someone, I felt disengaged. Empty. Deprived of that connection, the innate understanding that formed with years.

Nikolas and I... what we had wasn't exactly that, but it was something good.

His eyes half-opened. I froze. At least he'd kept his clothes on, and I was reasonably confident that my demon mark would have woken me if he'd touched it, but I'd been that out of it last night...

"I didn't want to leave you alone," he said, in a half-apologetic, half-worried tone. Not one I'd heard from him before. He made to climb off the bed, but I reached out and stopped him.

"It's okay," I said. "I want you to stay here, Niko." I grabbed the back of his shirt, pulling him back. My demon mark awakened at the close contact, and when he lowered himself onto the bed alongside me again, heat from his proximity seared my skin through the fabric of my shirt. The whole bed smelled like him—brimstone and heat, lightning and fire. Powerful yet somehow comforting at the same time. I shivered, feeling his shadowy magic rush over the mark, and shifted onto my back.

He leaned over me, our faces inches apart, and traced his lips over mine. At the same time, his hands delicately ran down my hips, moving towards my wrists—and my demon mark. I felt its urge to take in his power and pulled my hand back, shaking my head.

"It wants to steal your power, Nikolas."

"I don't mind at all," he murmured. He returned to stroking my hips, his hands slipping under my shirt. I moaned at the sensation, my skin tingling underneath his touch, and undid the clasp of my bra to allow him access. My fingers dug into the waistband of his trousers, pulling him on top of me. I could feel his readiness against me, but he busied himself exploring every inch of me, fingertips trailing over my ribs, circling my nipples, teasing until I was quivering all over, damp and trembling with need.

His mouth closed over my peaked breast, and I gasped, turning my head into the pillow as he moved his mouth to the other one, delicately nipping at the soft skin. When he eased down my trousers and underwear and kissed his way down the inside of my thighs to the wetness at my core, I lost all semblance of control. Lust surged through my veins like fire, drawing me to him, into him. I couldn't get enough. One breathless kiss followed another as he shed his clothes. A naked warlock was something to behold. Golden skin etched with hard muscle, faint shadows on his back where his wings sometimes appeared... and a condom in his hand.

"Glad one of us was prepared." My breath quickened as he straddled me, and I took the condom and rolled it onto him. With one powerful thrust, he was inside me, hands gripping my hips. I moaned, writhing beneath him as every thrust threatened to undo me, to send me over the edge. Pleasure sparked through my nerve endings with each movement, as we found our rhythm and moved against one another, torn between drawing out the pleasure and chasing it to its inevitable conclusion.

Tingles exploded through my body as I climaxed, gasping, my spine shuddering. He came moments later, and for a moment, shadowy wings appeared at his shoulders. Heat shimmered in his gaze as he climbed off me, removing the condom and throwing it into the bin. My demon mark, quelled for the moment, stirred when he lifted my hand and pressed his lips to the mark. I moaned again, the pleasant ache between my legs igniting once again.

"I don't mind if you borrow a little of my magic," he murmured against my wrist. Shadowy power poured down my arm, sizzling in my veins.

"You just want to be inside me again, don't you?" I moaned again. "Damn, Niko."

"Tell me when to stop." The power kept flowing, the heat kept building.

"Don't stop," I said, and pulled him onto me again.

12

By the time we emerged from my room, it was mid-morning, and we had a day to figure out how to hide a bunch of vampires and stop a war with someone who was, knowingly or unknowingly, working with an arch-demon to take over this realm.

So, you know, no pressure or anything.

Firstly, Nikolas, Rachel and I gathered to clean up the destroyed lab. At least the vampires slept during the day. Though if Javos came back and found out exactly what had transpired last night, he'd probably wake them all with a tantrum.

Fiona stumbled in, looking pale. I jumped to my feet, instinctively raising my demon marked hand.

"It's okay!" she said. "I'm not going to attack anyone."

I took a wary step towards her, guilt rising at the thought that I hadn't been there to help her yesterday. "Can you remember what happened?"

She shook her head. "No. I just blacked out."

"Ah, shit." The first celestial victims had been the same—losing all memory of attacking people. But what she'd done was something else entirely, and far beyond my area of expertise. I'd *killed* Azurial. No part of him should have survived.

I looked at the others. "Can you see her aura?"

"It looks human," Nikolas said, frowning. "Do you have a strange mark on your wrist?"

"No." She held up her arms. "Believe me, I'm as much in the dark as you are. I don't remember anything since you went to meet the vampires."

Ah. "Did the others fill you in?" After the morning I'd had with Nikolas, the state of everything didn't seem anywhere near so dire, but seeing Fiona reminded me of how I'd failed her. But if killing Azurial wasn't enough, there was nothing I could have done.

Her brow furrowed. "Yeah, they did. To be honest, I'm more confused than before."

The front door slammed.

"That'll be Javos," said Rachel. "I'll go and divert him. He'll flip out when he sees the state of the lab."

"Shit, yeah." I looked at Fiona.

"I'll go with her," Nikolas said, nodding to me. I took it to mean he'd explain the situation delicately, in such a way that wouldn't cause Javos to throw the vamps—and Fiona—out the window.

Seven hells.

"Is someone going to tell me why I can suddenly throw fire around?" Fiona asked. "Am I a demon?"

"Not according to your aura," I said, picking up one of the bottles which had survived being knocked to the floor. "I'm sorry. I really don't know. And you've probably heard our cure attempts didn't work out either. The last one I tried caused an explosion. And then I lost yesterday to angry warlocks, vamps and celestials."

"And you slept with Nikolas."

I nearly dropped the bottle. "Fiona."

She grinned and shrugged. "You're transparent as glass."

I sighed. It felt wrong to be happy when so much was going to shit. "I don't want to lose you to a demon."

"Believe me, I don't want that either," she said. "If it's too late... I can't believe the *guild* got taken. Not the inspector, anyway."

"I know. The celestial vamps are being turned into soldiers for the enemy. That won't be you, Fi. You're human. The worst that can happen is—"

"I'll turn demon vamp, and possibly go dark and attack people."

She was right. Unfortunately. And with the vampire bite victims apparently mobilising on the side of the celestials under hell's banner, it became clearer that someone had played everyone in the city for fools.

They're marking out souls. Souls were currency in the netherworld. I'd been chosen, and so had the others—but not by choice, and not on the same side.

Or are we? For all I knew, the arch-demon had intended me to fight alongside my allies... against the rest of Earth. *Not* a happy thought.

"Can't you go and find a Divinity?" she asked suddenly. "I know—I know it's stupid, and heaven knows I regret going on that website at all, but if you have a divine ally... maybe they can win this. Or a non-divine one. The person who marked you is on our side, right?"

"Maybe," I admitted. "But I don't know how the arch-demon answered me before, when he marked me. I've never been able to contact him since." Not for lack of trying either. "I don't know what to do. The arch-demon holds all the cards. I can take out the inspector, but the demon would just find another host. We're fucked."

"Not necessarily," she said. "Not all the celestials are

turned. The ones who weren't bitten. This city isn't the world."

"Maybe not, but if the demons get in, the other celestials won't be able to get them out. Not if the Grade Fours are compromised. No celestials here are a match for an arch-demon, even one using a proxy. And if they are, some of them would rather die than kill one of their own. They really will be their own undoing." Damian was right on that one.

"Actually… there were a few celestials' pictures on DivinityWatch," Fiona said. "From this city. People are curious. Since they broke the news of the attack on the shopping centre the other week, membership numbers have absolutely exploded. I reckon we can warn people that way. Anonymously."

"What, tell everyone that the celestial guild has been compromised?" I said. "The soldiers aren't there. Clover told me they relocated to the academy, so they don't all neces-sarily know what's happening. But the guild knows they don't ask questions."

"So make them ask questions," she said. "By some of the posts on DivinityWatch, I'm positive there's at least a few celestials who are members, under aliases."

Rachel skipped back into the room. "It's a good idea. DivinityWatch is one way of getting around behind Javos's back, too. He doesn't really do technology. So I made an account."

"When did this happen?" I looked from her to Fiona. "I thought you didn't know what DivinityWatch even is. More to the point, why sign up there? They think there are angels hiding amongst us. Not to mention about a quarter of the members are vamps looking to hook up with a celestial."

"Maybe," said Rachel. "But they're also on top of all things netherworld, and behind the celestials' backs. So I figured I'd keep an eye on them. There's a bunch of conspiracy theories, but I reckon you could get the truth out that way. The celestials who aren't working with the enemy would find out quickly—even the ones outside the city."

"True," I acknowledged. "There's not supposed to be internet access at the academy, but we used to sneak around that rule anyway. I suppose using DivinityWatch might counter the rumours that usually show up in the newspapers. The tabloids are already insisting we're all doomed. I'd blame that one on the arch-demon, too, but who knows." I shrugged. "I doubt the inspector's doing media interviews. He looks like he's staying out of the limelight. The whole setup relies on nobody finding that pentagram in the tower. I can't believe they haven't yet."

"If humans got too close, they'd disappear," Nikolas said darkly. "As would any celestial who got curious. It works because it's low-key, and from what you said, it sounds like he has Damian watching the place. Maybe others."

"Not to mention visiting the vampire queen and fooling her, too," I added.

"The DivinityWatch crew are already warning people to avoid being bitten by any vampires," Fiona put in. "Saying anyone might have the virus and that official channels can't be trusted."

"Good," I said. "I don't think we should tell everyone the virus kills celestials, but that's not relevant anyway. The important part is that they know the guild's compromised, there's a demon in their midst, and anyone who's been bitten might turn into a weapon. Get a warning to the celestials that way. But you know, they might not believe us. It's been forever since an arch-demon actually attacked this realm."

"Isn't your novice training about terrorising you into thinking that the demons are trying to corrupt everyone?" asked Rachel.

"Fair point," I said. "Yeah, there was a lot of talk like

that, but the inspector—people worship him, or are terri-fied of him. And as far as anyone's concerned, they're rounding up vampires for the safety of the public. That's the cover story."

"And humans?" Fiona asked.

I shook my head. "I won't hand you over to them, Fi, even if they demand it."

"Even if there's a demon in my head," she said quietly.

I winced, another possibility striking me. With the other victims, they'd flown into a frenzy and attacked people. I'd thought it was the demonic essence from inside the saphor demons controlling their actions. But if Fiona could use fire...

The virus is like the celestial power, except on the demons' side.

"It's okay," she said quietly. "If you want me to leave—'

"Not happening," I said. "Seriously. It'll take more than a blown-up lab to make me abandon you."

"But I destroyed all your research."

"There wasn't much anyway," I said. "Seriously—"

"DEVINA LAWSON." Javos shoved his way into the room, aura flashing with molten rage. "I knew I sensed another demon's presence in this house."

Shit. "Don't—"

"You aren't the one giving orders here, celestial," he snarled. "First the demons and now this. I will not harbour those who belong to the enemy. Those vampires are a liabil-ity, and now I hear that Madame White will wage war on anyone who helps them. I won't stand for it."

"Then they can come to my house," Nikolas said easily from behind us. "I trust that won't be an issue."

"The vamps are asleep," I said. "Seriously, you might have picked a better time."

"Like when Madame White is beating the door down?" Javos turned around and sloped away, the message clear. The vampires were out of the house one way or another, and so was Fiona.

Fine, then.

"Leave everything in the lab," Nikolas said. "I have all the ingredients we need at my house."

"Great," I said. "Anyone want to help with herding vampires?"

Twenty minutes later, we had the vamps loaded into the minibus again, Fiona and Rachel keeping an eye on them. I ran to my room, picked up my weapons and spare clothes and shoved them into a rucksack. I had a feeling I wouldn't be coming back.

Strapping on the last of my weapons, I left my room and ran smack into Javos.

"Not so fast, Miss Devina," he said, his horned head stooped under the landing ceiling "You still work for me."

You total prick. "I did my job. You just kicked out my best friend. So if you'll excuse me, I'm off."

He scowled, fury crackling through his huge body. Even the walls vibrated as his aura burned white-orange, and my demon mark switched on, eager for a fight.

"Fine," I taunted. "Kick off at me. Don't forget I can take in *your* power if I wanted to. I'm out of patience, Javos. Step aside.

I raised my demon marked hand… and he did. He moved, allowing me to pass. *Well, shit.* Maybe he really didn't want me to take his magic. That, or he realised belatedly that smashing me into a pulp would only give the enemy another advantage. Either way, I pelted downstairs to join Nikolas in the front of the minibus, my hands shaking with adrenaline. I'd never seen exactly what Javos's power did in battle, but it was enough for him to command respect from every warlock in the city. But he hadn't used it on me.

Nikolas was waiting, his gaze on the house. Shadowy

wings extended from his shoulder blades, while an opening into Babylon lay right behind him.

"He didn't hurt you, did he?" he asked, a warning note in his voice.

I frowned at the opening behind him. "No. What's going on back there?"

"Nothing, thankfully." His gaze passed over me, and I turned to see Javos briefly meet his eyes from the doorstep before firmly shutting the door.

What the hell was that, some warlock power display? *Oh.* Javos had probably thought Nikolas would bring an army through from Babylon to kick him in the head if he did me any harm. That explained why he'd let me go.

The opening into Babylon vanished and Nikolas boarded the bus without another word. I did likewise.

"I'm so screwed," I muttered. "No more demonglass."

"You don't think I threw away my own collection?" Nikolas said. "I have no shortage at my house."

I could have kissed him. But that might be too much for the poor vampires sitting bleary-eyed in the back.

"Good," I said instead. "Because if ever there was a good time to take matters into our own hands, it's now."

Nikolas drove, while I kept one eye on Fiona and one on the vampires. If the arch-demon intended to use her against me, I wouldn't hand her over without a fight.

"Fiona," I said. "I wonder—can I absorb your power?"

She frowned. "Maybe. I don't know. I'm not sure what it's supposed to feel like, but I don't feel any different."

If I had to guess, the demon was using her as a host in some sense, and its power was impossible to access when she wasn't using it. I turned to the nearest vampire, holding up my mark. It was the Asian girl I'd spoken to in the warehouse before. The mark didn't so much as flicker.

"What?" she said. "What are you doing?"

"I can draw demonic magic," I said. "I thought maybe I could take in yours, but I guess it isn't the same as regular magic."

Damn. It was worth a try.

Nikolas pulled over at the side of the road down from his house. It was a fairly ordinary four-bedroom house which I expected to look more neglected, considering he spent most of the time at Javos's place lately. He took my bags from me and carried them to the bedroom at the corridor's end.

"You can have the second guest room," Rachel told Fiona, pointing at one of the doors. "I usually stay in this one. Unless you want to be roommates in case you need someone to stop you starting fires in your sleep, but I sometimes shapeshift when I'm unconscious. Fair warning."

Fiona gave a nervous laugh. "No thanks. I think I'm good." She dropped her bags off in the spare room, arching a brow at me. "Nikolas seems certain you're staying together."

I shrugged. "Guess so."

Rachel gave me a grin. "I saw it coming. Even Javos did."

"Is that why he waited until now to kick me out?"

"Probably. I never understood how his mind worked." She bounded downstairs. "Come on. Let's get those vamps off the bus."

Between us, we relocated the vampires upstairs into the largest bedroom where they promptly passed out on the carpet—two of them mid-sentence. After locking the door, I met Rachel and Fiona in the living room downstairs.

"Not much of an army," said Rachel, settling on the sofa. "It's the three of us and a half-dozen vamps who might turn against us."

I sat down beside her. "Honestly, I'm willing to try anything at this point. Damian went through the portal into the demon realm, but he'll be back. And this time, I'll be ready to take the rest of the army off his hands. Where's Nikolas?"

"He went to check on the shadow realm, apparently," said Fiona. "Because that's a totally normal thing to say. Did I mention I have no clue how to explain all this to my parents? They want to fly over from Ireland and visit me, and I can't exactly tell them I might accidentally set them on fire. And now I'm pretty much homeless."

"Me too. I'm sorry." I sat in an empty chair, which smelled of brimstone and something warm and comforting. Like Nikolas. Oh, man. Sleeping together was one thing, but getting attached like this? Dangerous ground. "This is all my fault."

"Oh no," said Fiona. "I'm pinning this one on the demons. Always. The mind-invading bastards—"

Shadows exploded in the middle of the room and Nikolas reappeared. Fiona slid from the sofa with a shriek as his wings nearly hit her in the face. His shadowy aura was out in full force.

"Babylon is under attack," he said.

"From what?" I jumped to my feet, alarmed to see him bleeding from the arm. The wound, however, was already closing.

"Whatever it is, it came through a portal," he said. "I'd know the sight anyway. I need to assist my people."

"I'm coming," Rachel and I said at the same time.

Crap. So much for Haven City being the only target.

"Hold on," I added. "I'll get the demonglass set up. We need more than one way back. Where is it?"

Nikolas ran to the kitchen in answer. In this realm, his wings didn't appear completely solid, tucked away when he passed through the door frame and dug into a cupboard next to the shelves where he kept his collection of warlock tomes and ingredients for demon summonings. Returning with a jar of glass fragments, he scattered them onto the carpet. "Are you all armed?"

I checked my stakes and knives were in place, and nodded.

"Devi," said Fiona hesitantly. "Firepower would be useful in a fight, wouldn't it?"

"You—no," I said. "Sorry, but even with the arch-demon messing with you, that realm's dangerous. If you start to feel the demon's influence come on again…"

"Use this." Nikolas handed her another jar. "It'll knock you out. I can't say it'll work on the demon, but it's all I've got."

Panic and anger twisted his expression. Whatever he'd seen on the other side had been bad. Really bad. And that realm was tied up with Pandemonium—with the monsters who wanted to invade Earth.

Shadows blanketed the three of us. In another instant, we stood in a valley cradled between high cliffs. Not where we'd been before. I didn't know where we'd ended up. But even at such a distance from the castle, the light of a portal blazed, unmistakable. It appeared to come from somewhere below… *Zadok's tower.*

There weren't supposed to be working portals here at all.

The usually purple star-specked sky burned with the shadow of flames, while the castle gates were thrown wide. Too far to run to.

"They're down near the river," he said. "They came out of the water near—"

"The same place I set up the pentagram before." I swore. "It's got to be Zadok—or the link to Pandemonium."

He looked around. "I can fly—"

"But it'll be quicker to use the glass," I said.

He merely nodded. Shadows unfurled around us again, taking us back into the living room. This time I didn't hesitate before stepping onto the fragments of demonglass, the others behind me. Javos's lessons had actually helped.

My body seized up as pain racked through my spine, objecting to being forced to travel such an unnatural way. We landed in a heap, Rachel sprawled underneath me and Nikolas beneath both of us. I'd brought us into the castle's corridor with the demonglass pillars, and the sounds of fighting echoed from below.

"I should have warned you it's uncomfortable." I disentangled my legs from Rachel's, who groaned.

"Now I know where you got the courage to defy Javos," she said, stretching her neck. "I think I'd rather have the shadow power."

"This way." Nikolas beckoned, his wings shadowy and solid-looking now he was in the realm which fuelled his demon magic.

We moved in the direction of the noise, towards the door opening onto the bridge to Zadok's tower. Fiery light spiralled up to the sky. All around, demons did battle with warlocks. With a snarl, Nikolas launched himself into the air. His shadow passed overhead, a being of power and wrath, striking down the enemy with bolts of lightning edged in shadows. Lesser demons swarmed beneath the bridge and on it, too. The portal had definitely hit the same spot I'd used Zadok's pentagram on.

I caused this. Somehow.

Divine light leapt to my hand, and I ran into the fray.

13

Divine fire exploded from my hands, ripping the first row of demons to pieces. The light drew attention from other demons, who either cringed away or ran towards me with battle cries. I drew my celestial blade and cut left and right, severing wings and tails, sending dead demons toppling from the bridge into the surging current below. Rachel ran past in her demon form, tearing into anything that moved. As this wasn't their realm, the demons disintegrated into ashes... but not all of them did. Scorpion demons remained behind, dead stingers leaking venom onto the stone. Bat demons fell out of the sky. And the demonglass tower at the end reflected the gory scene back at us in three-dimensional vividness.

Someone in this realm is working with the enemy. Considering how close the nether realms were, it wasn't a surprise, but that someone had set up a portal again... I was almost certain it was Zadok, but I hadn't seen him since the last battle, and Nikolas had removed the pentagram I'd used last time. No signs of life came from the glowing glass tower. All attention was focused on the bridge, and the flaming light beneath.

A venos demon bore down on me. The scorpion's stinger flew wide, and its head followed. I climbed over its body, my demon mark thirsty for blood.

Fire roared beneath the bridge, but though the flames leapt close enough to touch, I didn't feel their heat. That meant one thing—it was demonic fire, close enough to the sort Themedes and Azurial had used. *Shit. Don't tell me there's another one.*

As if conjured by my thoughts, a winged figure appeared outlined in the flames, the shape of a person, highlighted against the fire. *Not again.* The figure appeared as female, clad in flame-coloured armour, and wielding a blade of fire. With powerful wingbeats, she landed in front of me.

"Who the hell are you?" I demanded. "Not Azurial's long-lost sister."

Actually… it stood to reason there'd be other fire demigods. She was no arch-demon. I'd know. But I'd only seen that type of fire magic on one person before.

"Celestial," she said dismissively, raising her blade of flames. "I've been ordered to eliminate you."

"You're late to the party."

I ran forwards to meet her, conjuring up my celestial blade once more. Oddly, no heat came from her, and her aura appeared more yellow than orange—albeit still like looking into the sun on a high summer's day. The combination of her blazing aura and the portal's light made Babylon's dark skies look bleached, washed-out.

I met her strike, sweeping her blade aside, but she struck back with ease, forcing me to parry. Damn, she was good. Better than her brother. The blade moved like an extension of her hand, and she didn't use the fire magic at all. She must know I was immune.

Time to end this.

I willed my demon mark to take in her power, and it glowed with fiery light. Then I conjured divine fire to my other hand. "Nice knowing you."

She disappeared into the flames. My attack seared through the air, but no screams came out of the fire. She was just—gone.

"What the—?"

White light grazed my back. I spun around, dodging aside, but she'd concealed herself in the portal's flames. *Dammit.* She was as much of a coward as her brother, apparently.

White fire pulsed from the twin marks on my wrists, not connecting with any target. My flames clashed with the portal below, and if anything, the flaming currents surged higher with each attack. Was I somehow making the portal stronger? Not good at all.

I have the power of an arch-demon. She's nothing.

The flames from beneath the bridge climbed by the second. *The portal...* dammit, I needed to shut it off, but to do that, I'd need to get down off this bridge—somewhat difficult when it was covered in warring demons and warlocks. Nikolas had disappeared from sight. Rachel, too. A spasm of fear shook me. The bridge trembled under the flames. Maybe demonic fire could even melt through solid stone. I didn't particularly want to be standing on it if that was the case.

"Get here and face me, coward," I snarled. "I'm immune to your fire."

A white thread of magic wrapped around my left hand. I swore, bracing myself. Rachel's shoes did their job, fusing me to the bridge and preventing the magic from pulling me off. The whip-like strand of magic squeezed tighter, and pain jolted through my celestial mark.

"Get *off* me." I grabbed it with my other hand, but too late.

Breath whispered on my cheek, the demigod's shadow appeared behind me, and a blade found its home in my back.

I dodged at the last second. If I hadn't, she might have stabbed me in the heart. At the same time, the bridge gave way. Stones crumbled over the portal and the crackling flames, and even Rachel's boots weren't enough to stop me from falling.

My right hand flailed, grabbing onto her magic—I bloody *hoped* it was her regenerative power I'd grabbed, because if not, I was dead.

And then I fell, towards churning water and raging fire.

The water hit me like a solid force, driving the breath from my lungs and rattling the bones in my body. I couldn't draw breath to scream before the current sucked me under. *Sure hope demigod magic can resurrect me from drowning* floated through my head, along with *What if I get swept out to sea?*

My arm struck something hard. A rock. I grabbed it, gripping as hard as possible. Both hands dug into its sharp surface, drawing blood. An excruciating pain splintered up my arm, suggesting broken bones. Dazed, shaking, I pulled myself onto the rocky protrusion as my blurred vision restored itself. Churning currents tugged at my battered body, threatening to drag me into the depths again. A cough rattled my lungs, and my numb fingers slipped on the water-slick rocks. I dragged my limp legs upright so Rachel's boots dug into the rocks, and I jumped.

I hit the bank, the boots absorbing the impact, then my legs gave way. *Come on, demon magic.* I'd have died several times over if the regenerative power I'd stolen wasn't working, but only a human could be in this much pain. A kaleidoscope of lights played out somewhere to my left—*the portal.* My vision blurred again, the tower not ten feet away reflecting light back at me at dizzying angles. *Demonglass.* So the whole tower *was* made of the stuff.

I half-crawled in that direction. Running away wasn't on my plan, but from what I'd heard of the creatures that lived near the river, I'd get eaten alive if I stayed too close to the water. Surging currents lashed the bank, masking the crackle of the portal and the noises of the bat demons dive-bombing the survivors on the bridge. *Rachel...* Nikolas had been in the air, but if Rachel had been on the part of the bridge which had given way...

My knees hit the ground again. Consciousness flickered in and out. *Not now. Move, Devi. You're too close to the portal...*

A shadowy figure melted into view.

"Stay away," I croaked.

"The ingratitude," he said softly. "Allow me to assist."

An angry retort died on my tongue as blackness darker than shadows dragged me under.

I came to moments later to unexpected warmth. A fire burned in a grate while a soft rug cushioned my weary body. I sucked in a breath and coughed water all over the rug, shuddering. From the absence of pain in my arm, the broken bone had healed itself, but my whole body was soaked and freezing.

I recoiled when a shadowy hand gently pressed to the demon mark. The pain in my bones receded, and even the coldness faded as sensation came back into my limbs.

A man with golden eyes and red-tinted hair grinned down at me. Zadok. *He's giving me his magic.*

I snatched my hand away. "Don't. I'm fine."

"You were minutes from death when I found you," he said. "That's how you thank me for helping?"

"I had it covered." I coughed again, pushing to my knees. Warmth licked at my back, and I resisted the urge to lie down again. I'd had enough fire-related close calls today already.

Zadok leaned against the wall. Like his lab, the room was

round, the walls dark and bare. "You needn't pretend to be invulnerable around me, Devi. I thought the two of us had an understanding."

I climbed to my feet. "You're just trying to piss off your brother, and I'm done standing in the way of your feud."

"It's not my brother who concerns me. It's you."

"You're not my type. Get over it." I shoved a tangled lock of hair over my shoulder. "I couldn't possibly be *less* interested, Zadok, so if you want to find something to fight with your brother over, you'll have to do better than that."

"I did say humans held no interest for me. There are consequences I'm frankly not interested in dealing with.' He tilted his head. "I assume he told you about them?"

"Nice try. I'm not pregnant with demon babies, so you can shove that mental image off a cliff."

He gave me a dismissive look. "That's not what I meant. I assume you're no longer concerned with the state of your soul, so perhaps it doesn't matter."

I rolled my eyes. "If you don't mind, I have yet another egotistical demigod to kill. Get rid of that portal and stop trying to overrun the castle with monsters, then we'll talk."

"You think I did that?" He gave me a wounded look. "You should know I'm looking out for my own interests. Destroying the castle and killing off every warlock in this realm doesn't further my goals."

"Please. You sent those fallen creatures to kill me the last time I was here."

"Simply to demonstrate the lies your lover hides beneath those walls, Devi," he said. "Those once divine beings… the fallen… they're his greatest shame. But I have a real army, and I have the impression you need one. Your realm is in quite a lot of trouble."

Major understatement. "The last thing my realm needs is another portal into an unstable realm."

"Not a portal," he said. "A bridge. I've studied the ways of the arch-demons, Devi… I know what they plan to do."

"A bridge?" I'd heard the term… a bridge was effectively a giant portal, merging two realms into one. Was that what they planned to do to Earth? *I'd say yes.* Specifically, Haven City. My home.

"No," I said loudly. "You don't get it, do you? The whole point of this is to stop the arch-demons screwing with my realm. Not invite more of them in. And for the record, Nikolas did tell me what the fallen are."

"He did?" He smiled. "And he told you that he's personally responsible for their imprisonment, did he? He didn't *have* to lock them down in the dark. He was too afraid to defy his father."

"I wouldn't want those monsters running around either. You can't turn me on him. Nobody can do that."

"Not even the one who marked you? He'll call your name…"

"And I'll tell him to go fuck himself. I'm a bit more concerned with the arch-demon who's trying to take over my realm, not the one loaning me his power. Besides, if I technically belong to another arch-demon, it makes us enemies, and if I ended up having to fight for him, I'd be as likely to kill you as anyone else."

"No," he said. "Like all arch-demons, it makes us potential allies or rivals. That is all. You might even have allied your-self with the ones who took that inspector of yours under their wing. Did he offer you the choice?"

Damian did. "His minion tried. But I'm opposed to people who try to take over my city and kill my friends. You've harmed my friends yourself. You tried to throw Rachel out the window and nearly killed Nikolas several times."

"The monster girl?"

"She's your sister, you complete prick."

"Not my choice," he said. "My brother always had an inexplicable soft spot for outcasts. I suspect that's why you get along so well."

"You'll have to try harder than that if you want to insult me."

"You're healing fast," he commented. "Do I get a thank you this time?"

"Thank you," I said. "I owe you nothing. And now I want to return to the battlefield before Nikolas roasts you alive."

"He won't." He smiled. "He knows better than to try. We're equals, separated by chance. And we're not so different."

"No, you aren't. He told me. I'm sorry your mother didn't love you enough to raise you on Earth, but it's nobody else's problem. Nikolas's included."

"That's not what happened." Rage ignited, his aura darkening into wing-like shapes. Just like his brother's. "He told you what he needed you to believe in order to think me the enemy."

"How many times do I have to tell you that your own actions are what makes you my enemy? You as good as declared yourself against me the second we met. You can't twist history. Let me out of this room. There's a war going on outside. Aren't you concerned they'll break in?"

"I have my own defences." He shrugged, his wings disappearing as quickly as they'd sprung into being. "Aren't you the slightest bit interested in whoever opened that portal?"

"Yeah, but I think I already know. The demigod I have to kill."

A smile danced on his mouth. "For a portal to open, there needs to be an equally powerful portal set up on this side. I wonder who did it?"

Nikolas had said there might be a traitor. But I owed this guy too much already, unfortunately.

"Don't we all. I think I have more chance of finding answers outside this tower, so… let me out."

"You're welcome."

Shadows folded back, revealing a door that opened out onto the bridge… or what was left of it. But the portal's lights had entirely disappeared. As I walked out, a winged figure passed into view, etched in shadow. *Nikolas.* Thank the Divinities—he was alive.

"Devi!" He flew to me, carrying Rachel. She was in her demon form, covered in blood, but not her own. "Did he—"

"He's not involved," I said quickly.

"He might as well be." His teeth bared in a snarl. The door behind me had already closed. *Damn.* "Whoever did it lives on this realm."

"Did you see the demigod I was fighting?" I asked. "It was Azurial's sister."

His eyes flared. "Emarial. I met her once. We need to get back to the castle. There's a traitor in our midst, and I intend to root them out."

14

Warlocks milled about inside the entrance hall. Some lay on the ground while others bound up their injuries with bandages. A sombre air covered the place. I stood with Rachel, knowing I was lucky to be alive myself.

"The enemy's in here?" I asked quietly. "They sure don't look like traitors."

"Maybe, but I don't trust them," said Rachel. "What did Zadok want?"

"To recruit me. Same old. He's hinting that he holds all the secrets, et cetera. Don't worry, I'm not listening to him."

"Good," she said. "It's *not* good that he's fixed his attention on you. I think he's looking for allies. He's lonely."

"He shuts himself up in the tower and attacks anyone who goes near. It's his fault." I shook my head. "I'd say he has a crush on me, but I don't think it's that. He seems to think his brother's corrupting my mortal soul."

"Only if you believe in such a thing." She shrugged. "Mine's damned anyway. So are all of ours. But we're less doomed than those poor souls under the castle."

"He claimed to know secrets about them, too," I said. "He said Nikolas imprisoned them on his father's orders and has no intention of letting them out."

"Now he's talking crap," she said. "Sure, it's true that they locked the fallen underground because the shadow demon said so, but they're also corrupt, immortal, and attack everything they meet. They'd be just as dangerous outside. Here, they have some measure of protection. But they didn't do this. They wouldn't have the strength to open a portal even if they could."

"Do they still have celestial magic, or…?"

She shook her head. "No. Not like you do, anyway. I don't know much about them. I found out because they attacked me the first time I came here, probably on Zadok's orders. He hates that Niko pretty much adopted me as a sister without his permission."

"I thought it was something like that. No excuse to throw you out a window, though."

"I sometimes think Zadok assumes everyone's as invincible as he is."

I frowned. "He doesn't act like it, hiding in his tower all the time. You'd think he'd have come and helped. I mean, this is his realm, and they were right outside his tower."

"Hmm. Maybe he's scared of fire demons. Or demigods. He has no trouble trying to smite Nikolas on a daily basis."

Good point. Not only had he sat out *two* battles, he'd stopped trying to kill me after my encounter with Themedes had caused me to take on his power. Might his weakness be fire? Not that I was scared of the guy anyway, but that was knowledge that I might put to good use.

"No wonder he helped me right after I figured out how to use divine fire," I said. "He was probably hiding from Emarial. But she disappeared. And she can't be pulling the strings. Someone sent her to kill me."

And she'd almost succeeded. I cast another look around at the warlocks, wishing I could see auras which might give away who'd betrayed us to the enemy and set up a portal here. Of course, that was assuming it hadn't been Zadok. But destroying his own tower didn't sound like him, and nor did sitting out of the action. Then again, he hadn't directly participated in the fight with the vampires' king either. Hiding in the shadows... from the fire.

Sure would help to know Azurial's sister's weakness, though. Not to mention the arch-demon behind the curtain. Themedes had had a weakness, so arch-demons weren't completely invulnerable. But who had let them into this realm? Had someone from here been responsible for the arch-demon getting to Earth, too?

Nikolas finally joined Rachel and me. His clothes were torn, bearing the obvious marks of regeneration. But none of his army had those same abilities. Some would die.

"Any luck?" I asked.

"Nobody in this room has the resources to set up a portal," he said in a low voice. "That makes it Zadok by default, unless someone got through from Pandemonium before, during the attack. It's certainly possible."

"Damn." And the portal had gone, taking all proof with it. "I don't think it was Zadok, though. He wouldn't have wanted to destroy his own realm."

The obvious solution was to go into Pandemonium to see who'd launched the attack. But we were exhausted, injured, and needed to make sure everyone at home was safe.

"How'd this realm end up cut off in the first place?" I asked.

"I don't know," Nikolas said. "Nobody does. My brother claims to, but he claims a lot of things. If I had to guess, I'd say it's because the vast majority of higher level demons died out here. With them gone, so is the ability to make portals."

"Until Zadok did it." I bit my lip. "He did it to catch Azurial and the vampire king, supposedly. I think he was looking for an excuse to. And I was that excuse."

"He'd have schemed the same whether you found him or not. He wanted…"

"An easy target? Everyone seems to think that."

"No. Not at all. No humans are made to stand up to the gods, but you… I think if anyone can, it's you."

I gave a shaky laugh. "After that? I don't think the gods particularly care if I'm still in one piece when they throw me out onto the battlefield."

He scowled. "Then maybe the gods need to face up to the fact that they're not the only players in this game, and their pawns have a life of their own." A shadow passed over his gaze. His wings weren't visible anymore, but his shadowy aura was ever-present. Nobody in their right mind would make him into a pawn.

Maybe he saw the same when he looked at me. After all, I'd held the power of the gods in my hands.

"Who are you and what have you done with Nikolas?" I asked teasingly. "First you defy Javos, now this. Next you'll be carrying illegal demonglass to transport us around the city."

"Technically, I do have some of that," he said. "Speaking of which—I think you and Rachel should head back to my house. I have a few things I need to sort out here."

"Okay, but come tell me if the portal comes back."

"Deal. It's that way to the hall with the pillars." He pointed through an open door on the hall's right side. "It's best not to linger here."

"No kidding." I approached the door, with Rachel. Her human disguise came back as quickly as it'd vanished, bright pink hair clashing with the bloodstains on her clothes.

"You're getting good at arguing with him," Rachel said.

I glanced back over my shoulder at him. "He wanted us

out of harm's way. But I need to check on Fiona. And the vampires. I don't believe for a minute that demigod is finished with us. Or whoever's behind this."

We reached the pillared corridor, and I nodded to Rachel before stepping through the glass with her at my side.

Fiona slammed into me, so fast and unexpected that I lost my balance, stumbling into the wall. My elbows scraped against plaster, and she smiled a smile utterly unlike Fiona. Dread gripped my heart, freezing my nerve endings even as flames danced from her palms, scorching the walls on either side of me. The heat told me I wasn't immune—and her eyes blazed with a familiar fire.

"Hello, Devi," purred Azurial's voice.

"What... the fuck?" I massaged my throat. My elbows stung, and my head rang with pain. Not enough for a concussion, or anything that might hint at this being a mistake. The fire warmed my arms, singeing the already-torn sleeves of my coat.

"Surprised to see me again? Your friend is an interesting host."

Bile crawled up my throat. "What the hell are you doing, possessing her?" *It's not possible.* Especially when he was *dead.* I'd seen him die, torn apart in my own divine fire.

He gave a terrible laugh, driving his fist towards me.

Even in shock and faced with my best friend, my instincts switched on. Pivoting out of the way, I pulled out my celestial hand, punching him back. Fiona's head snapped back and I hesitated, not wanting to hurt her. There was no way he could actually be here in person, and he wasn't a shapeshifter, so it was definitely Fiona's body he was using.

Rachel launched herself forward. Fiona spun around with incredible speed, far more like a demigod or vampire than a human. *Shit. It's the transformation.* But turning into a vampire was a world away from a fire demon speaking to me through her mouth.

He smiled. "You can't burn me out, celestial. Not without burning her, too."

"Get out," I snarled. "Whoever you are, get out of her head, *now*."

He laughed again, fire dancing from Fiona's hands. Then the light went out of her eyes and she collapsed onto her front.

"Fiona. *Fiona.*" I shook her. She groaned a little, her voice unmistakably hers.

"What… happened?"

"You were…"

"Azurial." Rachel backed up, holding a knife. "Don't move."

"Whoa," I said. "It's really her this time. Did that happen when she lost control before?"

"No," Rachel said. "Well, yeah, but she didn't speak like him."

"I lost control again?" asked Fiona.

"Worse," I said. "You spoke like—" I cut off my words. Telling her the demigod from her nightmares might be living in her head… damn. I hadn't the fortitude for this conversation, not after the day I'd had already.

Rachel didn't move. "Prove it's actually you."

"What…?" Fiona looked between us in confusion. "You're all wet, Devi. And freezing. Are you hurt?"

I shook my head. "No. We were lucky. But Babylon's a mess, and… Rachel, put down the knife. It's her." I gave her a look telling her to pick up the subject later when Fiona was out of the room. She'd gone into hysterics at the mention of Azurial's name for a while after her kidnapping.

And it was clear he'd done worse than kidnap her. From beyond the grave, apparently. *Impossible.*

Rachel gave me a suspicious look. "I'll give her the benefit of the doubt, Devi, but you can't keep someone like her here and not expect to draw attention. Even more than the vampires."

And she left the room, presumably to change out of her bloodstained clothes. I needed to do the same, but Fiona's dilemma was paramount.

"I'm okay," Fiona said. "Except I'm missing a few memories."

"Shit." I walked around the living room, looking for anything out of place. I doubted Nikolas would have left anything lying around which could backfire, but I still checked. All the bottles containing ingredients were sealed, and so were the books.

"Okay." I breathed out a little. "How many memories are you missing?" I asked Fiona.

"A couple of minutes. Nothing else."

"Then how did he know I was coming back?"

"How did who know?"

I'd sworn not to lie to her again, but given the trauma of her experience with Azurial… I needed to check it was even possible for deceased demigods to take up residence in someone's head before I sent her into a panic.

Nikolas chose that moment to materialise behind me, bringing a freezing-cold breeze from Babylon along with him.

"That was fast," I said. "You flew, didn't you?"

His wings disappeared. "Your ability would have made it easier." He frowned, his gaze immediately going to the burn marks on the walls. "Did Fiona—"

"Yeah. Again. We're okay now."

"No, we're not," Fiona snapped. "Devi's not telling me something. What did I do, start speaking in tongues? I know I attacked you."

"She—you weren't you, Fiona," I said to her. "You were…" Seven hells, how was it even possible? "Azurial."

"No." She sank back, pressing her palms into her eyes. "No. No…"

"You're certain?" Nikolas asked.

"It sure sounded like him."

Fiona sank to the floor. "No. I'm not possessed by *that*. I can't be. You said demons can't do that!"

"They can't," I said. "And that's why I didn't tell you. I know those TV shows have people being possessed by demons, but it's not—the most they can do is put ideas into your head. Even incubi and that type of demon can't pass on their powers to a human. Unless you can remember Azurial doing anything else to you when he captured you? Aside from the vampire bite?"

She shook her head and moaned into her hands. "No. I don't know."

"You don't have a demon mark," Nikolas added. "If it's more than the vampire virus… I need to look into this."

Fiona whimpered. "He's going to kill me. He has my soul."

"Soul." Nikolas's gaze snapped onto her. "That must be— but it's incredibly rare, and not at all stable."

"What do you mean?" I asked.

"His soul's attached to hers," he said. "Demigods… the reason we're hard to kill is because our souls are half-arch-demon. Arch-demon souls keep regenerating if they're killed. So we have the same ability, to some extent. Attaching part of one's soul to a person… I'd say it isn't possible, but Azurial was working with the former inspector, who bore a demon mark. He could steal abilities from others, including those parasite demons."

"But they're less than Grade One," I said.

"Yes, but the way the saphor demon virus works is by attaching a piece of their consciousness to a person. It's the only ability that matches. If someone gets bitten, part of the demon's soul is transferred over that way."

"So the vampire king bit Fiona, and transferred… Azurial's soul over?" My head swum. Fiona's face was chalk white and she looked ready to pass out.

"A small piece of his soul," Nikolas said. "Otherwise there'd be nothing of Fiona left."

"The fucker," I said quietly. "How do you get a *soul* out of a person?"

"You don't," said Fiona. "I don't know why he did it. Maybe he knew you'd kill him."

"No, he wanted to screw with us," I said. "Unless he was being influenced… unless the arch-demon behind all this planned it that way. The same side has a new demigod. I'm starting to get the impression someone wants to stack the playing field against us."

"That's how arch-demons work," Nikolas said. "But you forget… any of them could reset the playing field any time they wanted to. They can kill as easily as they revive, take powers away as swiftly as they are granted. The humans who foolishly serve them will meet a terrible end one way or another."

Including the celestials. Didn't I know it. One battle won, and yet it felt more like a defeat than a victory. All I'd accomplished was a near-drowning and giving Zadok another opportunity to get under my skin. And now Fiona… *dammit.*

I scrubbed a hand through my hair, grimacing when my fingers snagged on matted curls. "I need to change, get a shower, and figure out how the hell to resolve this one."

And we hadn't even started to tackle the vampire problem yet. At this point, if the vampire queen showed up, I'd shove her through a portal into Pandemonium and let her fight it out with Emarial.

With the vamps blissfully napping upstairs, no lab to

speak of and the knowledge that nobody had a cure, we had very little to go by. Fiona didn't remember any more of what'd transpired since we'd left, not to mention her ordeal in Pandemonium. Which meant our next logical step was to go back there, not knowing what might be on the other side.

Being one step behind the enemy was wearing very thin. I was on the brink of marching right to the arch-demons myself and demanding answers. Pity I didn't know the name of the realm I'd been in when the arch-demon had first marked me, and it might not be the fallen Divinity's original realm either. The generic wasteland description matched a hundred desolate realms ravaged by demons. Even if I wanted to meet the arch-demon who'd 'made' me, I didn't even know where to start.

After showering and changing, I returned downstairs to find someone had ordered takeout and the others had gathered in the living room around the demonglass I'd scattered on the carpet. I joined Nikolas on the sofa and helped myself to a plate of takeaway pizza, thanking the Divinities for small mercies. Nikolas himself held a book in one hand, one of the demonic tomes he kept on the shelves. It was in a language I couldn't read. I never did get the hang of demonic languages, even if I knew how to speak a few.

I recognised one word though... *soul.*

Fiona sat on the floor, her back to the sofa, typing on her phone. Possibly telling her family she was possessed by a demon. Or not. They didn't even know how deep in the netherworld we were involved, let alone the most recent shit show.

"You okay?" I said, leaning closer to her.

"I'm on DivinityWatch," she mumbled. "I know you think it's stupid, but it helps. There are other humans out there... people who think this is crazy, but are coming up with ways of coping."

"No, it's good."

"You might want to check it out." She held up her screen. My own face covered it… on a wanted poster, photographed at the guild. Wanted for colluding with demons.

"You have *got* to be kidding me," I said. "The inspector's walking around with an arch-demon's mark completely unchallenged, and *I'm* the one they put an arrest warrant out for?"

"He must have worked out you went into the guild," Nikolas said.

"Damian told him." I groaned. "Obviously. I don't regret telling him to fuck off, but even DivinityWatch is against me?"

"Actually, they're calling you a hero," Fiona said. "They're saying the guild are corrupt."

"Wait—they believe you?"

"Some do. They've started to respond," she said. "The celestials—I don't know what he did with the Grade Fours, but the others have started questioning his orders. He keeps sending them to round up vampires. I put out the message that they're sentencing innocent people to death, and I think the celestials might have helped the vamps escape."

"No way."

"Apparently."

I blinked. "That… sounds too good to be true. I know not everyone blindly follows his orders, but the Grade Fours do, and they can execute any of us in a heartbeat. But I don't know whereabouts they are."

"Good question," Fiona said.

And not one I wanted the answer to. If the arch-demon turned *them,* they'll be more deadly even than the infected vampires.

"How many Grade Fours are there?" asked Nikolas.

"Maybe a dozen," I said. "Enough to kill a hundred vamps, anyway. Why?"

"I'm trying to work out how big the enemy's forces are," he said. "All the enemies, not necessarily the ones on the same side. Pandemonium lost a lot of their vampires in the fighting. Even when they attacked Babylon, they sent mostly demons. I didn't see any vampires at all."

"Hmm." I frowned. "I don't know. Does DivinityWatch have any clues about whether the inspector's gathering any more vamps, aside from the celestial ones?"

"No, they're mostly repeating what Rachel and I told them," Fiona said. "The celestials are compromised. Every vampire or human who was bitten is in danger." Her voice wobbled. "And the inspector's the villain. But as I said—there are actual pictures of people helping vampires. They're not all evil."

"Good." I closed my eyes. "Okay. So assuming some of the celestials will stand against the others... I don't know what they'll do when the truth comes out. It depends how deep under the influence the inspector is. If he realises he's creating an army of celestial vampires on the orders of a Divinity, or if the mark is actually controlling him. Like... like the virus."

"Most likely, he believes he's doing the right thing," Nikolas said. "If he's like the vampire queen, following the enemy's orders without realising they're intended to wipe his own people out... they'll start a war without needing to lift a finger. If the celestials destroy one another, the demons need not be involved at all."

"Then we need to get a warning to the Grade Fours," I said. "That's what we should have done from the start, but they have an arrest warrant out for me, and heaven knows what'll happen if they're actually fully complicit in this. If they are, we're outnumbered."

"I don't think they are," Rachel said. "But I'd hold off on going near them until we have the full picture."

"Damian's definitely complicit," I said. "He set up the portal. Which I need to close, but you know, there's a sleeping army of celestial vampires on top of it. And Pandemonium on the other side. If Emarial has the same ability to use fire to travel between realms as her brother did..."

"Strange how he never used it," said Rachel. "I mean, he tried to, but once the vampire king dude stepped in, he stopped his whole *conquering Earth* plan."

"Because he didn't need it any longer," I said. "None of them is acting under their own power. They've all signed over their souls to hell."

"Is it possible to repair the damage to a soul?" Fiona asked tentatively.

"I don't know," I said, thinking of the celestials. Divine magic didn't repair. It only destroyed. "But really, the Divinities alone care about the state of your soul, and from what I hear, they're not exactly reliable anyway."

They're just as likely to fall as anyone. They were scared not for their souls but for their lives. And in the end, coming out of this with my soul intact was meaningless if everyone was killed. A pure soul was also a dead soul.

Nikolas pulled his phone out of his pocket. "Javos is calling me," he said.

He left the room. Fiona looked up at me. "I'll share the truth on DivinityWatch, for what it's worth. They're on your side, Devi."

"Good, because all we have are the four of us and six sleepy vampires. Wonder what Javos wants."

Nikolas came back into the room, his expression incandescent with rage. "The celestial Grade Fours have made a list of warlocks suspected of bargaining with hell. They're planning to arrest us all—or declare war."

15

"What—they're going to Javos's place?" I asked. "Do they have a death wish?"

"Apparently," he said. "Javos said that according to our back channels, they're planning a raid on the Harpy's Nest tonight. This will end in bloodshed, make no mistake."

I swore. "Do they not know they're taking the orders of a demon? Has any one of them actually set foot in the guild to check the person giving them orders is actually who they think he is?"

Of course they wouldn't. Because any excuse to make trouble for the preternaturals was acceptable, and they'd never believe the truth.

I looked at him. "There's no chance of negotiation. We're in an open conflict with a demonic dimension and the Grade Four celestial soldiers are on the wrong side. I need to take them proof that the person they're working for is on the enemy's side."

"You want to talk to them?" Scepticism tinged his voice.

"Has that ever worked before? They can see your aura, can't they?"

"Yes, they can. But they can also see the inspector's, which means they can't have actually spoken to him in person recently. Unless the enemy got them, too. And to be honest, I wouldn't notice if they did."

I wouldn't forget what Farrell had done to the celestial vampires. They were unrepentant murderers without a conscience, believing they were carrying out the divine will of the Divinities.

"Then what do we do? Kill them?" asked Rachel.

Warlocks. "I don't think that's the answer," I said. "They're the strongest celestials here. If this realm is invaded, they're the last line of defence. If they and the warlocks destroy one another, the demons will have an open shot at the city."

"They also want you dead, Devi." Nikolas scowled.

"There is that. But if we prove the inspector's evil..." I trailed off. No camera could capture a person's aura. We'd need a face-to-face confrontation to stand a chance of convincing them that they followed the orders of a traitor.

"They're not the type who'd take your word for it," Rachel said.

I bit my lip. "Let me think... Rachel, can I borrow your power again?"

"Oh, here we go." She rolled her eyes.

"I go in there as a regular celestial. Better—I find some of the ones who helped the vampires, and go in there as a team to talk to them. We work out a way of avoiding violence, gently break it to them that their boss is a murderer, and march on the celestial guild. If we take out the inspector, it'll slow the demons down, if nothing else."

"But what if they're under the arch-demon's control, too?"

"I don't think they are," I said. "They haven't taken the so-called cure. If they did, there's a good chance they'll die. Most don't survive, do they? So maybe… maybe the arch-demon wanted to keep them alive on purpose, with their magic intact."

"But the inspector isn't," Rachel said. "He's marked."

"That's the point I was making," I said. "Grade Four celestials can see auras. We need to *show* them, by taking them to the guild in person."

"They'll see you coming," Nikolas said. "Certainly with this arrest warrant out. And their portal might bring any manner of demons over to fight on their side."

"True." I paused. "Hang on a second. Do you still have that pentagram?"

"You mean, Zadok's?" Wariness flitted across his face. "Why?"

"The inspector is a demon by definition now," I said. "Might we theoretically use the pentagram to summon *him?* I know his name. That's all you need, right? We summon him directly to the celestials, and there's no way they'll be able to deny what he is."

Nikolas's mouth tightened. "Bringing that pentagram out risks the enemy getting hold of it again."

"The celestials already have their own active pentagram," I said. "The Grade Fours don't know what they're up against, and I doubt they'll agree to follow me over to the guild without a fuss. I could use demonglass to take them there myself, but I doubt I can carry all of them at once. Besides, they're likely to attack the second I show up, and if I leave a trail of bodies behind me, they won't care what I have to say. We need to back them into a corner the same way they did to me. Give them proof. If the inspector breaks out of the pentagram, well, there are a dozen Grade Four celestials whose powers are made to take out demons. Not to mention me."

Nikolas listened to my words in silence. Then he nodded slowly. "I may be able to doctor the pentagram so that it can only be used once," he said. "But it'll take several minutes, and it's risky using it either way."

"What—seriously? You can do that?"

"You forget my brother and myself came from the same place, as much as he'd like to believe he knows more than I do about the netherworld's workings." He smiled grimly. "I'm just a little more restrained in how I go about using that knowledge."

Two minutes later, we'd crowded into the living room again. Fiona and Rachel on the sofa, me in an armchair, and Nikolas kneeling over the pentagram, a book open at his side. I watched, oddly mesmerised by the swirling patterns inside the pentagram. And I had one eye on Fiona in case a certain demigod made a reappearance. *Hope he can't see every-thing we're doing.* It was too late to hide our plans, anyway. The inspector wouldn't be able to resist when I called him, demon mark or none.

Anticipation burned inside me. *You can't resist the demon's call.* The notion of using the arch-demons' own methods against them… I couldn't deny it was appealing. The inspector's whole game hinged on him being in control. Summoning him in front of his own army would remove that control and put him at the mercy of the people he'd ordered to torment vampires on command. As for them, having to kill their idol would be punishment enough.

If they all survived the conflict.

I, meanwhile, had a few potions to brew of my own. Aura vision, for a start. And a couple of minor traps in case my own allies attacked me. It seemed dangerously suicidal to think of the Grade Four celestials of anything other than a loose cannon, and heaven knew I wanted to put Farrell in his place—possibly with a full-body blister attack. But I wouldn't resort to outright attacking them until I had no choice. No matter how much demon power I had, a dozen high-ranked celestials could fry me. And if it turned out I *could* burn them with my divine fire, I'd be weakening our realm against the demons. Hell, the one who marked me might even have planned this. Ultimately, I'd be set against my own people. Win or lose, the demons would be the victors in the end. Unless I outsmarted and overtook them.

I downed the aura vision potion, concealed various traps on me, and met Rachel in the living room so she could transfer some of her power over to me. Then I turned to Fiona.

"Call Clover," I said to her. "I'll give you her number. She might not be able to stop the demon but she can at least stop you hurting anyone if you-know-who takes over again."

I think.

"That's not reassuring," she said. "If he takes over again—I shouldn't be anywhere near the battle. I don't want to hurt anyone."

And I don't want to accidentally kill you. Azurial… damn. I didn't know how to go about detaching someone's soul from a person, but I'd add that to the ever-expanding list of questions to ask when I finally got hold of someone who knew what the hell was going on.

"Are you sure the three of us will be enough?" asked Rachel. "If the best case scenario happens and the celestials take down the inspector, I'll bet there's someone else at the guild ready to act in his place."

"Damian," I said, nodding. "That's why I think we should head to the guild immediately afterwards. With an army."

She frowned. "Who?"

"The other celestials?" Nikolas asked.

"Yep," I said. "One of Javos's demonglass fragment collections is two roads down from the academy where the celestials are based now. I can walk there in person. They can't see my aura, so you guys don't have to be there. But if you can bring the minibus, we can take it straight to the Grade Fours. If I can't persuade anyone to come with me, at least I tried.'

"I don't like this," said Rachel. "We're exposing ourselves to people who might turn us in."

"That's why I'm going in alone," I said. "To the academy, anyway. I'm on their wanted list. I'll warn you if anything goes wrong, okay?"

Nikolas stood rigid, his jaw tightening. Then he drew me into his arms. My mouth parted in surprise beneath his, briefly, then he brushed his lips over mine and took a step back.

"We'll be there," he said, releasing me.

Rachel raised an eyebrow at us. "Yeah, we will. But if you two decide to screw one another on the bus, I'm driving."

Fiona choked on a laugh. I grinned at Nikolas, drew back, and leapt through the demonglass fragments. Despite the world-bending sensation, I managed to land on my feet this time, on the edge of the roof I'd nearly fallen off the first time. Inching towards the gutter, I climbed over and carefully lowered myself to the ground.

My boots pounded on the pavement, carrying me towards the academy. Before I reached the door, I activated Rachel's power and turned into Inspector Deacon.

"Hey!" I shouted. "Let me in, immediately."

"Inspector!" said an alarmed-sounding voice on the other side. "Come in right away. It's him!"

The doors opened. I slipped inside, and then switched on the miniature sleeping potion I'd brought. The security guard slumped in a heap without a word. Then I channelled Rachel's magic and transformed back into Devi. Much better. I was running a risk coming here as me, but hopefully enough of them had been keeping up with DivinityWatch that they'd believe my story. And if not, I'd deal with the Grade Fours one way or another.

Thumping footsteps drew me into the main corridor, where all the celestials were in the middle of running into the hall. Like novices assembling for a surprise announcement. Old habits died hard. They didn't even notice me until I slipped into the hall ahead of them.

"It's her—Devi!" someone shouted.

"What the hell?"

"She sneaked in?"

"Hey!" I waved my hands to capture their attention. "I need to talk to you and it was the quickest way in."

"You used demon magic," said one of them accusingly.

"Listen," I said. "The Grade Four celestial soldiers are planning to ambush a bunch of innocent warlocks with the intention of blaming them for the events of the last week. But those orders didn't come from Inspector Deacon. An arch-demon has marked him. The people you're taking orders from are no longer trying to win the war against demons. They're trying to ignite a war of their own in which nobody will come out alive."

Shouts and accusations rang out. I let them all wash over me. I hadn't come here to be praised or exalted. I'd come here to find an army.

"You're talking nonsense," said a novice. "The inspector can't be a demon."

"And you've seen him recently? You've seen proof he's repaired the damage to the west tower and closed the demon portal?"

I held up my phone and showed a photograph someone had uploaded online of the celestial guild from the back. The ruin of the tower reflected light that plainly wasn't from a celestial. Whoever posted on DivinityWatch was thorough, I'd give them that.

"Why leave the portal open if they're not working with the netherworld?" I asked of the stunned crowd. "Have any of you even been back there since the battle? Of course, I guess the inspector asked you not to. You'd have seen the truth pretty quickly if you'd disobeyed."

"Of course they have netherworld allies," said the same novice as before. "That's their job. Spy on what's happening over there. The portal's controlled, right? Nothing can get out."

"It will," I said. "And it already did. There's an arch-demon in this city, and I think you know there's been something wrong at the guild ever since Damian Greenwood blew up the tower. There's a portal in there, and it's a direct link into the demon realms for the purpose of aiding them in their quest to take this realm."

"Damian?" asked a couple of voices.

"Yeah, he faked being a victim so nobody would notice his demon aura," I said. "Then he came back from the dead— possibly—and tricked the inspector into letting hell put a mark on him."

Sceptical expressions mingled with shock and horror.

"You've been there." A shout rang clearly. "You've been into a demon realm yourself."

"Obviously." Impatience burned within me. "Look, you can choose whether to follow me or not, but I'm about to prove to the Grade Four celestials that the inspector is really a demon. If you want to come with me to see the fallout of *that,* not to mention help me fight whatever's behind that portal, then come with us. I get the impression some of you are getting bored with being shoved aside. They're not telling you a thing."

"You're luring us to our deaths," said an accusing tone.

"I can't deny there might be fighting," I said. "I don't know how many Grade Fours might have been compromised, either. But if we stop them attacking the warlocks, we stop a war. How is this any different to stopping them from massacring innocent vampires?"

Some people amongst this crowd had helped save them at the risk of their own safety. I saw a couple of subtle looks exchanged. They weren't all blindly following orders. They had their own agenda, too. The inspector hadn't taken away their free will.

"Okay," I said. "Tell you what, imagine nobody was giving you orders. What choice would you make then?"

"Warlocks are higher levelled than most of us," said the male celestial at the front. "And even if they weren't, the Grade Fours—they could execute us."

"What if I said I can stop them? I can hand over damning evidence that proves their boss isn't what he seems. But remember—you're likely to have to fight some of your former allies when this comes out. Fair warning. If you want to fight them now, come with me."

I stepped down off the stage and left the hall. Footsteps came from behind me as two celestials I knew from my own year group followed. Then others. By the time I reached the reception area, a good fifteen celestials stood behind me.

I didn't blame the others for staying. If the Grade Fours *were* compromised, the only people with the strength to fight them were other Grade Four celestials. Or warlocks, technically. But there weren't a huge amount of arch-demons' children. The Grade Fours… they could easily put the city under siege without the need for demonic involvement. And while nobody *liked* Inspector Deacon, the notion of the demons infiltrating our highest order undermined everything we'd been taught to believe.

I just had to hope that the group of us would be enough to make the Grade Fours pause and listen before attacking—

and that they'd leap on the most likely target when I called the inspector.

I stopped outside, seeing the minibus approaching. "That's our van."

"There's a warlock driving!" someone shouted.

"They're our allies," I hissed. "If you have an issue with that, go inside, but don't draw attention."

"You've been hiding out with him?" a celestial asked accusingly.

"Clearly, we're not hiding," I said. "That's Rachel."

"I saw her bite someone's neck, but she didn't look like that."

"Look, are you going to get in the bloody bus or not?"

This was why I hated supervising novices. But despite their grumblings, apparently the desire to see me summon the inspector won out. At least we hadn't brought the vampires, though now the sun was setting, they'd be waking up soon.

We drove for a short while, halting outside the hotel whose address Rachel had found. Apparently the Grade Fours were living it up in luxury. Only the best for the guild's elite soldiers. Glass windows reflected the fountains splashing in front, while expensive cars were parked nearby.

I picked up the pentagram, nodded to Nikolas, and led the way to the doors.

Farrell was the one to meet me. Because of course he was. Several others followed behind him. I scanned them, using my aura vision to search for any demonic taint. All their auras were pure white. As though the Divinities themselves stood before me. *What a lie.*

"So you've come to hand yourself in here instead of at the guild?" Farrell asked loudly.

"Nope," I said. "I have someone else who you might like to meet, though."

"The warlock." His lip curled. "You both deserve to be arrested for giving us the slip."

"Thought it was for hiding illegal vampires. I'm losing track of all my supposed crimes, to be honest."

"You never did have any respect for authority."

"Authority never did have any respect for me." I pulled out the pentagram. "And we're here to prove to you that the person whose orders you're following is a demon in disguise. Did you ever stop to question why the inspector never ordered you back to the guild, or fixed the damage to the tower? There's an open, active portal right there, and an arch-demon got through it."

"What are you babbling about?" He reached out a hand for the pentagram and I threw it at his feet.

I looked up at him. "I summon you, Inspector Deacon."

16

For a moment, everyone stared at the pentagram. It flickered with fiery light, perhaps confused by the command to summon someone within this dimension. Nikolas had bound it so that nothing in any other realm could be summoned that way.

I really hoped it worked.

Light gleamed, reflected in the glass. Then he appeared, wreathed in fire and shadow, a hulking figure materialising in the middle of the pentagram. His aura swam with darkness, masking the light entirely.

"What is the meaning of this?" he shouted.

Go on. Show them who you really are. "Just thought I'd demonstrate why you're no longer fit to lead the celestial soldiers. They can see your aura, Deacon. And it's dark as the deepest shadows of hell."

The inspector shrugged, stepping out of the pentagram so there was no mistaking the dark aura swirling around him. Not like shadows, more like blotted ink clinging to his body. Then he waved a hand, and all the Grade Four celestials turned to me instead. "Look at her aura!" one of them shouted.

Oh hell. "Maybe look at him first? He's the one whose orders you've been following for—"

One of the soldiers ran to me, conjuring his celestial blade. I reached for my own by instinct, raising it to deflect his. If I used my demonic power, I'd win—but the other dozen Grade Fours would smite me on the spot. I didn't want to find out if twelve handfuls of celestial light were enough to dissolve me like a regular demon—and more to the point, the inspector had begun to run away.

Nikolas got there first. Demonic lightning sparked from his hands, blocking his path. But no celestials moved to his side to help. *You bastards.*

I pushed against the celestial soldier's blade, his light swamping mine. When a celestial soldier ascended to Grade Four, they gained abilities beyond the rest of us. I might have been close to that level myself once, but I hadn't gone through the final stage of the process. For all the divine magic I possessed, it was still one grade below them.

"Attack *him*," I snapped. "For the Divinity's sake, don't tell me you don't even know the basic rules. You can summon any demon by calling their name. That's exactly what I just did."

"Might the demon have assumed his name and form for their own purposes?" asked another of the celestials. "That's what they do."

Damn. Of course. I should have figured they'd come up with a reasonable explanation. Anything to avoid facing the truth.

I grabbed a smoke bomb spell and threw it into the air. Fog descended in a cloud and I ran past the celestial, aiming for the inspector. Nikolas's lightning had slowed him, but not enough. He reached me first, tackling me to the ground. Muscular arms pinned me down, cutting off sensation in my limbs. I brought my knee up into his groin and he snarled, moving enough for me to shove him off me. Light spun from my hand and I blasted him with it. He barely staggered.

If he wouldn't expose his demon power, I'd drain it out of him.

My demon mark glowed, and I willed his power to rush towards me the same way I'd done to the others. But no answering tingle came from my demon mark, nor any flood of magic.

What? Can I not take his power?

The celestials surrounded Nikolas and Rachel. My heart sank. Even our allies weren't enough to stop the Grade Fours. I'd been so sure they'd accept the evidence before them, however loyal they were. It was like my words meant nothing.

Celestial light blazed from my hand, and demonic power surged from my right. Screw being careful. I was a wanted woman one way or another, so the best I could do was use the power I had to bring the enemy down with me.

The inspector laughed and... changed. He shrank to child-sized, then grew, turning into... Javos.

He was a shapechanger? That was his power? No wonder it wouldn't work for me.

Two could play at that game.

I transformed into Rachel, using my smaller form to wriggle out from underneath him. Then I brought out my blade again. He dodged, smirking. Damn. I'd never faced a full-grown shapeshifter before—the super-powered version of Rachel. The demon mark was just a ploy. He must have come through the portal in person and taken the inspector's place.

"Take on your true form, demon," I growled.

My hands glowed, one white, one red. I brought them together in a clash of power which sent him staggering back. He screamed, the flesh burning off his bones. Divine light consumed him, turning his body to ashes.

And a dozen celestial blades pointed at me.

I raised my hands slowly. "Whether he was actually the inspector or not, he's the one whose orders you've been taking. The warlocks are innocent, and so are most of the bite victims you were sent to slaughter. If you really want to do your divine duty to protect this realm, then come to the celestial guild and get rid of the portal this madman opened."

None of them moved. "Come with us, Devina," Farrell finally said. "If you use that power again, you're dead."

His voice wavered. I'd never seen him afraid of anything. But they were all scared of my power. Divine and infernal fire. Even Grade Fours would never have seen anything like it before. And their instinct would be to destroy what they didn't understand, just like the inspector.

"Come on, Devina," said Farrell.

"Good luck running a trial when your master's dead," I said to them.

"Luckily, we have the authority to do that ourselves," said Farrell. "It'll be quick. You want to protect your warlock friends… then it's your own life which will be put on trial."

Light shone around him, reflecting in his eyes. He was anticipating the moment he got to stab me and burn out my soul.

So that's how he wanted to play.

Drawing on Rachel's magic, I transformed into Farrell.

He blinked and stared for a moment, and that was all I needed. I spun around and pelted for the bus. The others were quick on the uptake. Nikolas had already snatched up the pentagram and taken it with him, while the other celestials still sat in the back. I dove through the open door, Rachel close behind, and Nikolas put his foot on the pedal.

"The guild?" Nikolas asked, as we picked up speed.

I grabbed the back of the nearest seat for balance. "You've got it. Time to shut down the portal before another inspector clone comes through."

"That type of demon is rare," Rachel said. "It must have come here alone, but I don't see how it's possible."

"What, you mean shape-shifting demons?" Rachel herself was one. But there was little information on her demon magic in the guild's files, and I couldn't load them on my phone while hanging on for dear life as Nikolas drove. Several crashing noises and yelps from behind told me the celestials were having difficulty keeping their balance, too

"Zarth demons," Nikolas said over the roar of the engine. "Very rare. They're generally under direct control of their master—an arch-demon."

"So he really wasn't the inspector." I winced as tree branches scraped against the bus's side with a deafening sound. "He was a demon the whole time. They must have made the switch while the guild's defences were down.'

"The good news is that I know which arch-demon it is now," he said. "There are very few shapeshifter demons with those capabilities."

"Who?" I asked. "You know what, tell me later. We need to figure out what the hell to do with the guild first. Their leader's dead, and the only other people qualified to take over are following us with deadly weapons. Told you the inspector wasn't the worst of it."

"Let's get that portal shut down first," Nikolas said.

"That was the plan. I'm not cleaning up the guild's mess, and I'll be lucky to get out of this alive, let alone without making enemies of the rest of them."

Unless everyone who thought I was an evil demon was

killed in the conflict, there was no way the guild could continue the way it was after this. There were too many conflicts and divisions, and I'd hate it if the upper levels punished the celestials who'd agreed to fight with me. But all of that could wait. I needed to find out how many people had been replaced with demons. Even Damian Greenwood—he'd lied about fooling the inspector. Maybe he wasn't human at all.

Nikolas parked down the road from the guild, and I turned to speak to the celestials in the back.

"The celestials in the infirmary are totally gone—they're infected with the demon virus," I told them. "They'll attack you if they see you. What we need to do is shut down the pentagram in the west tower, but I don't know if Damian's anticipated us coming and planned an ambush. Either way, don't go near it if you aren't prepared to fight demons of Grade Three or higher."

Shapeshifter demons were Grade Three, for sure. But if an arch-demon got through... *it can't. No portal is that strong, not even the guild's.*

Light shone over the brick walls and sloping roofs. Not natural light. The portal must be active. They knew, all right.

I approached the guild from the front. Several windows were broken, and a horrific noise came from inside, like crumpling metal and plaster. Glass shattered, and a gigantic tail lashed out, missing us by inches. I pulled out my sword and swung it, but the giant demon's thick armour deflected the blade as though it was a rolled-up newspaper. Bristled spines prickled all over its hard skin, and its huge maw contained rings of serrated teeth.

The Mother. The inspector had left a friend behind.

Rachel froze next to me. The Mother's body had crushed part of the roof, next to the place where the comatose celestials had been held. Crap.

The giant worm wrapped around the roof, half-buried in the collapsed building. Beyond it, hisses and snarls came from other demons spread throughout the guild. There might be people alive in there. *We have to kill that thing.*

Lightning fired from Nikolas's palms, bouncing off the beast's spiked armour. Footsteps came from behind, and to my surprise, several celestials ran from the bus to confront the smaller demons crawling from the guild's ruins. Despite their obvious fear, their calling was to kill demons, and a whole bunch of them had trampled on our turf.

Divine light sizzled from my palm and bounced off the giant worm's armour. To do any damage, I needed to get at its vulnerable head. Problem: the top of its skull was covered in spikes, and snapping rows of teeth blocked my path every time I took a swipe. I ducked and swept low, willing my demon mark to activate. Fiery light poured from my right hand, hitting the already shattered window instead.

The Mother writhed, her tail slapping down. I took the blow on my sword's edge, staggering back a few steps. A human-sized figure crawled from the building's ruins, straightening upright.

"Grace!" shouted one of the celestials. "You're alive!"

"Don't," I warned, too late. The girl turned on him, dark eyes gleaming, and ran at us with a vampire's speed. Her aura wasn't white, but greyish-black. I raised my sword, fending her off, but just going near my blade made her skin smoke like a demon's did. No humanity shone from her gaze at all. She was gone—entirely demon.

My blade sank into her chest, and she slumped down.

You'll pay for this, demons. The blade burned out anyone with the demon's mark, and if I had to destroy my former allies to stop the virus infecting anyone else, so be it. Every time the other celestials hesitated, it cost them. I had to end this.

"Fight me," I growled at the Mother.

I had no reason to fear her barbed touch like the others did. I slammed my two marks together, and let them burn.

17

Celestial and hellfire clashed between my hands, sending a torrent of white-hot flames towards the giant worm. At the last second, the worm thrashed out of reach, and my attack slammed into the building instead. *And I'd thought carving my name into the wall in the quadrangle was bad enough.* I'd fantasised about burning the place to the ground so many times, but felt no triumph to see the guild consumed in an inferno. From the state of the place, there was no way anyone was left alive inside it. Who knew how many the demons had killed.

Energy crackled overhead, turning the sky neon orange. No way would the humans not notice. Innocent people would get caught up in this if we didn't shut down the portal.

I caught Nikolas's eye, and he nodded. He understood my plan. Shadows cloaked his body, reforming into shadowy wings, and he flew at the worm. Its head reared, snapping at him, taking its attention off me. Its dark red aura pulsed, indicating it was definitely gaining some kind of power from the portal. *Then I'll destroy it.*

I ran for the wrecked building, skirting the edges.

Vaulting heaps of rubble, I kept my gaze on the blazing light behind the ruins, sword high and demon mark at the ready.

A person stumbled onto the bloodied floor of the former quadrangle.

"Get out!" yelled Sammy. "Stop terrorising us and get out."

"*Me?* Not the giant worm?" I waved over my shoulder, hoping the others were holding it off. The portal was barely ten metres away, for crying out loud. "Maybe let me destroy the giant blazing portal behind you before you accuse me of anything? Get out of the way."

Unbelievable. I'd bet he'd believed his inspector was innocent up until the end.

"I won't," he said. "You're disobeying the law."

"Fine. Come and see the demons with me, and I hope one of them eats you."

I took one step, and he moved to block the way. He smiled a familiar smile, his face changing, warping before my eyes. It was the same demon who'd posed as the inspector. It must have regenerated into a new body. That, or it had a sibling. Crap.

The worm screamed and thrashed behind me. It sounded like the others were giving as good as they got, yet it refused to die. As long as I didn't shut down that damned portal, it wouldn't.

Hellfire and celestial flames danced across my palms, colliding in front of him. He laughed, and I think he said, "You're wasting your time, celestial," but his words were lost in the crackle of flames as he turned into ashes.

I climbed over piles of debris, approaching the blaze of light. My demon mark itched, drawn to the dimension beyond. The tower door hung from its hinges, and I ran towards it.

A demon leaped from the portal, colliding with my celestial blade. Holding it one-handed, I continued to walk. The roar of flames became louder the closer I got, pushing against me with the force of a strong breeze. Unlike home-made portals, the pentagram needed no bloodstones to fuel its power. It'd keep burning until I switched it off. Sammy had been a decoy. Worse would await me inside that tower.

Power boiled from the pentagram, making my teeth chatter. So much... crackling in my demon mark and raising every hair on my body. Fire demanded to leap into my hands, but unleashing that sort of power would only make the portal more powerful. *Focus, Devi. One foot in front of the other...*

A head poked out of the pentagram. Lava-coloured and covered in spines, it spat venom at me. I recoiled, grimacing when it splashed on my shoes, but kept walking. Swinging my celestial blade, I decapitated the beast mid-jump. *Whatever you throw at me, I'll kill it.* I knew who waited behind the pentagram before he appeared, smiling the way he had before. Not a friendly smile. More like the look of a demon before it tore up its prey.

"Hello, Devi," Damian purred, positioning himself in front of the pentagram. "Wouldn't you like to give me a taste of that remarkable magic of yours?"

No. He was trying to lure me into using my power on the pentagram, to make it even stronger.

Rather than using my celestial blade, I drew a stake and threw it at him. He raised his arms and blocked, the weapon clattering to the floor. I squinted at him. Though the pentagram's roar drowned out any other noise, he wore a plain leather jacket. The stake shouldn't have bounced off like I'd thrown it at the armoured worm.

He's using magic. I'd known he wasn't Damian—hell, maybe Damian himself had been replaced a while back. Like the inspector, he was an impostor. But what level of demon might he be? The beast thrashing in the building's wreckage was Grade Four—miles above all our levels. The inspector, maybe Grade Three. He had a weakness somewhere, but my priority was switching off that pentagram.

Drawing another stake, I feinted, then hurled it at his neck. Again, it bounced off an invisible shield. The same noise had come from the Mother when I'd tried to hit her. Might *she* be a fake, too? If there were no limits on what shapeshifter demons could turn into, anything was possible. But... that meant the portal was fuelling *his* power, too.

Fire swirled behind him. Definitely Pandemonium. *Think, Devi.* In my demon mark, I carried Rachel's magic as well as the fire, not to mention Nikolas's lightning power. Shadow magic wasn't from that realm, so it wouldn't give the portal more fuel. And I'd seen Nikolas knock doors down and blast holes in walls with that power.

Dark-edged lightning exploded from my right palm, over Damian's shoulder. He grinned, not realising I'd missed on purpose. For all its power, the portal wasn't nailed down. It was attached to the pentagram, and I already knew how to turn it off. I just needed to access the switch.

A second palm of lightning sizzled from my fingertips, through the tower door, aiming at the floor. The pentagram shifted, momentarily lifted off the ground, and the fiery inferno tipped over, warping the tower around it.

"You can't break it, Devi. This is only the beginning." His voice boomed, slipping into Higher Chthonic. The demon language of Pandemonium.

"Who the hell even are you?"

I aimed the lightning at Damian himself this time, drawing a knife. *Shielding is one of his powers.* But it wasn't a primary demon ability. Neither was shapeshifting. He must be...

A demigod.

I leapt, lightning surging from my hand in twin streams. One bounced off his armour. The second collided with the pentagram's side, sending it crashing into the tower's wall. If I'd aimed right, it should have hit the switch.

The fire disappeared, going out. Damian made to run towards it, but I jumped, kicking him in the face with Rachel's boots. The momentum sent us both crashing to the ground, but he transformed first, turning into Rachel. I pinned the fake Rachel beneath my knees, and he turned into Damian again. Blood trickled from the corner of his mouth.

"So who's your arch-demon parent?" I asked, holding the knife to his neck.

He laughed. "One who cannot die. I am dust and ashes, and I cannot be destroyed."

"We'll see." I cut his throat. Invincible or not, the blade sliced through flesh easily enough.

His body dissolved beneath me. I waited, knife in hand, but he didn't reappear.

This isn't over. I'd killed the inspector, but he might even have been the same demon. For some reason, killing him— even reducing his body to ashes—didn't destroy him the way it did to other demons.

But the portal was gone. I walked to the tower door, reached inside, and picked up the gold-edged pentagram. Fire tingled along my palms, but no inferno appeared. I wasn't sure I could even destroy it with my magic without opening it again. I'd just be providing another source of fuel for its power.

There was a deafening crash, vibrating through the floor. Dust flew over my head and I whirled around. Nikolas's winged form brought the giant worm's body crashing to Earth with another tremendous thud. Shards of lightning whirled around his hands, piercing the worm's armour.

Horrible screaming noises gurgled from its throat. Then...
silence.

I turned my back on the ruins of the tower and
approached Nikolas. His wings remained out, dark and shadowy. Thick demon blood stained his arms to the elbows, and
he was bleeding from cuts which had presumably come from
the monster's spiked armour or teeth.

"It's not dead," I said. "The pentagram might be, but the
portal isn't. It's still active on the other side. In
Pandemonium."

"I suspected so," he said. "But I've never seen one like that
before. Portals are usually static. If I had to guess, a force on
the other side was constantly pumping power into it. That's
an incredibly dangerous thing to do. If there's not an equal
force on either side, it can cause ruptures in the weaker
realm."

"Meaning this one," I said. "Shit. I wasn't too late, was I?
What sort of side effects are we talking about?"

"Dimensional rifts opening and spitting demons out,
higher levels of demons coming through weaker portals...
that sort of thing." He eyed the pentagram in my hands. "Not
ideal, but survivable."

"Assuming the celestials rebuild," I said. "It's a global
collective, but if there's that level of corruption elsewhere...
not to mention the ones who helped me will have to explain
this crap to the celestials' council. Because I sure as hell
can't." The celestials' leaders generally had the same ability to
see auras as the Grade Fours. As much as they needed to
rebuild, as much as this realm desperately needed the celestial army to survive... I couldn't be a part of it. Not as long as
I was marked.

"The Grade Fours haven't caught up yet," he said. "There's
nobody else living in this building. Either the demons drove
them out or they killed them."

I shook ashes from the pentagram. "Where's Rachel?"

The celestials who'd fought alongside us stood in a huddled group, but there was no sign of Rachel.

"She went to scout for survivors." He jerked his head in the direction of the east wing, which was mostly intact. The front of the building had taken most of the hit. "Like the real inspector."

"There's no way he survived," I said. If I was a demon, I'd have finished the job, anyway.

A celestial from the group at the academy tentatively approached us. Sandra Yun, who'd survived more than one assault at the demons' hands, not to mention losing her partner a few weeks ago.

"Hey," she said. "Devi… is the portal closed? Is it where that *thing* came from?"

I nodded. "Yeah. Damian, too. He was a demon in disguise. And the inspector. I don't know where the real guy is, but I think you're going to have to nominate a new leader until backup from outside the city arrives."

Before the Grade Fours take power.

I didn't know if she heard my unspoken words, but she dipped her head. "I know. There might be one or two… it's just so confusing." Her gaze passed over the dead bodies of the vampire celestials, her former comrades. "Were they under mind control?"

"Sort of," I said. "The parasite—that was its final form. They lost their minds to the virus. There's—there's no cure." My throat closed up. "I'm sorry."

"Who did this?" she asked quietly.

"An arch-demon," I said. "I can't say I know which. Or where it came from."

"Hey!" Rachel waved at us, crossing the bloodstained pavement from the wrecked building. "No more demons in there. But I'd shut down that pentagram, permanently."

"That was the plan." I looked at Nikolas, then at the celestials. They not-so-subtly moved away from Rachel, possibly because she had her extra set of teeth out. Like a pink-haired girl with an unhinged jaw dripping blood everywhere was the weirdest sight they'd ever seen.

"And us?" asked Sandra. "We can fight if called for, but since we don't even know who the enemy is…"

"Normally I'd say they won't attack the guild again," I said, "but the source on the other side of the portal is still active. So if they try to get through again, they might use the same route. Because this part of our realm is weaker. The guild's headquarters directly overlaps with the place they keep making portals."

"How… how do you know that?"

Nikolas stepped in. "We shouldn't linger here," he said.

Ashes blew away on the breeze. The giant worm was beginning to disintegrate, as demons usually did when killed in this realm. I pulled out my phone and snapped a photo of it, for all the good that did.

"Proof," I said. "Not that the Grade Fours will accept it, but someone needs to see what happened here."

"I agree," said a male celestial with dark skin and dreadlocks. "But—all we have is half an explanation. They're saying you've fought demigods and met—Inspector Angler? The guy who died four years ago?"

"Later," Nikolas said. "I'll drive you back to the academy, on the condition that if the Grade Four celestials or anyone else asks how the guild ended up being destroyed, you tell them the truth—about the demon and the portal."

"Who *are* you?" asked the dreadlocked celestial, as though he couldn't help himself. Even with his wings gone, it was plain as day that Nikolas was unlike any warlock the celestials had ever encountered before. It wasn't like they generally hung out at places like the Harpy's Nest.

"Nikolas Castor. Warlock," was all he said.

"I take it you believe me about the guild now?" I added.

Several nods followed.

The drive back passed much smoother than our hair-raising arrival. As much as I wanted to ask Nikolas if he had any clue who the arch-demon was, I took the opportunity to give a proper account of recent events to the celestials instead. I didn't know how much they took in—some were in shock, others in flat-out denial. But when we dropped them off at the academy, subdued and covered in blood, some of them even thanked me.

Another quick drive found us back at Nikolas's house. My chest tightened as I looked up at the full moon, an echo of the one in Babylon. Orange streaks tinged the sky from the site of our battle, but no other signs of it remained. For now.

Nikolas unlocked the front door and led us inside.

"Devi," said Fiona, who waited in the living room. "I saw the fire. Are you okay?"

I flopped onto the sofa. "There's a lot of celestials who are much less okay than I am. I'll live."

Nikolas came in, with Rachel behind him. "How are the vamps?" asked Rachel.

"They keep coming down and asking questions," Fiona said. "Like if I'd let them bite me, for instance. I told them I was possessed by an evil fire demon who'd burn their faces off."

"Good," I said. "I forgot about them, to be honest. They're probably on the verge of being blood crazed. I don't know about you, but I'm not volunteering to donate."

"Don't worry," said Nikolas. "I have genuine bloodstones somewhere here. I can't say I know if Madame White will show up here tomorrow morning, but it'll keep them quiet until then."

"Shit," I said. "I forgot about her, too."

"So how'd it go with the Grade Fours?" Fiona asked.

"Badly." I gave a brief rundown. "So the Grade Fours think we set them up," I finished. "Because they wouldn't believe the inspector's a demon."

"They were listening to propaganda for years," said Nikolas. "You didn't find the real inspector. He might still be alive."

"Not much chance of that," I said. "If so, he's probably in Pandemonium."

"So who *was* the fake one?" asked Fiona.

Everyone looked at Nikolas. He picked up the book he'd been reading before, flipping it open. "Once I heard it confirmed we were dealing with shapeshifters, I knew who was behind this."

I raised an eyebrow. "Want to give me a clue?"

He turned the book's page. "The arch-demon's name is Abyss. She's a shapeshifter, but her own true form is too powerful to hide. So she uses proxies to infiltrate places. Governments, whatever. On demon realms and otherwise. She's vicious and cunning. She's brought down several realms without lifting a finger herself, sending in her own people instead."

"Shapeshifters," I said. "There's something I don't get about the whole thing. The act was so convincing. He *was* the inspector. An arch-demon who's never been to this realm wouldn't have had time to learn everything about him, even with Damian passing on information."

"That's their power," he said. "They're also not simply shapeshifters. They take in the memories of the people they imitate, and actually take on their characteristics. That's what makes them so convincing."

Damn. "Then why did Damian lie and say he was raised from the dead? To throw us off her trace?"

"Yes, I suspect so," he said. "We were never supposed to figure out it was her. She thrives on chaos, and her actions have stirred everyone up in this city. She likes destroying things, but has no interest in ruling."

I frowned. "Then what's the point in this setup? To screw with us?"

"Essentially. She's ancient, and arch-demons have a tendency to get bored easily. But I can't say I know what turned her onto our realm in the first place. The vampires' former leader had his own grievances with Haven City, and perhaps it struck her as an easy target."

"Not on my watch," I muttered. "Great. So we know who she is, and possibly where she is… You said she sends in her minions rather than coming in person. So might she not be in Pandemonium at all?

"Her goal is to watch the destruction from a distance, usually," Nikolas said. "I can't say I ever had the pleasure of meeting her in person. However, the portal has closed. The problem, of course, is that I don't know exactly how the shapeshifters revive themselves, or how they choose who to imitate. Their regenerative magic doesn't work the same as ours does."

"Damian said he was… ashes. Like he can be reborn that way. So he might still be here?"

"Possibly, but I doubt it. She has no shortage of servants."

"Great," I said. "How are we supposed to track her down? How *do* you find an arch-demon?"

"Inside their own realm?" Fiona suggested. "Like—like the one who marked you? He must know about this, whoever he is."

"I don't even know if the realm where he marked me is actually his," I said. "I never even figured out which realm it is. They all look the same."

"Bringing another arch-demon into this conflict wouldn't

be a wise move," Nikolas said. "It's not possible to track one down, anyway. Not if they don't want to be found."

Zadok had said… if the demon called my name, I'd have to go there. I wouldn't be allowed to resist. Finding the demon on my own was all but impossible.

But giving up wasn't an option. And who knew, maybe the arch-demon had no intention of calling me at all. Maybe I had to find him first.

Exhaustion seeped into my bones. I looked up at Fiona, wishing I could rip the demon out of her head and rid her of his awful presence.

"I didn't ask for this," I said quietly. "I've literally no freaking clue if I'm supposed to fight for heaven or hell, but it seems the people I care about suffer no matter which I choose. I win the war, and we get locked up for life. I lose, and this world is destroyed. Who in the netherworld volunteered *me* for the job? I want to resign."

"You and me both," said Fiona. "I don't know what that creature will make me do next."

"I know it's worse for you. I'm sorry."

I was scared—terrified—that the dark Divinity would turn me on my friends and force me to fight on the enemy's side. Fiona was braver than me for confronting those fears directly rather than hoping to get through the confrontation without having my mind manipulated by a demon. Even a former Divinity. It raised me from the dead. Maybe it could bury me as easily. But I owed it to the others to try.

"I'm going to bed," Rachel announced. "Wake me up if the vampire queen knocks on the door."

"That reminds me," Nikolas said. "I need to reset our defences."

Once they'd both left, Fiona turned to me.

"I never asked… are you and Nikolas definitely a thing? If I'm going down in flames, I deserve to know that, at least."

"I think we are," I said. "Honestly? I didn't think that far ahead. Kind of stuck on the war, to be honest."

But I'd moved on from Rory. I wanted Nikolas, and not just because my demon mark was drawn to him. He was magnetic, yes, but he'd also saved me in ways I'd never expected. And if one thing in my life came without complications—aside from Babylon, that is—I was glad it was him.

I slipped outside after him. The warlock district usually wasn't quiet at night, but the only sound came from the front lawn, where the celestial guild's pentagram was hooked up to what looked like—explosives?

"You're blowing up the pentagram?"

"Just taking it out of commission." He circled it, sprinkled some powder onto the edges, and snapped his fingers. Lightning sparked, and the pentagram turned black around the edges, its golden sheen dulling to grey.

"The guild will arrest you for damaging a priceless artefact if we survive this."

He shot me a grin. "It originally belonged to a warlock, actually. Nobody alive now… it's been decades since its creation. But I'm disabling it so it only works on a Grade One level if at all. It's too dangerous to risk the guild getting hold of it again. I know it won't stop them making another portal, but…"

"We have to do something." I moved to his side. "I know. I feel pretty helpless, to be honest."

"I wish I knew more," he murmured. "I wish I could lie to you and tell you I know a way to win this."

He stepped back from the pentagram. My gaze followed the movement in the dark—the shadow of wings extending from his broad shoulders, the curve of his neck, the golden tint to his eyes even when I couldn't see his aura. Maybe I'd always been destined to fall, when I saw beauty in chaos. Even in the demon dimensions.

I inched closer to him. "Thanks for coming with me to find the celestials. Even considering everything that's happened."

"Not at all." He took my hand. "I had to check you weren't wearing your trap."

"I can't promise I won't forget to take it off one day and accidentally use it on you."

His answering laugh sent warm shivers down my back. "I'm much too careful for that," he said, drawing me into him, kissing me long and deep. I grabbed a fistful of his shirt and pulled him closer, as though by holding on tight enough, I could keep the world from spinning out of control. The taste of him exploded against my tongue, his brimstone scent awakening all my senses. Hot desire filled my blood with every stroke of his tongue over mine, every touch of his hands on my bare skin. Moonlight reflected in his golden eyes.

"All I want now is you," he murmured. "Deal?"

"You bet." I wrapped my arms around him again, seeking comfort in his touch, knowing it wouldn't be nearly enough. One night wasn't enough.

One night was all we had until the vamps came to kill everyone here.

Possibly less time than that until Armageddon. So you'd better believe I'd make the most of tonight.

18

Nikolas wasn't there when I woke. The bed was cold, and the covers had fallen onto the floor. Gathering them, I went in search of my clothes. Not a sound came from the rest of the house. Since the sun was up, the vampires would be asleep. Doubtless Madame White would send a contingent later to ruin our day, but where in hell had Nikolas gone? *If he's gone to Pandemonium alone, I'll kill him.*

I strapped on my last dagger and left the room.

"Hey, Devi," said Rachel, peering around her bedroom door. "You're up early."

"Nikolas has gone," I said. "Have you seen him?"

Her brow furrowed. "No. Maybe he went to warn Javos. He was concerned about warning the other warlocks about the shapeshifters."

"Shit," I said. "Yeah. I know. Who else might they have been imitating? They do such a convincing job, you wouldn't know they were fake."

"Exactly." She shivered. "But I wouldn't have thought he'd

just—leave. Unless he was more concerned with the vampires."

Dammit. "Tell me he didn't go to confront her alone."

"I wouldn't have thought so." A note of doubt entered her voice, and my mind. Maybe he would. Last night... had he thought we were saying goodbye?

"It's okay. He's probably in the shadow realm. Wouldn't be the first time."

"No, but that place isn't exactly the safest. What if that portal came back? We never did find out who did it."

"Zadok?" she asked. "Or—maybe one of them was an impostor, too. Anyone might have been."

"Not a comforting thought." I dragged a hand through my hair, fear slicing through me. Anyone might be replaced. We hadn't been nearly careful enough.

A whistling noise came from behind the closed bedroom door opposite. Fiona's room.

I looked at her. "She didn't turn again last night—right?" Maybe we should have locked the door or set up more precautions. But with Nikolas's ability to sense demonic magic, he should have picked up on it if she'd woken up as Azurial. And I was a light enough sleeper that I'd have woken, too.

"I don't think so," Rachel said. "Niko would know."

"Fiona?" I knocked on the door. No response came. Then I knocked again. The door opened a little. Not locked. Tension gripping my spine, I pushed it fully open.

She wasn't there. But a pentagram lay sketched on the floor, its edges charred to ashes. In the middle was—

"The demonglass from downstairs. Azurial stole it."

How had I slept through that? More to the point, Nikolas was usually careful about putting things away. The guild's pentagram was no more. But there must have been enough demonglass fragments left on the floor for Azurial to scrape together a portal, using Fiona.

My demon mark burned insistently, angrily. "They took her. But Nikolas… fuck."

I ran from the room, taking the stairs two at a time, and careened into the living room. No signs of Nikolas, or Fiona.

"Where the hell is that demonglass?" I ran to the shelf, finding the jar intact. And protected by a spell, to stop Azurial getting his hands on it. He must have dug right into the carpet to find every missing fragment he could. *Dammit.* It wasn't like any of us had thought to clean up the floor, considering everything else we'd had to deal with yesterday.

Grabbing the jar, I threw its contents down on the living room floor. Then I picked up a handful and shoved them into my pocket, just in case.

"Wait!" said Rachel. "Who's going to watch the vampires?"

"No clue. Their door's locked. I can't leave Fiona. It's not like anyone can arrest us if we're not here. The celestials will have worse to worry about if whoever took Nikolas comes here."

Unless he'd left of his own volition. But Fiona clearly hadn't.

"Javos needs warning," Rachel said. "The enemy knows his weakness, right?"

"Shit, you're right. The list had almost every warlock's weakness. Not Nikolas's, though—even I don't know that. But I think I should go alone."

"Not to Babylon," she said firmly.

"I'm going to find him," I said. "I have allies in that realm. And I know Zadok's weakness. I can bring him over to our side if necessary."

"I don't know. He'd throw his own brother under the bus to save himself, and always sides with the one likely to win."

"Perhaps, but he claims to know who's pulling the strings

here. So I reckon I can get answers out of him if need be. We do know who's likely behind this. Abyss."

She shook her head. "We know the name, but not what she's planning to do now we're onto her."

"I can guess. She wants to make a bridge between our worlds. Possibly involving Babylon, too. If there are more demons attacking, then I'll stop them coming here."

I stepped through the demonglass, and the ground fell away beneath me. Too startled to scream, I flailed, desperately searching for something to grab. *What—?* I'd aimed for the pillared corridor, but someone had blasted a chunk out of the castle's side. The pillars lay in shattered ruins. I landed on the smashed flagstones, Rachel's boots cushioning my fall.

Venom dripped onto the floor from the stinger of a dead scorpion demon, adding to a thick river of blood. A battle had taken place here, and from the number of twitching venos demons' bodies lying around, Zadok's demon army had come off worse.

I ran, leaping over the cracks in the stone. I'd absorbed more knowledge of the castle than I'd thought, because in no time, I found my way to the bridge across to Zadok's tower. As I'd suspected, the portal was open again, a torrent of achingly bright light blocking the path. Preventing me from seeing if Zadok was still in the tower or not.

"Zadok?" I asked uncertainly, wondering if he was in the shadows nearby, or one of his spies was. Stars speckled the sky, a picture of beauty and terror. And no sign of Nikolas *or* his brother.

I backed up, and ran down the corridor, aiming for the stairs. The sounds of fighting came from below. I jumped down the last step and nearly collided with a bloodstained warlock, the fork-tailed succubus I'd seen before.

"Have you seen Nikolas? Is Zadok here?"

She shook her head. "Not Nikolas. He left us. Zadck commands us now."

"He didn't leave you," I said, but she'd already turned her back and stumbled down the corridor out of sight.

Zadok had taken over. And with an imminent invasion, the warlocks would have had no choice but to accept his rule. I didn't have a clue how to handle this without Nikolas. This realm wasn't mine. But I *did* know Zadok's weakness. Whether he and Nikolas had ever been close or not, I needed to take him down. Nikolas would want me to. But where *was* he?

I about-turned, running for the shattered pieces of demonglass again. Maybe it was a coward's choice, but when it came between the warlocks who'd nearly killed me and saving Nikolas's life, I'd pick him every time. Zadok would have nobody left to rule over if the people on the other side of that portal got their way. I ran into the corridor—and stopped.

Inspector Angler stood there, like he'd been waiting for me. *How did he get there?* Half the corridor was destroyed and the rest in ruins. He might as well have walked out of the wall.

"Oh, for fuck's sake," I said.

He tilted his head on the side. "Is that any way to speak to an old friend?"

"I think we both know you're not actually him. You're nothing but ashes."

"Aren't we all?" He smiled.

I called the infernal fire, sending it towards him in a wave. He raised his right hand, and the power rushed into him. Harmless. *What? It can't be.*

It could. He was no shapeshifter demon. The archdemon… really had raised him from the dead.

I re-summoned my blade, ignited in celestial fire. "Nice party trick."

"Isn't it just?" He smiled. "Lythocrax sent me here, you know... He would also like to request that you stop interfering in his plans."

"Who the hell is Lythocrax?"

"Our maker."

"That's the name of the arch-demon who marked us?"

"One of his names. Names have power here."

"Tell me something I don't know. You might as well be a shapeshifter in disguise. You demonic pawns are all interchangeable." I spoke to cover the horror dawning inside me. Nikolas was wrong. The arch-demon *did* have the ability to raise someone from death. And now I had his name. But was that enough to find out who he really was?

Rage flashed across Inspector Angler's expression, his mouth tightening at the corners. "You're lucky to be alive, Devi. The only reason he hasn't come to confront you is because you aren't important to him."

"I don't care. Someone in this realm screwed over myself and my friends, and it looks like it's your unlucky day."

I jumped at him, magic flaring from my right hand. He sprang out of reach, his own mark glowing with power. Shadows surrounded me in dark shades, blocking me from attacking. He'd stolen Zadok's ability. Which meant he'd broken into the tower. Not to mention he'd apparently learnt his lesson from our last battle.

I braced myself, pushing at the shadows, but they didn't budge. Damn him. I'd defeated him in the same manner before, using the shadows to trap him before using my divine fire to turn him to ashes. But he'd come back. The arch-demons had zero concept of playing fair.

"Why the hell are you doing this?" I snarled. "You know you're letting Abyss's minions into this realm, right? They've already taken Pandemonium. You're no longer the ruler of that world."

Instead of answering, he sent another wave of shadows at me. Every attack I conjured was absorbed into his demon hand. The bastard had me trapped. How much extra power had the arch-demon given him?

"Sorry, Devi," he said. "You're a loose cannon and too unpredictable. I'm here to make things fairer once again."

"There's nothing remotely fair about a war where one side has the power of a dozen armies of demons at their beck and call," I told him. "And I told you—the person who raised you from death has no concern for your well-being at all. This Lythocrax doesn't give a crap about you, Kenneth."

Shadows rolled in, like solid clouds, wrapping around my legs. They held me in place. Try as I might to break free, the shadows crept up my back and held my limbs still. I cursed and struggled, writhing against the bindings, trying to reach the shattered pieces of demonglass not five metres away—

He grabbed my hand and pressed his demon mark to mine.

My demon mark ignited. Pain splintered my arm, sending shards of agony through my body. A flash of light dispelled the shadows, and I landed on my feet, backing away. The pain faded, leaving nothing but echoes. I winced, but drew back my fist and landed a solid punch on his face.

He just laughed. "You can't hurt me, Devi."

My hand twinged with pain. The arrowhead remained etched on my wrist, but no light shone within it. Lythocrax's power no longer resided within me.

The arch-demon had actually deactivated my mark.

"It's for the best, Devi. You weren't supposed to come this far. You've interfered in the gods' plans."

"I'm being punished for winning?" I couldn't believe what I was hearing.

"For defying the master."

"He is not my master."

The former inspector smiled. "Lythocrax made and remade you, just like me."

I blew out a breath. "Taking my mark off me is handing victory over to the enemy."

"Not at all. Victory will be ours, but on the master's terms, nobody else's. It'll go a lot easier for you if you wait until your time comes rather than making trouble for everyone."

"I'm not blindly following orders, unlike some people," I said. "What's he want me to do, let him take over Babylon through you, and then... go to war with Pandemonium? I thought you were working *with* the other demons."

"Not anymore," he said. "I never intended to let them take Pandemonium for their own."

"You're talking like you have any more say in this than I do," I countered. "We're being set up. You all but said it yourself. So who decided you have to switch sides? If you really wanted Azurial to replace his father so you could sneak into Babylon and take over the castle, which I'm assuming was the cover story, that sort of ignores the fact that none of your thoughts or plans are your own. They're all someone else's."

"The power I gained is mine alone." Shadows unfolded behind him. He'd stolen Zadok's power, all right. Now the arch-demon, Lythocrax, had the run of the place. But if he'd wanted it so badly, why not have me take over as a proxy, not this guy? Because I'd screwed up his plans by getting in the way? Or because he had something else in mind for me entirely.

No. Divinities, no.

The truth slammed into me like a full-speed train. Earth was the site of the final battle. That's why they'd used me—to get to Earth, a realm untouched by darkness. The perfect prize. A victory in a dead-end realm like this one wouldn't be half as sweet in hell's eyes as a victory in a city teeming with life. Millions of human lives, fuel for hell's battlefield. Winning was all that mattered to hell. Not the lives they toyed with, and not those who they trampled in their quest for domination.

Of course they wouldn't permit a human to run around with their power and use it indiscriminately for their own purposes. Instead, they'd cut it off. Like I'd never had it.

The shadows crowded me again, and the floor gave way beneath my feet.

"Go down below, celestial, where you belong."

The former inspector's cold laughter pursued me beneath the earth.

Falling was peaceful. Landing, not so much. I fell through what seemed like a tunnel, though it was too dark to see, coming to an abrupt halt on a stone floor. I had enough trained reflexes—not to mention Rachel's boots—to land on my feet, in the darkness. A cold, empty space. Inside the castle… or beneath it?

Oh, no.

Cold hands scrabbled at me. I conjured up celestial light, relieved *that* was still working. The demon had taken my demon mark, but not my celestial power. No demon could take that away. Not even from the blinded, clawed creatures surrounding me.

I was locked in with the fallen—the children of the dark Divinities.

I didn't move. The light remained burning bright, and they cringed away. *Huh?* Of course—their own Divinities' light had long since departed, and now burned them as badly as the demons.

I lowered my glowing hand, warily. They didn't move to attack. We stared one another out. Their eyes were blood-shot, their pupils pale and dilated. Most were hairless and had long, claw-like nails. They wore only rags, their emaciated bodies exposed to the elements. It was as cold as the ninth circle of hell down here. They'd died, been cast down, and nobody had come to rescue them. If they were going to attack me, they'd have already made a move in my direction. Instead, their eyes followed the movement of the celestial light in my hand, reflecting a longing too deep for me to comprehend.

"I don't suppose you know the way back to the surface?" I asked.

Nobody answered.

"Seriously," I went on. "Things are pretty dire up there. You've probably seen. The demons are coming…"

But they'd already taken the castle, and locked them deep in the shadows. I doubted anyone in this room particularly cared what happened on the surface, given what they'd suffered already. To be immortal yet cursed as they were was a special kind of hell. They held no worse threat to me. Not now.

I took a step forwards. They closed in.

"Celestial…" one of them whispered, gazing reverently at my glowing hand.

"Yes," I said. "You were… like the celestials here?"

He nodded. "They fell, and they dragged us down with them, and they hardly cared."

"Sounds like them." I was certain that he meant the Divinities. Not the arch-demons, though they were one and the same. "I need to get out of here, though."

"There is no way out."

I looked around. He was right. I'd fallen down a sheer tunnel, and the opening to the surface was high up in the wall. Otherwise, there were no doors or windows. A hellish dungeon with no exit in sight. My stomach twisted.

"We cannot see the light. No light at all, in the world above or below."

"I'm sorry," I said. "I—I wish I could help you, but I'm needed up there. My world is about to get overrun by warring arch-demons. And the celestials... there's not enough of them."

"You carry the light inside you, too, celestial. The celestials were our disciples. When we fell, they died. Except those who were chosen to ascend."

I blinked. "What, the Grade Fours? In my realm... they're monsters."

"You have power like theirs."

"Some good that is," I muttered. My demon mark had been my best asset—in fact, considering I'd used it to kill more than one demigod, it had actually been higher than Grade Three. But I was only Grade Three in celestial training. Even if I was qualified to ascend, it didn't mean a thing, locked down here.

"But if my Divinity fell, why can I use divine power at all?" I asked. "You—you're saying I'm... like the Grade Fours? I can't be. I can't ascend, not when I've been kicked out of the guild."

"The power was gifted to you. I do not know the rules of your world, but you have been chosen to carry the light."

Despite everything I'd done, I still carried the celestial light. Somehow my divine power was the key to winning this. As a celestial, I'd been disobedient at best. Not to mention the slight issue with my Divinity being a fallen angel. But in terms of skill, I'd been on the brink of a promotion. And if I figured out how to ascend... the Grade Fours had *direct contact* with the Divinities. Not the fallen ones, but the true angels.

If not for Rory's death, we'd have gone through the ceremony together. But the guild were tight-lipped on what it actually involved. A meeting with the Divinities? Surely not, but I had to wonder.

Maybe… if I couldn't use my demon magic any longer, I might be able to gain the highest rank of celestial magic instead. Unlike my demon mark, it wasn't the arch-demon's. It was mine.

My back straightened. I must be losing my mind. I was prepared to bargain with heaven to save my realm from hell.

"Thank you," I said to the fallen. "Now… I need to get out."

My celestial hand lit up again. The fallen parted to allow me to pass, but there were no doors, nor any other way out. Except…

I shone my celestial light into the shadows, getting a closer look at the opening high up in the wall, hidden in the darkness. Recalling how Zadok had once set the inhabitants of this dungeon loose, I moved in that direction. He must have released them somehow. But the door was too high up.

Wait… the boots. The walls were sheer, but my boots could stick to the walls like velcro. The former inspector hadn't counted on that.

I'm coming, Nikolas. Fiona. I promise.

Time to get out, back to my realm, and find a Divinity. Then get answers.

Easier said than done.

19

I emerged in Nikolas's living room, after passing through the demonglass again. The former inspector, mercifully, hadn't been there. He'd probably gone to attack the warlocks. But the way I was now, I couldn't oppose him, not even to save Nikolas and the others. I needed power beyond his.

The power of a Grade Four celestial.

"Oh, thank the nether realms you're alive," Rachel said. "I thought I was going to have to fight this one alone, and let me tell you, I really don't think Madame White wants me to chew on her neck."

"She's not here yet? I don't have time for this. I'm going to find the Grade Four celestials again."

"Why? Is Nikolas—?"

"Pandemonium," I said. "Has to be. And the vampire king deactivated my demon mark because I'm apparently ruining the fun by trying to end the battle too early."

Rachel's eyes widened. "Wait—what? You lost your demon mark?"

"Not for long," I said. "He threw me into the dungeon

with the fallen—it's complicated, but they helped me. Point is, the demon realms are at war, Nikolas is probably a prisoner, and we're next. The arch-demon who marked me can summon me at any moment, but instead of doing that, the bastard took away my powers. So I'm out for revenge."

"What in hells do the Grade Fours have to do with it?"

"I'm going to speak to them about the secret ceremony where they upgrade from Grade Three to Four. If I can upgrade my celestial power, it might make up for being handicapped. Best case scenario is I get to take my disapproval right up to the Divinities themselves. I can't fight this war without my demon mark."

Rachel bit her lip. "The Divinities. Are you sure?"

"Nope," I said. "No idea what this ceremony involves. But I'm qualified. If I'd stayed at the guild, I'd have been tested at the very least. And I've been able to use my celestial powers the whole time I've been demon marked. Now I don't have demon magic any longer, I can try. I have to."

"Well… you have an easy way there," Rachel said. "During our little confrontation at the hotel, I took the liberty of sprinkling down some of your demonglass. I figured we might need it."

"You're amazing, Rachel."

"I do my best."

"Now we just need to get the Grade Fours to answer my questions." I still had my weapons—even my anti-warlock trap had miraculously survived intact. And Rachel's boots. "Can I—crap, I can't use your powers this time. I need to capture one of the Grade Fours in a trap. A simple one. They're immune to anything fancy."

Rachel's brow furrowed. "I show up as the inspector again, you throw a net over their heads?"

"I don't have a net." I paused. "I do have a spell which can knock someone out. I'll have to move quickly, though. And you'll have to be prepared to tie him up."

"You have someone in mind, don't you?" Her eyes glittered. "I'm in. I'll get some rope."

Two minutes later, I faced the demonglass fragments once again, calling to mind the image of the Grade Four celestials' hotel.

"I'll be ready," she said, and I vanished.

I emerged in front of the hotel, where the minibus had been parked yesterday. This time, nobody waited for me. I scanned the gleaming exterior of the hotel, then summoned my light, as bright as it would go.

Sure enough, within two minutes, Farrell stalked towards me from the hotel, conjuring his blade. Its light whistled through the air, and the lack of response from my demon mark almost made me pause for a moment. It never missed the chance to jump into a fight. *I will get it back.*

"Hey, Farrell," I said, then slammed down the spell.

The blast of herbs caught him in the face, and he collapsed. I ran, grabbed him by the shoulders, and was through the demonglass before any of the other celestials could reach me.

Rachel was waiting. Between us, we bound his hands in rope. Again, the simplest traps worked best. He might be powerful, but I knew all his secrets, and the other celestials would never reach here in time to catch us. This would be a quick conversation. I was counting on it.

Rachel passed me a glass of water, and I threw it in his face.

He woke up with a yelp. "DEVI LAWSON."

"Sorry, but not sorry," I said.

Farrell yelped and flailed, totally stuck. Panic flashed in his gaze.

"Tell me, Farrell," I said. "What's the process for ascending to celestial Grade Four?"

"Like I'd tell you. Let me go. This is against the law—"

"This isn't optional. What is the process? Whereabouts does the ceremony take place?"

I shone my celestial light in his face, warningly. With his hands bound, he couldn't conjure his blade, and his light couldn't burn through plain old rope.

"You can't ascend to Grade Four without the inspector," he croaked. "You need recommendations, and the tower is destroyed."

"There are celestials all over the globe who follow completely different traditions to you," I said. "They get along just fine. Try again. It's not the ceremony that matters. And it's definitely not the inspector. Who gifts you with your powers?"

When I'd been promoted to Grade Three, the celestials had given me one of their wristbands infused with celestial energy in order to enable me to access my blade for the first time. But the Grade Fours carried no props at all.

He shook his head. "You won't be permitted entry."

"You know I can take you into any realm through that glass, don't you?" I asked. "Any realm in the netherworld. I can think of a few demons who are dying to meet a celestial. Did you know I've actually met an arch-demon?"

He breathed shallowly. "The realm... you can't go through the ceremony here. It doesn't take place in this realm. It's..."

"Go on."

"Purgatory!" he gasped. "The ceremony takes place... it takes place in Purgatory. Any pentagram will give you access if you ask to speak to the angel's representative."

"Now we're talking. So I go there and ask, and they're obligated to give me a trial?"

"No. Nobody ever gets in there who isn't invited. They'll kick you out, or kill you for daring to steal an angel's power."

"We'll see," I said. "So there's a test, right? You meet a representative of the Divinities who gives you your new powers?"

"Yes! What more do you want, woman?"

I had the information I needed, even if I didn't know what the Divinity's representative would do to me. I did know they couldn't knock me any lower than they already had. Purgatory sounded like a breeze in comparison to the demon realms.

"Leave him here," I told Rachel.

"Or feed him to the vampires," she suggested. "They're interested in fresh blood."

"Nah, celestial blood tastes foul to them, and his is probably worse. Tell you what," I said to him, "I'll toss you back to the guild. Let you see what a state it's in." I nodded to Rachel. He'd break the ropes eventually, and I had no interest in supervising him forever.

I grabbed his hands, pulled him towards the demonglass, and yanked him through with me, into the ruins of the former inspector's office. The combination of the thrashing worm and the magic I'd thrown at it had blasted the roof off this part of the building, leaving shattered brick, broken furniture and little else.

Farrell stared at the blackened ruins of the celestial guild like he'd never seen it before.

"It's gone," I said. "Thanks to your boss. Believe me now?"

"No," he snarled. "Aren't you going to untie me?"

"Oh, I'm not feeling *that* sorry for you."

And I jumped through the glass again, landing on my feet beside Rachel.

"Mission accomplished," I said. "He was really understanding in the end. Nice guy."

"You call *me* scary," Rachel said. "So what's the plan? Talk to the Divinities? I'd come with you, but I don't want to get burned to a crisp for being a warlock."

"It's okay. I should probably talk to them alone. I mean, I don't know if it actually is the Divinities, but I'd like to have words with them either way. They let this Lythocrax guy put a mark on me—two marks. What do you think the endgame is here? Because I don't see it. The Divinities must know."

"Most likely, they probably don't care," Rachel said. "I wouldn't know."

"Nor me, but I think you're right." My memory of the fallen trapped on Babylon was clear enough. "The Divinities don't give a crap. The demons see it all as a game. Maybe they took Nikolas because he's powerful and might get in their way. Same reason they took out my powers." I took in a breath. "I need to set up a pentagram. A regular portal won't do, and I've no clue if there's any demonglass in Purgatory."

Now to ascend… and hopefully not end up eternally banished to hell. I didn't know what happened to the people who *failed* the tests. Maybe this wasn't such a great plan. It'd seemed much simpler than dealing directly with the arch-demon who apparently hated me so much, but he'd marked me for some purpose so he probably wouldn't kill me right away.

The Divinities were a different story.

Between the two of us, we created a crude pentagram in the room's centre, using Nikolas's store of ingredients. He'd taught Rachel well. My hands shook when I used my celestial light to ignite the marks around the edges. I half expected it to burn my hands, but with the demon mark deactivated, the pentagram's blazing edges caused me no pain.

The arch-demon had been sending a message, for certain. He'd been saying that he had the run of this realm all along.

All the realms. And me. I wouldn't take it. I'd scream the truth in the faces of the divine overlords.

The pentagram flared up in white light. I gritted my teeth, not switching off my hand.

"I am Celestial Devina Lawson, and I wish for access to Purgatory in order to take the test for ascension to a Grade Four celestial soldier."

Silence reigned. Then a cold voice resonated through my bones: *You are not welcome here.*

"I'm qualified," I said loudly.

A blast of cold air blew at me, and the curtains fluttered, the furniture shaking. I inched closer, and met a solid barrier. A human-like form appeared in the pentagram. Winged, deadly, and shrouded in light.

My skin broke out in goose bumps, and a primal fear shook me. I'd seen demons of all levels. Angels, though? I wouldn't describe him any other way. Feathery white wings at his back, and an indistinct masculine form. Achingly bright light haloed his body, too bright to look directly at. Another blast of cold air numbed my hands. The gates of heaven were as cold as the ninth circle of hell, apparently.

"YOU ARE NOT WELCOME," said the angel. I didn't have a clue what language he'd spoken, but I understood clear as day.

And I wasn't having any of it.

"Tough shit. I summoned you." I folded my arms, my hands so cold they burned. "And can you turn down the air con? It's not necessary. Neither is the shouting. There are a bunch of sleeping vampires upstairs I don't want to wake up."

He didn't respond. Just hovered there, feathery wings glowing faintly.

I peered past him into the light. "Interesting. That's Purgatory? We're between heaven and hell?"

"It is the grounds of the testing," he said, in a slightly

quieter voice. Still no distinct language. I'd heard the tongue of the angels was universal. Holy crap indeed.

"Neat," I said. "That's exactly where I was trying to go. So if you don't mind, I'd like admittance to your testing. I'm a Grade Three celestial soldier ready to advance to Grade Four." I held up my left hand to clearly display the arrowhead mark. He scrutinised it with narrowed eyes.

"Your aura is marked."

"We all have our demons." I shrugged. "Doesn't erase my mark. According to the rules, I'm allowed in."

"No demons are, and you are tainted."

"Ooh." I looked into the light. "The fallen. Heard of those? If you don't want word about them to spread amongst all your soldiers, I'd suggest you do as I say. I need access to ascension. I'm more than qualified according to your system. You remember Babylon?"

Cold fury flashed in his gaze. His aura was too bright— far too much to look at. Wrathful and terrifying—yet he'd recognised the name. I'd guessed right. The Divinities knew about their fallen kin. This guy surely wasn't one of the supreme overlords, but I didn't know if you could grade angels on the same level as demons.

"Then come."

Pain ignited in my left hand. Then light swarmed over my body, bearing me away into the pentagram.

20

Silence and emptiness descended. I stood, or hovered, against a white backdrop the colour of pale clouds on a summer's day. Except bloody freezing.

Was this death? Had I walked into the afterlife? Surely not... but the celestials confided nothing about the ceremony. Shivers ran down my back. My bravado only went so far. If I was about to face an interrogation on all the times I'd broken the celestials' rules, there wasn't a whole lot you could hide from an angel.

"Hello?" I called. "Angel?"

Crap. The pentagram had gone. Wherever I'd come, there was no visible way out.

His voice echoed—"You're no true celestial."

Two small lizard-like demons jumped out of the clouds at me. I raised my celestial hand in defence, automatically. The Grade One demons were no danger to me. I'd seen this before, in my first test in celestial training. Light flared up and the demons dissolved into ashes.

There was a moment's pause, then two biter demons appeared in their place. *This is the test? Child's play.*

I spun around, guiding the light to burn every demon that crossed my path. My body fell into familiar movements, the weightless sensation of standing on empty air receding as instincts took over. Time became meaningless, the demons disintegrating to ashes the instant I killed them. Nothing in this realm existed but me and my celestial blade.

Then an armoured body appeared, a vaug demon. The beast which had dragged me into a demon dimension for the first time. Did the angel know that? Maybe. But I had no reason to fear it. Thanks to that realm, I'd become something the demons should fear. Arch-demons included.

And I will *get my demon mark back.*

My sword materialised in my hands again, and I charged. The vaug demon's earth magic was useless in this between-realm, but its armoured body deflected my attacks. Still, I'd faced it before, and knew its weak points.

My blade came up, shattering the armoured scales over the weaker joints in its arms. Slamming the sword to the hilt under its arm, I withdrew the blade, pivoted around its back and stabbed the back of its neck. The vaug demon crumpled into ashes.

A shadow appeared. *Another demon.* After Grade Three… I knew what was coming. It must be a Grade Four. To ascend, I needed to beat the demon of the same level I wanted to be. Without my demon magic. My heart skittered in anticipation.

The demon revealed itself, emerging from the clouds like a beast from a nightmare. Sharp bones covered its body in a ghastly exoskeleton, while beneath were what looked like dark-coloured scales.

The demon towered over me, and I faltered. Its aura was a vivid blue, like the overwhelming sky on a day too hot to breathe.

He was one step below an arch-demon. I'd never faced

one like it. Never alone, armed with a Grade Three weapon and nothing more. *Oh... crap.*

The demon raised its hands and I was lifted off my feet, slammed into the cloud-like floor. My ears rang, my body contorting in pain, and for a second I lost myself in agony. When the pain pulled back, I scrambled to grab my sword.

The beast jabbed at me with a bony hand. I rolled out of reach, sweeping my celestial blade, but it bounced off the creature's site. I swiped high and low, trying to get an opening. Its bone-like armour was tough as rocks, and I didn't know its demon species to guess its weakness.

Blade-like wings poked from its back like a mockery of a fallen angel. Even in imminent danger, the trained celestial part of me was trying desperately to categorise him, to remember the files... but there was no information on any creature like him.

"It doesn't have to be this way, Devi," the demon whispered. "It's oh so easy to fall..."

I beat him back, blade smacking off its armour. It'd be just like the angel to assign me an impossible task. Kill a demon far beyond my level. My human spells did nothing. Not that it hurt to try. Grabbing an explosive in one hand, I threw it. The charm bounced off the fallen angel's face. *So much for that.*

I kicked it instead. Pain exploded in my foot where it made contact with the demon's armour, while my blade glanced off no matter where I struck. *Is this really the test?* I'd never heard of any Grade Fours failing, so there must be a way to win. Unless, of course, they wanted me out of the way.

"Tell me," I growled. "Was that the plan? Wear me down and lock me up in this world forever? I'm not letting that happen, demon."

Light burst from my palm, flooding the celestial blade,

and I whirled around the demon, slicing across its back. My blade caught the tips of its dead, blackened wings, and it hissed in anger. Another strike, and I thrust the sword through its spine.

The demon gave a coughing laugh. "I can't die by any physical blow, celestial."

Another figure walked into view beside the demon. Despite myself, I glanced up—and froze.

Rory watched me with sad eyes, standing beside the demon. Unmoving.

I couldn't move. *It's a trick.* The demon must be using some sort of illusion magic.

"Give it up," I said. "I know it's not actually him."

"But I can make it so," purred the demon's voice. "I can give you whatever you desire. Life and death are immaterial to me. I am a god."

"You can't do that. Never. You're a liar and a cheat. And I'm not afraid of you."

I whipped the blade from the demon's back and threw it at the illusion of Rory.

The spinning sword went through his chest. He looked down, still wearing that same sad expression, and something fractured inside me. *It's not him. It can't be him.*

"Devi..."

I screamed in rage, summoning the blade to my hands again, and cut off the demon's head.

The demon and Rory disappeared at once, leaving nothing behind but silence.

I breathed in and out, blinking tears from my eyes. Had I done enough? I didn't know. I wouldn't go a day in my life without mourning Rory's loss. It was unthinkable to forget him—and unwise to trust in a demon's illusion. They couldn't bring him back.

The demon reappeared, standing up. I jerked backwards.

His head was back in place, not at all like I'd dealt him any wounds, but he didn't move to attack me. Instead, the demon regarded me with disconcerting intelligence. Wings flickered behind his back in the place of the blackened stumps, and his aura softened a little, lightening.

The angel looked at me, as golden as before, but without the achingly bright light.

"You?" I asked. "You were—you're fallen?"

"This is my fate." He dropped his gaze. "I'm no longer fit to set foot in heaven, so here I remain."

The angel facade had been an illusion. Of course it had. That's why he was stuck here in Purgatory, testing celestial soldiers... and I couldn't help wondering if he'd ever shown himself to the other Grade Fours in the same way.

"Do I have to kill you?" I asked.

"No. I think you've proved your worth. I really did think you'd say yes."

"You don't know me."

"I suppose not, Devi," he said. "You see me as I truly am, as you will anyone you come across, in any realm. Your weapons will never fail you from now on, no matter where you are."

Wow. No wonder the Grade Fours thought they were the centre of the universe.

"Lastly, I will grant you one favour of your choice. You saw what I'm capable of."

Rory's face flashed before my eyes, his expression pleading. Desperate. *Oh no.*

I saw what he would do. He'd raise Rory with a sting in the tail. Half dead, or a demon. Or not as himself but as someone else. Not my best friend who'd died in that cave. The real him was dead and buried. They would create a copy, a fake, and not the person I'd once loved.

Pain twisted in my chest, a knife opening wounds that

would never heal, only fade with time. Nothing would erase my memories of his death—but this was all a lie. A demon lie.

The demon's whisper caressed me. "If you don't want to save him, what about the city you love so much?"

Rory disappeared, and a new vision overtook me. Startling, bright images. Fire ripped through Haven City, tearing off roofs and devouring everything in its path. Roads split and demons crawled out, small and big, tearing through shrieking humans. The screams and the smell of burning and brimstone caught my senses and held them captive. Nikolas fought, snarling as the demons tore at his wings and dragged him into the earth.

Fiona walked, Azurial's fire blasting from her hands and obliterating everything in her path. Rachel dissolved in fire, screaming—and then Fiona turned to Nikolas.

Cold sweat trickled down my back. Sure, I knew it wasn't real—but it could be. The demons were setting things up that way. And the message was clear... if I said no, they might die.

Visions continued to parade before me. My friends dying in any of a hundred ways. Humans burning. The celestials falling. Earth becoming like so many other demonic dimensions—uninhabitable, ruled over by amoral fiends who cared nothing for the destruction they wreaked.

With one word, I could ensure my world was safe forever.

But if my own realm was safe, others wouldn't be. The demons would find another target. I wouldn't stop them from achieving dominance, and innocent lives would be lost one way or another. They might kill a thousand worlds to keep their word. They would cause as much destruction as possible. I wouldn't be responsible for that.

No... there was one remaining question to ask, and if the demon was honest...

"The name of the arch-demon who marked me," I said. "I

need the name. His *true* name. I need it to summon him, don't I? The name Lythocrax isn't enough."

The demon stared at me for a moment. "What possible reason would you wish to summon *him*?"

"He and I have a score to settle. You promised me one favour… and I ask for his name. If you lie, I'll come back and make your life more of a hell than it already is. You can give me the name or I will stay here until you do, and it won't be comfortable for you. Haven't we spent enough time together?"

"One name, celestial. The demon's true name is Altheare."

The word resonated somewhere inside me, and my demon mark shivered. Not quite alive, but not dead, either.

"Thank you."

The light backdrop faded, the clouds brightening until nothing but dazzling celestial light filled my vision. Then the pentagram reappeared around my feet, and the glow dimmed, revealing Rachel perched on the sofa, gawping at me.

"Whoa," Rachel said. "Your eyes are glowing."

"They are?" I looked down at the pentagram, and the lights went out.

"So you're one of them?" she asked, her voice slightly awed.

"Basically. We came to an understanding."

I had the demon's true name, and from that, I could find his dimension. And then…

Get my demon power back. Save my friends. It sounded easier when I recited the list in my head. Not so much in reality, knowing Nikolas and the others were held captive in another realm. The celestials weren't a unified force, either. We had no army on this side. Nothing but scattered, desperate forces, half of whom didn't truly believe there was any war at all.

It might be too late for Haven City, but I'd defend it to my last breath.

"So you know where to go?" she asked.

"I know the demon's name. That's enough."

BANG. A hammering noise came from the front door, which trembled in its frame.

"Shit," Rachel said. "It's Javos."

"Oh no."

We both ran from the room, too late. The door flew aside as he tore it from its hinges, shoving his way through into the hall. I'd forgotten how terrifying he was. And I had no access to music of any sort. What I *did* have was my new celestial power, but even that faltered at the sight of his blazing orange aura. My new aura vision made it a little difficult to ignore the tremors that indicated his magic was seconds from breaking free.

"Do you have an explanation as to why you failed to deliver the vampires as promised to Madame White?" he asked.

"Hold it," I said to him. "In case you haven't noticed, Nikolas has disappeared, and Pandemonium is attacking Babylon as we speak. Just pick a side and make this easier for everyone, okay?"

His aura trembled again as he turned on me. "My choice is to defend my people, against the celestials if necessary. They are the biggest threat to the warlocks at the moment. And they will act on Madame White's command."

"Only a dozen fanatics," I countered. "I tried to tell them, believe me. Even killed the impostor inspector—did you know Abyss's people are going around shapeshifting into others? Also, Azurial's ghost is possessing Fiona. So you're gonna have to come up with a better excuse than that. There are a dozen better enemies for you to target. Like the demons trying to unleash Armageddon on this city, for instance."

"You mock me for the last time, Devi." The whole house trembled under his power, his dark orange aura burning like the surface of the sun.

"I don't want to kill you, Javos," I said sharply. "This realm needs defenders, even reluctant ones."

"Those vampires will *not* leave the house alive. I won't risk my people on this."

"The Grade Four celestials are looking for their leader, who I left tied up at the guild," I said. "I wouldn't worry about them."

He stilled. "You did what?"

"I did say I had the case in hand." I smiled. "So if you don't mind, I'm off to get my demonic magic back, so I can use it to save your ungrateful neck, and everyone else in this realm. Yeah, that includes the celestials, too. But the demons *will* come. No matter what I do. So be careful."

"Don't lecture me," he snapped. "If you go into the demon realms, you won't come back."

"I went to Purgatory and got away in one piece," I said. "One question, though—which demon sired you?"

"What?"

"Just a question. Because I have a feeling they took Nikolas off the playing field because he was too powerful. They might do the same for you... or your demon parent might claim you."

His face went a furious purple. "You, Devi, are no warlock."

"Nope." My hand glowed. "But whoever said I had to be? I'm off."

"Where are you going?"

"To meet my maker."

And then it would be time to get Nikolas back from the demons. No matter what.

21

The pentagram glowed. My heart pounded in anticipation. Finally, *finally*, I was on my way to find the one whose rogue demon mark had sealed my fate and controlled my life. *It's in my control now. And I know your name.*

I raised my hand as I stepped into the pentagram. "I summon you, Altheare, otherwise known as Lythocrax."

Fire came first. Molten orange crested the horizon, gilding the dark ground with bright stripes in stark contrast to the lifeless landscape. *Whoa. That was fast.* The scene around me had changed in a split second, turning into the demon realm where I'd been marked in exchange for asking for the arch-demon's help. The demons had scourged this place and burned the remains to ashes. No life remained here... but there was little doubt the arch-demon had heard my call.

The world trembled. An aura shifted across my vision, along with the shadow of a great winged beast descending. The dark shadow brought a gust of warm air that seared my skin, filled my nostrils with the scent of brimstone, and a roar that drowned my ears in noise. A rumbling crash, an earthquake and tornado rolled into one. The winged figure that dropped out of the sky was like an exclamation, a shout the world could hear at full volume.

Primal terror gripped me in a vice. All sense and reason fled in its wake, and the impulse urged me to curl into a ball and wait for the storm to pass.

Maybe this wasn't such a good idea after all.

Focus, Devi. You knew it'd be overwhelming.

The beast descended. Ash-coloured wings extended from its shoulders, and its vaguely humanoid shape was otherwise the colour of molten lava. He was midnight sky, burning sunshine, a tornado, a snowstorm, a torrent of nature contained within an aura hardly visible to my own eyes. Too much. Even for demons. Power radiated from its very being, a demand that I kneel and worship it, or perish.

I refused. Digging my heels into the ground, I planted myself in front of that embodiment of divine and infernal power, and gave it my mightiest glare.

"YOU." The voice rumbled through me, the echo of power unimaginable.

"Me," I said. "Surprise."

"You're not allowed here," boomed the arch-demon.

"I don't make the rules, and it sounds like you don't either," I said. "Otherwise you wouldn't have marked me in the first place. I summoned you. You'd better believe I can banish you again. And I know your true name."

"The one who gave you that knowledge will pay with their life."

"Too bad I won't tell you. You might think you're all powerful and all knowing, but you're not. I see through you. Deep down, you're nothing at all. The Divinities make the rules, and when you fell, you gave up your divine magic. But mine remains intact."

The arch-demon's aura surged, ashy darkness blotting out the sky, but he didn't move to attack me. Maybe he believed I really would use his name against him.

"What do you want, mortal?" he snarled. "If you like, I can offer you a different kind of deal to your angels."

"Now you're asking me for a deal? No thanks. I had enough of demonic bargains when you got me marked. You put me on a platter for the celestials to kill."

"It's not my concern if your own people saw you as a danger and took matters into their own hands to deal with you."

"You sure seemed concerned when I started using the power you marked me with to do things you didn't like."

A hiss escaped him.

"Sorry, didn't catch that," I said. "Maybe you should think before you commit to your decisions rather than trying to backtrack. Because I'm not going to forget what you did. You let me believe I killed my best friend, Altheare."

He let out another low hissing noise. Not in anger alone, but pain. Somehow… using the name hurt him.

"You have something of mine, which you took from me without my permission," I told him. "Give me my demon mark back."

"Did I not gift you with life, the power of the heavens?"

"You're not the same person you were back then. Besides, you don't own me. Either give my power back or I'll keep going right to the leaders of heaven. I've already spoken to one of their angels. I have *their* power, Altheare."

He took a step back, his aura surging. "Don't speak that name, mortal."

"Would you prefer 'Lythocrax'? Too bad. You can't force me

to respect you of my own free will, and you can't order me to sit out the battle because it suits you. Ruling in hell's working out well for you, is it? Or would you rather be in heaven?"

The demon roared. Earth trembled, the sky boiled—and yet none of it touched me. Somehow, my use of his name insulated me against harm.

I rolled my eyes. "Nice little display. Maybe throw in some fireworks at the end for that extra special touch. Give me the power back." I raised my demon marked hand. "That's all I ask for. If I ruin your plans, then you shouldn't have marked me to begin with. Or you know, you could try showing up to the battlefield in person."

He spoke through gritted teeth—*"The Divinities take your soul, celestial. Let them burn you."*

Fire flared across my vision, then it was replaced with Nikolas's living room. My demon mark tingled, awakening. *I hope.*

Rachel screamed. "Devi! Holy mother of all demons, I thought you were dead."

"He didn't kill you." Javos didn't sound either relieved or disappointed, just neutral. No more than I'd have expected of him.

"Nope," I said. "I had it covered. Any new events I should be aware of over here?"

"It looks like your celestials have taken back their base," Javos growled.

"There isn't much left of it. Which ones?"

"The Grade Fours," Rachel put in. "You were gone—at least an hour."

"What? Seriously?" I blinked, frowning at the ashy remains of the pentagram's centre. "It was only a couple of minutes for me, if that. What happened to the celestials?"

"They went to join their leader at the base," she said,

bouncing on the balls of her feet. "Did you actually get into hell?"

So the other Grade Fours had found their leader. I wasn't worried about them anyway. They could be dealt with after the war, assuming any of them survived. Serve them right for blindly accepting orders that screwed the rest of us over.

"You used the demon's name," Javos said, still watching me curiously. "How did you know to do that in the first place?"

"I didn't. I inferred from something Zadok said that the one sure-fire way to summon a demon is to use their name. Their true name. So when I had the chance to get it, I figured it couldn't hurt." I looked at Javos. "I suppose I have a name, too? A demon one? And nobody knows it?"

He paused before saying, "You're a blank slate, Devi. If you haven't claimed a name, they can't use it against you."

"But—" Zadok had seemed certain. Had it all been an act? He hadn't thought they'd summon me at all? Or had he been hinting that I was the one who had to go to them? Who knew. Demons, warlocks and demigods of any level were bloody incomprehensible. Maybe he'd been helping me, maybe he'd been screwing with me. It didn't matter.

The demon Abyss and her minions were my true enemies. Now I truly carried the power of heaven and hell, but she had me beaten by experience, not to mention knowledge. I might have recovered my powers, but I'd lost all the magic I'd borrowed through the mark.

Including...

Crap. Oh no.

"What is it?" asked Rachel, as I lifted my hand, turning it over.

"One second." I took a step back, activating my demon mark and calling the fire to my hand.

No fire appeared.

"The bastard." I lowered my hand. "The thieving bastard." Of course the arch-demon would have got the last word in by swiping the power Themedes had given me, and my infernal fire along with it. No wonder he'd been so quick to comply.

"You need more of my power?" asked Rachel.

"Possibly, but he took the infernal power I've been using all this time." I swore under my breath. "It's okay. Maybe I can steal more from Emarial."

Javos turned to me. "You're planning to leave. To find them on Pandemonium."

"Listen, I know you care about nobody except yourself, but this war is coming to Haven City whether you like it or not. I'm going after my friends, and then I'm going straight to Abyss to end it. Deal with it. And don't kill the vampires. We need them."

"The vampires will turn, in the end," Javos said.

"They haven't fully turned yet. And I was supposed to be claimed, but I told the person behind it that isn't happening. So are you coming to Pandemonium or not?"

"Certainly *not*," he said. He jerked his head at Rachel. "I assume you're going with her."

"I assume you're not going to stop me." She looked at him defiantly. "Because you know deep down this is all your fault. If you'd let Devi use the bloody demonglass from the start, we might have known the enemy's plan before they came after this realm, just like they did to my home."

A flash of some emotion crossed Javos's face, but he didn't move to strike her. Weird. Wait—might he have a soft spot for Rachel? He'd sort of adopted her, but I'd honestly thought he had no feelings towards anyone at all, family or not. Then again, I didn't understand demons. They were far more complex than I'd thought.

I looked down, regarding the demonglass fragments. I

had weapons. I also had full aura vision without the need for a potion. What I *didn't* have was time to stall.

"I intend to contact the other warlocks," he ground out. "Our allies are scattered, unreliable, and most look out for their own interests alone. The Wingless Warlock *might* answer my call, but if you expect my people to make a showing like the Castors' army on Babylon, you'll be disappointed."

"I'm going to find Nikolas," I told Javos, stepping close to the demonglass again. "Try not to let the city fall to pieces while I'm gone."

I took one final step, and let the demonglass pull me through.

Empty air replaced the carpet. Dizziness swept through me as the blood rushed to my head, my hands scrambling to grab onto anything solid. Below, the pentagram glowed red. Above, the torrent of light pierced Babylon's skies. Shit. I'd fallen through the open portal—and this time, I had no regenerative magic at all.

No. I can't die like this.

A pair of clawed hands caught me. I spun upside-down, gasping when the spinning stopped. One of Zadok's bat demons had fished me out of the portal. Except I'd ended up on the wrong realm. The portal had screwed up all the demonglass, apparently. Even Zadok's tower reflected the swirling lights and nothing more. *Dammit. I need to get to Pandemonium.*

The bat demon placed me on the side of the broken bridge. "Thanks," I said. Apparently, it'd figured I wanted to be on the side of the bridge closest to the castle.

I ran for the wooden door, my feet pounding against stone. Inside, the corridors were empty, even the ruins of the demonglass one. Inspector Angler was probably fighting, or doing whatever he thought he was supposed to do in this war. He didn't think he had any choice in the matter at all.

Too bad for him.

I went downstairs, my footsteps echoing. *Please let someone be alive in here.* I needed allies. Desperately.

As I'd suspected, the warlocks had gathered in the entrance hall. The doors were barred, though the warlocks surely knew that with the castle half destroyed, the enemy would be able to find them no matter what.

"It's the celestial!" someone shouted, and all heads turned to face me.

"You wanted someone to lead your army?" I asked. "Allow me. I'm going to kill the person responsible for that portal, arch-demon or none. Why are you hiding?" Not all of them were injured, though they were clearly shaken.

"We do not set ourselves against the arch-demons," said the warlock who'd welcomed me to the castle what felt like forever ago. "You know nothing about us. If they want our realm, then we will stay here."

"Okay, then imagine I'm the shadow arch-demon telling you to go and fight him. Would that make you change your mind? Or would you prefer I steal your magic and use it against the enemy? I can do both, even."

Light flared from my left hand, striking inches from his feet. He swore and jumped back into his neighbour.

"Pull yourselves together!" I snapped. "You're *letting* yourselves get invaded. Would your leader really tell you to lie down and take it? I don't think so. Nikolas is alive, and in the enemy's hands."

"If he's alive, he's already lost," said a familiar voice.

Shadows folded away from the corner, revealing Zadok. Several people gasped, presumably unaware he'd been hiding there. His features were drawn, ravaged with exhaustion.

From the amount of blood on his hands and his torn clothes, he'd regenerated after suffering life-threatening injuries.

"Nice," I said. "Way to hide like a coward."

"What you're proposing is a fool's errand. This realm is poised to fall." He spoke matter-of-factly, but his aura surged with dark energy. Rage pulsed from his very being. Something had happened to push him out of the fighting... and I had the feeling it involved a certain fire demigod. Sure enough, those were burn marks on his arms, open and weeping blood.

"Way to be a downer." I took a step closer to him, out of hearing range of the others, and dropped my voice. "If you want to keep that weakness of yours under wraps, I'd suggest you listen to me."

"What weakness?" he snarled.

"You know which. Azurial knows. And I'll tell them all. Everyone in this room."

"You lie," he said. "Azurial is dead."

"You know demigods don't die easily," I said. "It's your choice. I'll even let you lead part of the army, if you like. I'm more concerned with getting Nikolas back onto the battlefield. It's your choice. Who knows, you might redeem yourself enough that Nikolas doesn't kill you for stealing his army."

With every word, his eyes widened. "Nikolas wouldn't have wanted this realm to fall into ruin."

"There you have it," I said. "Point proven. Either you tarnish his name or you admit you wanted to claim his army for your own."

"Everyone knows that," he snarled, shadows unfurling from his body in the form of wings. "I've never hidden what I am, Devi. And I will not bow down to these invaders."

"Then come with me."

I held my demon mark high, clearing a path through the hall to the doors. Then I turned around again.

"I have the powers of heaven and hell in my hands," I said. "You can follow me into battle or die here like cowards—your choice."

Without waiting for an answer, I pushed the doors open.

The portal's light cast an eerie glow all around outside. The velvet sky appeared starless and distant as though every source of light in the world had been pulled into the pentagram. It shone, a beacon in the wasteland. No sign of any arch-demons or demigods… yet. But demons had assembled in front of the portal, waiting to strike.

Celestial light blazed from my hands, and the demon army faltered. But they weren't my targets. I shone the light directly at the castle, and drew on the power from the warlocks behind me, particularly the ones who hadn't elected to follow me. My demon mark blazed, and the castle trembled, bits of rock falling from the side.

"What are you doing?" demanded several warlocks.

I didn't answer. I'd seen the castle from the outside enough times to know where the fallen were kept imprisoned. Half of it had collapsed already, and needed little encouragement to clear. The way out was open. If they wanted to leave—or help us—they could.

Power exploded from my hands. I didn't even need to draw my blade. Demons fell, buckling beneath my power. Shimmering rays of light continued to spiral up into the sky from the portal.

As though on cue, the warlock army surged towards their enemies. Zadok took flight in a way not unlike his brother, dive-bombing the enemy from above. Wherever I walked, demons fled from the light, back into the portal.

Good. Now to follow them.

Letting the light die down, I approached the portal at a

run. Light blinded me for an instant, and I floated. *Pandemo-nium. Take me to Pandemonium.*

I opened my eyes. At first I thought I'd landed on another world entirely. Demonglass pillars were shattered and reformed into sharp protrusions, like a barbed fence surrounding a cage. And… tunnels. The entrances to Pandemonium's tunnels had been brought to the Earth's surface. Maybe when the Mother had crossed into our realm. It'd been totally levelled in the space of a few days. Or hours. Nothing like demon magic for large-scale destruction.

"Show yourself," I shouted. "Abyss. I know you must be here."

I didn't have her true name and couldn't summon her in person, but she must be close if she'd manipulated the realm to this degree. Even Emarial couldn't have done it.

I walked, my footsteps crunching on shattered glass and broken rock, and a disturbing number of bones. Every time a demon crossed my path, I blasted it aside and kept going. My aura vision warned me they were coming. But nothing darker crossed my vision, no hints of an arch-demon's presence.

I reached the edge of the palace's former entrance hall, which had once been a balcony, and gasped.

The city had become a true maze, houses rising to form tall, sharp walls. Now I stood on ground level, the sky was entirely blotted out. Had it been put in defence mode, or had the arch-demon done it?

"Devil!" shouted a familiar voice.

I spun around. "Rachel? I thought you weren't coming?"

"I couldn't leave you to fight alone," she said. "I used a portal. I had to see… I had to find him." She looked around, a distraught expression on her face.

"Abyss," I said. "She must have done this."

She shuddered. "Yeah, I know. Javos—he left, he said he

needed to warn the other warlocks. I think he knows Haven City is their target. But—but I can't find Nikolas. No arch-demons either. If she did this, then she came from Babylon."

"What—seriously? How?"

"Babylon's damaged," she mumbled. "From what happened before. I don't know Abyss—I don't know her magic, but she couldn't have got in any other way. She turned it to ashes. And now she's going to do the same to Babylon."

"Not yet," I said. "Zadok's fighting, for what it's worth. They won't die." My voice rose. "Show yourself, Abyss."

"She isn't here." Inspector Angler stepped out in front of me, radiating power from his hand. Dark lightning collided with the floor inches in front of me. Nikolas's magic.

"You're the one who took him?" I should have guessed.

"The children of arch-demons cause too many complications."

"Then I'll have to take it up with Lythocrax again."

"You'd better believe it," said Rachel, her voice deepening as her demon form took over.

He laughed. "A disgraced celestial and a bastard hybrid. How convenient."

"What the fuck is even going on?" I demanded. "You're supposed to be at war with Abyss. You're on Lythocrax's side, right? Aren't you meant to be fighting, not stalking me? Or do you have to wait for your master's command before you blow your nose?"

"You still aren't taking this war seriously. I'm here to set the stage for the battle, on Lythocrax's orders. No more."

"This petty little war of yours nearly cost me everything, so you'd better believe I'm taking it seriously. Doesn't mean I'll come and meet you on your own terms, dickhead. Tell me what you did with Nikolas."

"You're failing to see the bigger picture."

"What, the part where you make a big performance,

rather than doing the sensible thing and taking care of your little feud in the infernal realms, not Earth?"

"Your realm contains so much more potential," he said. "So many of these realms are already lost. Not yours. Look how easily you were marked, gifted with divine power and darkness both. Imagine others like us." He grinned wickedly. "You're the bridge, Devina Lawson. And you'll help me bring the battle to the city you love so much."

22

"No," I said. "I wasn't even supposed to get my powers back, according to Lythocrax. But I won't submit to him. I *told* him that."

"You never spoke to him, you lying human."

I summoned the swirling current of magic I'd taken from the warlocks. "Not lying. He reactivated my mark."

"Then he must have decided it was worth the risk," he said. "Since the end is so very near… what entertainment you must be. They're enjoying watching you scuttle around like an ant avoiding a magnifying glass."

"You are *such* a creep," I said. "I keep forgetting you're not one of the shapeshifters. So they're coming, but not Abyss? Are both arch-demons sitting this out? Cowards."

"Merely practical," he said. "Does a king need to conquer in person to take a throne?"

"You're not—" I stopped. "There's only one demon army, right? That's it. Lythocrax and Abyss are on the same side. Those attacks were just their attempt to take out Babylon."

A smile curled his lips. "Right you are. Why do you think

your realm has remained safe for so long? Babylon's presence protected it. No longer."

Hate exploded inside me, at the same time as he lunged forward with preternatural speed. Divine light surged from my left palm. Let him see the fire he'd rejected used against him.

He dodged, ducking behind a smashed pillar. The divine light bounced off it, dissipating. *Dammit.*

The former inspector laughed from behind the pillar. "You cannot destroy me, Devi."

The power pouring from my hands never touched him. Instead, it veered to the side as though dragged by an invisible force. Towards the portal.

Dammit.

They'd set me up. Both sides. Earth would be their battlefield one way or another, and I'd take the fall. The conniving bastards.

"It won't be so bad," he said softly. "This is how it's meant to be."

With a guttural snarl, Rachel leapt on him from behind, pinning him down. Lightning shot from his hand, narrowly missing her. Recent. He'd seen Nikolas, not long ago.

As though my thoughts had conjured up the image, my celestial hand lit up, a tugging sensation pulling me towards one of the open tunnel entrances. Right—I had advanced tracking magic now. Was it telling me Nikolas was underground?

Rachel flew to the side, landing on her feet beside me. Lightning surged towards us but I absorbed the power and threw it back at him. He flew back several feet, tumbling head over heels. Inspector Angler shouted a curse, and jumped into the portal.

"Dammit," I said. "Nikolas is in one of those tunnels."

"You're joking," said Rachel.

"Nope. You don't have to come. Seriously."

"I'm not sitting behind like Javos wants me to." She scowled. "*Now* he has an issue with me fighting. The hypocrite."

I stood over the place where the lightning had struck. Nikolas's magic. Its echo passed over my demon mark, but it was my celestial mark that glowed, honing in on its presence.

"I can track him," I told Rachel.

We entered the tunnel side by side. The path ahead was clear, branching off into several other tunnels. There must have been a whole labyrinth underground while the palace had been standing.

Several venos demons leapt at us. I burned them to cinders without a thought, concentrating on the echo of Nikolas's magic inside my demon mark. My celestial power honed in on it, telling me which tunnels to head down. Rachel followed close behind, her body tense.

Then I stopped. Inside the cave ahead of us, Nikolas was tied to the wall with crude ropes, and he wasn't alone. The inspector was tied up beside several other celestial soldiers. At least half a dozen. *So they brought them here from the head-quarters?* No wonder it'd been so easy for the demons to seize power.

"You shouldn't be here," said Fiona's voice.

She sidled into view from behind the prisoners' slumped bodies. But it wasn't her gaze that looked at me, nor her aura that burned like fire.

My hand buzzed, the light bending in her direction. I clenched my fist and the light hit the floor instead. Sensing Azurial's presence, my divine power was trying to kill her. *Stop it. Now.*

"Go on," Azurial said softly, cracking a smile.

Shit. Shit. Was it like this for the Grade Fours all the time?

No wonder they were so trigger-happy. I clenched my fist, willing the light to die down, but it burned on relentlessly.

"I wish we'd had the chance to know one another better, Devi," Azurial said. "We might even have ended up on the same side. I know everything about you. I took all the knowledge from her head. All your hopes and fears, everything you confided."

"Get out of the way," I said. "And get out of her head."

My celestial hand vibrated intensely.

"She said you were considering appealing directly to the arch-demons," Azurial said. "Did you? You could have asked for anything, you know… you could have asked her to be freed."

My heart sank. I *could* have. But the demons would have found a way to twist my words, and as much as I cared for Fiona, she'd slap me if she found out I'd sacrificed the world for her sake.

The only way to be rid of Azurial was to use my celestial power and kill her in the process.

My celestial hand ignited, insistent. Reaching for her.

No.

I grabbed her with my demon-marked hand instead, letting my grip tighten. Furiously, like she was the enemy.

"All right then," I snarled. Divine power thrummed in my blood. "So be it. Sorry, Fiona."

"What are you doing?" Azurial asked.

"Isn't it obvious? I'm burning you."

I raised a hand—and Fiona's terrified gaze stared back. I pulled my hand away, and she collapsed into my arms.

"My *head*," Fiona moaned. "He's going to kill me."

"You're okay." I sagged with relief. I hadn't really believed it'd work. Azurial would be back eventually, but we needed to get the others out of here first.

"No," she said. "I'm not. You should have killed me, Devi. Otherwise—"

"He'll find someone else," I said. "Or disappear. He shouldn't have survived in the first place, but he's drawn to fire, right? So he can just find a new vessel."

An idea sparked. Light grew in my palm, and she yelped, veering away.

"Sorry," I said. "Look—this is about as bright as it gets. What if I 'persuade' him to take up residence somewhere else?"

"I don't—"

The rumble of a force like an earthquake passed through the cave. Then the world tilted sideways. Literally. I fell onto my side, my arm bruising on the floor, Fiona slipping from my grasp.

"What now?" she asked, her voice half-hysterical.

Nikolas's head snapped upright, his eyes opening. "It's a side effect… of the bridge."

No. We were too late.

"Nikolas?" I crossed the cave to him. "Are you okay?"

"Yes, but we need to get out of this cave before it collapses."

Rachel stood beside the celestials, as though unsure what to do. "Should I free them? These are the good guys, right?"

"Except that guy." I jerked my head at the inspector. "He's out cold, by the look of things."

"He's been here the longest," said the celestial nearest me, his voice faint. "What—what are you doing here, Devi?"

"Rescuing everyone, assuming the world doesn't turn on its head." *And assuming there's anything of Haven City left.* "Inspector Angler must have opened the bridge. How the hell do you close it?" I addressed Nikolas.

"You don't." His forehead pinched. "When worlds collide

like that… they change, warping, merging together. Even if we win this…"

Earth as we knew it would be gone.

Molten fury rose in my veins. "Then I'll slaughter every last one of them."

I examined the chains that held him, and blasted them with Nikolas's own lightning power. The chains broke, freeing his hands and feet. He immediately staggered backwards, cursing under his breath.

"He drained me," he said, his fists clenching. "Even my regenerative power—I need access to Babylon to recharge."

"I can take you there, but Fiona—"

"I'll take her," Rachel said quickly. "I can handle Azurial."

I doubt it. I swallowed down the words. The ground vibrated, a steady thrum that pulsed in my bones and blood. The portal.

"You're not leaving us here!" shouted the celestial.

"Depends if you'd like to jump through a demon portal into a war," I told him. "You too, inspector."

He didn't stir at my words, but several celestials moved in to help him.

"You're welcome to follow us," I said. "Don't go any deeper underground. There are monsters down there."

We left the cave via the same route I'd come in. Several times, the whole place trembled, knocking people off their feet. Thanking Rachel's shoes for sparing my dignity, I kept going until we reached the palace's shattered ruin on the surface.

The portal was a mass of swirling light across from us, masking the view of the city beyond, and the realm on the other side. Or realms. Was Babylon there—or Earth? Damn it all. The palace's demonglass must be fuelling it, but the boundaries between realms had been weakening ever since the first portal had been set up here.

I moved closer to Nikolas, instinctively. His wings weren't out. Drained of power, he couldn't fly directly into the portal to Babylon without passing directly through the battlefield. Or use his shadow power. *Oh shit.* I needed to get him back to Earth, but the portal had expanded to cover half the demonglass ruins.

"Want me to take you back so you can shift through to Babylon?"

He shook his head. "No. I won't sit this one out." Now the chains were gone, his dark aura had begun to return, shrouding his body. Being close to Babylon was recharging his magical ability.

"What the devil..." The inspector's voice was faint, but unmistakable.

I turned to him. Two celestials carried him awkwardly between them.

"Hey there, Deacon," I said. "I wasn't going to say 'I told you so', but well. Judge for yourself." I waved a hand at the portal. "You guys are welcome to follow me. I can't say I know what'll happen when we reach the other side, but I'll clear the road."

"And I'll be right behind," Rachel said. Fiona was draped over her shoulders, while the celestials helped one another. My body hummed in tandem with the magic surging around the portal. Celestial fire kept burning my palm, and I didn't dare help carry Fiona in case it burned her.

Instead, I ran towards the portal.

Demons cringed away as I tore a path through them, leading the others. Picking up speed, I ran towards the swirling currents of fire, already seeing echoes of those awful visions the angel had shown me. My city, alight in fire. Pandemonium and Babylon transplanted on top of one another, on top of Haven City. I'd never seen anything like it before—never thought it might be possible.

The world tilted under my feet. One second I stumbled on the ruined demonglass of Pandemonium—the next, I was on a tarmac road in which terrified humans fled from a venos demon. As I stabbed it, the beast disappeared, and so did I, the street replaced with a narrow opening between towering stone walls. Pandemonium—inside the maze. I summoned my celestial blade and cut down the demon. As it died, Babylon's violet sky replaced Pandemonium's pale grey one, and the huge facade of the castle loomed overhead.

Crap. I'd lost sight of the others. Nikolas better have made it here. But that road—it'd been Haven City. The three realms were colliding. Any of the unlucky humans living near the portal were effectively trapped between three worlds, and now I was, too. My steps should have carried me closer to the portal's swirling centre, but the wind knocked me sideways. It was like walking into a tornado.

Dammit. I need to end this. But I never had found the one responsible for creating the portal. Emarial, and the shapeshifter children of Abyss. If the arch-demon herself wasn't here. It was all her doing.

But I knew who *would* be here, standing in the portal's centre like the world literally revolved around him.

Inspector Angler.

"Mind stepping aside?" I called to him. "Or maybe you'll stay dead this time."

"You can't shut down the portal," he said, his mouth twisting in a smile. "You can't stop me, either. He'll just raise me again."

"Why you? You're nothing special."

"I'm unique." Celestial light blazed from one of his hands, and demonic light from the other. Killing him wouldn't help, because the arch-demon would resurrect him on the spot.

Of course, there was one thing he didn't have—a direct blessing from an angel. But to be honest, I'd rather have the arch-demon on my side. Another minute and the wind would take me off my feet.

"So you're supposed to stand there until Abyss shows up?" I called. "Is that it?"

The world tilted and holes appeared in the sky, ripping through the worlds. Demons materialised through, slamming down on the pavement, on the palace ground, on the waste-land where Zadok's army fought the oncoming horde—

I failed. They already wrecked the city, and now they're going to trample on the remains.

A whirling demon hit me in the face. I grabbed him by his throat. "Dienes?" I said in disbelief.

"HELP!" he wailed, clinging to my sleeve.

"This is your doing," I bellowed in his ear. I'd bet he'd been lurking near the palace to see how shit went down. With all the times he'd been hopping in and out of this realm, of course he'd got caught up in the portal. "Your fault. I should leave you to get kicked between realms forever."

He wailed again. "I didn't want this... tried to stop them..."

"Don't bother with excuses." But maybe he could give me a clue. Steadying myself against a lamp post, I asked, "What's the deal with the fortress? Is Pandemonium expecting Abyss to show up in person? Let me guess, you're serving her."

He shook his head frantically. "Nobody. I just wanted to live, Devi."

"Don't we all," I said. "Where is she? And where are those servants of hers?"

"You'll never find her. She's not—Pandemonium." He shrieked as the tempest yanked him from my hands again.

With fierce concentration, I thought about Haven City, about solid ground beneath my feet. And I walked.

Tarmac became wasteland became road again. Debris blew past, and I had to draw on my demonic power to summon a shield. A car bounced off it, striking a nearby building. Around me, my city fell apart, the sky burning.

Then—it stopped. I staggered against a wall. I must have left the danger zone. But demons filled the street, ripping into anyone they encountered. Vampires tore into the rest. I didn't need to look closely to see their auras, pulsing dark, demonic. Demanding I unleash my fury on them. An angel's fury, enough to consume a whole world.

I let the celestial power roll over me, guiding my hands. Pulses of white-hot energy seared every demon in my path. The tidal wave of the portal had swept up the celestial guild and the surrounding streets, which left the warlocks' areas untouched.

A deafening roar came from the portal. Several warlocks fell on a vaug demon, ripping into its armour with clawed hands. A vampire dangled from the hands of another, dead. I stopped, staring into the portal. *Rachel. Fiona. Nikolas...*

Auras clashed in the corners of my vision, my new senses drawing me to every demon in the vicinity. If I followed that sense—it'd lead me directly to her. Abyss. But my blood-thirsty celestial mark highlighted every dark aura, demanding I burn them all.

I closed my eyes to the sounds of battle, and concentrated on the new divine power pumping through my blood. The angel's gift, however reluctantly given. Words trickled through my memory—every warning I'd heard, from Javos and Zadok and even Nikolas to some extent, that I didn't understand the nature of the war, every derogatory comment that I was an ignorant celestial serving a lie—and my eyes flew open.

It wasn't the arch-demons directing this war. The Divinities were. Our struggles were entertainment to them.

As cold rage chilled my blood, my demonic sense awakened. *There she is.*

23

As I pivoted, a roar shook the Earth. Javos stampeded past, several warlocks on his tail. Even the furred warlock who'd thrown a paintbrush at me threw himself into the fray, claws tearing into the demonic onslaught. Looked like the local warlocks had shown up after all. And the vampires. Even Alec, though he hung behind the others, tentatively hitting out at a demon whenever one got close.

"Where's Rachel?" Javos demanded. His hands were stained in blood, and a piece of unidentifiable demon was stuck on one of his horns.

I shook my head. "Somewhere in there. The portal's gone crazy, and keeps flipping between all three worlds. I need to find Abyss—"

"Traitors." The vampire queen stalked towards Javos and me. Her dark hair was tied back, and she wore dark warrior-like gear, such a contrast to her usual appearance that I hardly recognised her. But her fluid movements and effortless grace were unmistakable—and so was her appalling sense of timing.

"Hey, Madame White," I said. "In case you haven't noticed, there's a war on. A massive one. And half your people are turning into demons."

"They all need to be purged," said the vampire queen. "You could have brought them to me, and I'd have taken care of the problem before it'd come to this."

I tensed. "You should know the celestial guild wasn't acting under its own power. They had no intention of killing the vampires. They wanted an army, and now they've got them. So get your priorities in order. If you have an issue with me, come talk to me when the world isn't ending."

"Of course the guild's hopeless," she said. "I've been here a long while. You don't think I've seen a demon or two in my time?"

"What—you knew they were compromised? And you played along... *why?*"

"Survival." Her teeth bared. "As you should know well."

A venos demon spat venom at us and she faced it, knives whirling in her hands. Trusting her to finish the job, I ran to join the cowering vampires. Alec and two others huddled in the entryway to a shop, its glass shattered.

"If I were you, I'd get away from the portal," I said. "The demon might still have you turned." If they hadn't turned, the demon couldn't be in this realm. Which meant I had to walk into the portal again.

I turned around—and someone grabbed me from behind, wrenching my arms behind my back. My celestial light came on, but my attacker was no demon.

"You?" said Farrell. "The angels gifted you?"

"I persuaded them." I squirmed, snarling. "Let me go, you bastard."

"You're not worthy to fight at our side, you traitorous little bitch."

My shoulders screamed with pain. I stepped back onto

his foot, driving the heel of Rachel's boot as hard as possible. He grunted in pain. Pulling my arms free, I spun around and kicked him solidly in the chest. He flew back, doubled over, then straightened up with pure murder in his eyes.

Farrell stalked forwards. "You fight alongside these vermin, and you'll die with them."

"So whose side are you on, the possessed vampires—or the warlocks and the non-possessed vamps? You have to pick one. You can't kill both."

"Who said we can't?" he said. "This is the Divinities' will, to cleanse the Earth of these vermin. When they're dead, there will be nothing left."

"You're deluded. You know that portal can't be closed, right? This city is permanently attached to two demon realms. You can't kill the entire population of two planets. They tend to call that 'genocide'."

"Cleansing. So the gods will. The angel told me."

Damn. Had someone told them... *of course.* He'd either spoken to the inspector or someone else the shapeshifter had impersonated. Should have figured.

"First the inspector and now this," I said. "Tell me—do you never use that useful aura-sensing power when you take orders from someone? Because the angel who gave me this gift had the power of illusion. He was a demon."

"I am a vessel for god." Power surged from his hands, right at Alec and the other vampires. I shouted a warning, too late. They died, screaming, in celestial fire.

"You *bastard.*"

Farrell spun on the spot, his hands aglow, and zeroed in on Javos. *Oh no you don't.*

I tackled him from behind, sending both of us falling into a heap. He snarled and kicked, but I held him pinned down.

He twisted to glare at me. "You know that warlock? You like him?"

"We can't stand each other." I slammed my hand into his head, and he rolled over, shoving me off him. On his feet, he fired celestial power directly at Javos.

The demigod shook his head as though an annoying fly had swatted him. Then he clapped his hands, his teeth bared.

Farrell was lifted into the air, as though pulled by invisible strings. He shouted and fought, but Javos's power held him captive. The huge warlock rampaged over, picked up Farrell and snapped his neck.

"That's one taken care of," he said.

"So much for being blessed with the power of an angel." I rolled my aching shoulders. "So that's your power? Levitation?"

"Amongst other things." Javos dropped Farrell's body, glaring at the vampire queen. She bared her fangs back, and continued tearing into a demon's neck.

If I didn't know better, I'd think the two of them had reached some kind of unspoken mutual understanding. I'd never understand warlocks *or* vampires, probably as long as I lived.

"Since when were you immune to Grade Four celestial power?" I asked Javos. "He should have obliterated you."

"Why else do you think I was chosen as the warlocks' leader?" He shook blood from his hair. "It wasn't for my diplomatic manner or good looks."

I blinked at him. Warlocks—and demigods. Bloody incomprehensible. "Okay... I don't suppose you know where Abyss is? I think she's *on* the portal, somehow—either as herself or in disguise."

He laughed. "You didn't think they'd come in person? This is a game to them. They're watching, through the portal —watching three worlds tear one another to pieces."

"It's not just entertainment," I countered. "Not for them. She's here. I sense her."

A fresh wave of demons appeared, and Javos splayed his hands, sending them flying twenty feet into the air. Others fled before the world-breaking power he usually kept restrained. I ran alongside him, and skidded to a halt.

Behind the demons were... celestials. I knew them all by sight. Lydia. Even Bad Haircut Sammy. All had flat black eyes and moved with eerie grace they'd never had before.

They all must have been bitten, and the transformation by the virus had been accelerated. Celestial power surged from their hands, yet darkness shrouded their auras. Others fought without their celestial light, throwing themselves out of the line of fire. Several burst into flames of their own accord, their own power betraying them.

The virus tested those who'd been infected, and killed the ones that weren't worthy enough.

Their auras swarmed my vision, light and dark, and one flaming red. Fiona stood in the middle, her eyes blazing, Azurial's power at her hands.

The scattered forces of the warlocks and non-turned vamps would have looked helpless—if not for Javos's domineering presence. He ran straight at the army, the ground trembling. *"Don't kill Fiona!"* I screamed after him, and light exploded from my left hand. My newly evolved celestial power, demanding to be used. Demanding to burn the army to ashes. It took all my concentration to call on my demon mark instead, to only burn those too far gone to be saved. And to concentrate on the portal behind, and the pulse of the more powerful aura coming from behind it.

I'm so sorry, Fiona.

To end this, I needed to kill the arch-demon.

As the armies clashed, the ground trembled, the effects of the portal spiralling outwards. Every second threw the road into a wasteland—into the palace surrounded by spiked walls—and again, in rotation. The sharp blade of Zadok's tower gleamed at its centre. The demonglass in each realm held the portal open—but without an equal force inside this realm, it'd be torn apart.

Demons burst from the earth, pouring from Pandemonium's tunnels directly into Babylon's wasteland and Haven City's streets. I held my divine blade, cut down any enemy who crossed my path, and kept walking. The road tilted sideways, and it felt like I was climbing a hill which got steeper by the second. The warlocks from Babylon swarmed, pushing the army of demons back. But the portal remained, a whirling untamed vortex. A winged figure flitted across my vision. *Nikolas. Or Zadok? Or...*

Emarial landed in front of me, her body blazing with fire. Her aura unfurled like a pair of flaming wings.

"So you're Abyss's stand-in?" I said loudly. "Or is she disguised as you?"

No... the pulsing aura didn't come from her, however formidable hers might be.

She raised a hand, and fire surged along the pavement, cracking the earth. Warm air rose and smacked into me. I flipped and landed on my feet, blasting her back with celestial power. It barely fazed her. She must be the same level as Javos. No wonder I'd hardly been able to do any damage before.

"Get out the way," I told her. "I'm going to kill the one who started that portal."

"You won't find her," she said. "Not before I bury you."

Fire blazed over her body, but its heat didn't touch me. "Yeah right," I shouted. "It's all for show, isn't it? I already buried your brother."

Celestial light blazed around my hand, while in my other, I threw everything my demon mark had at her. She raised her wings, and arms, and the attack rippled across her skin.

For a second, her aura slipped, revealing a blazing red glow—not fire, but something else. Something familiar.

"You're not Emarial," I said. "You're one of Abyss's children, aren't you?"

She wasn't a fire demon at all. But I couldn't think clearly beneath the noise of the battlefield dulled to a hum beneath the roaring sound of the portal. Abyss didn't want to take part in the battle. I'd take it as laziness, but if she was this close and couldn't be bothered to lift a finger—either she was drained of power, like Themedes had been...

Or her weakness was here somewhere. Close by. Too close to risk her coming in person.

Remembering how Zadok had reacted... even Themedes and Javos... they didn't like admitting weakness. And bringing down an arch-demon was nigh on impossible. But it *had* been done. Themedes and Azurial were proof of that.

Emarial shook herself, and the aura of fire slid away, to be replaced by a shimmering red haze.

"You can't imitate magic," I said. "I *knew* it didn't feel like Azurial's."

"Pity you won't get to enjoy your victory," she snarled.

Her attack slammed into me in a rush of energy that sent me flying off my feet. I landed in a crouch and leapt at her, celestial blade at the ready. She blocked my first strike, but I pushed back, the blade weightless in my strengthened arms. Despite the rippling energy pulsing through the blade, humming through the twin marks on my wrists, she didn't give ground. The portal was too strong, and must be fuelling her power. She wouldn't die unless I cut it off. Just like the giant worm. They were the same, after all. The only difference was that I couldn't see the pentagram this time. Zadok's tower, a beacon to the sky, reflecting the multi-coloured energy swirling around the portal. Through blurred vision, it looked like the power was held within...

I can absorb power.

Can demonglass do the same?

His tower must be fuelling the portal. But he wasn't inside it. He hadn't been there for a while. Zadok, terrified of fire, had been swept into battle anyway. But the tower was the central point of the pentagram. The direction all the swirling power came from.

She's in the tower. She's hiding on top of the portal itself No wonder nobody had been able to detect her.

Once again, the false Emarial's power blasted me off my feet. I landed in a forward roll, the movement jarring the weapons in my pockets. I reached for a knife, my fingertips brushing sharp fragments. *Demonglass.* I'd grabbed a handful from Nikolas's place when I'd tipped out the jar.

Looked like I had a shortcut to the tower after all.

Nikolas appeared behind me, wings out, and crashed into Emarial. With a sweeping gesture, she flung him aside. The scene changed to Babylon proper, giving me a close up view of the whirling portal on top of the tower.

Dark energy pulsed from Nikolas's hand as he stood, spitting out a curse in the demon tongue. Then he launched into the air, at Emarial, and the two collided with one another at speed. Power rippled from their auras, masking my view of the portal.

I took my chances, pulled the demonglass from my pocket—and the wasteland turned to jagged demonglass, then became shattered brick, the ruin of the celestial guild.

We were winning, but the world was losing. All three worlds. The castle crumbled on one side, warlocks lay bleeding alongside vampires and celestials, and if not for my aura vision, I wouldn't know who was on which side. And in the centre of it all, the perpetrator hid from view.

Her weakness is somewhere in this realm.

Whatever it was, she'd believed she'd run into it. So it

must be common. Or on the battlefield itself. But without seeing her, I wouldn't know what it was.

I raised my hand, threw down the demonglass, and leapt through, emerging from the tower's side, on ground level. The portal wasn't directly on top of the tower after all but beside it, a swirling vortex dragging at me. I staggered drunkenly towards the tower, even as the vortex threatened to draw me away.

Inspector Angler approached from the direction of the portal. "Devi Lawson," he said. "This is your end."

He raised a hand, and my demon mark ignited. Power rushed from me to him—all the magic I'd taken from the warlocks in the castle. His aura was bright with power. He'd been feeding on the portal. Even my celestial flame seemed dim by comparison. *Dammit. I was so close.*

Shadows slammed into him on either side, abruptly cutting off his attack. Zadok appeared in front of the tower, wings spread wide like his brother's. They might have been twins—angels of destruction, cloaked in shadows. Bat demons flew in Zadok's wake, dive-bombing the battlefield.

Raging light tore strips in the universe, the roaring wind threatening to rip me out of this world with every step, but I took my chance to run for the tower, press my hands to the demonglass and vividly pictured the room inside.

A barrier slammed into me, launching me into the air. I landed on my feet and tried again. Same result. She'd sealed the place, and it wasn't like I could ask Zadok. I glanced behind me and saw the vampire king holding his limp body, his neck snapped. *Oh hell.*

Skirting the tower, I searched for the place Zadok had opened the door last time. My vision had been blurred due to my injury, but his shadow power concealed things. *Wait.* I switched on my celestial light, willing it to dispel the shadows.

Aha. A door lay hidden in shadow. Had Zadok left it for me?

The handle turned beneath my grip. *I think he did.*

I didn't know if he was still alive back there. But I wouldn't get another chance. Quickly, I slipped into the tower. A spiralling staircase was all that awaited. I'd never been in this part before. Shadows filled most of the space, and above all—a pulsating dark aura that wasn't entirely masked by the portal outside.

The door slammed behind me.

"Hello, Devi," snarled Abyss. "It's time for you to die."

24

I climbed the stairs, towards the voice. She stood in the demonglass room, or lab, I'd been in before. Her wings were bat-like, but the real surprise was her face. She looked hardly a day over twenty, her tanned features glowing with youth. Her golden eyes glittered, while her slim body was cloaked in golden armour. But for all that, here she was, hiding from the battlefield.

"You can't hide forever," I told her. "Sooner or later, your weakness will make it into this room. I guarantee it."

"Who said anything about weakness? This world is mine, and yours will soon join it."

"Scary words from someone too afraid to claim her prize." I tilted my head, using my celestial vision to see her aura. Dark, edged in red… no hints at her power, aside from shapeshifting. As an arch-demon, she'd have more than one. She'd also be near-impossible to kill, unlike Themedes. And taking her life wouldn't save my world. It was too late for that.

I hadn't come here to take her life, but to bargain.

"I spoke to Lythocrax," I said. "I assume you did, once. Guess he's hiding for his own reasons."

"Are you going to tell me what you want from me or do I have to start making you scream?" she enquired.

"You know what I want. This war needs to stop. It's not achieving anything. I know the gods find it amusing, but frankly I think they're arrogant shits who deserved to fall. You probably agree with me on that, right?"

Her eyes narrowed. "You presume to speak of gods as though they exist on the same sphere as us."

"You'd know," I said. "You *were* one. And honestly, this is all a sham. I don't particularly want to kill you. I will if I have to, but I think they probably want that. They'd like to watch you smite *me*, too. Because they obviously have nothing better to do with their time."

She rose to her feet, her aura surging. "You might be able to burn out any other demon, but I'm of a race beyond yours, and beyond the pitiful creatures that carry the divine power. They will all expire, and become fallen like the others in time."

"The celestials? I don't know, you don't really give humans enough credit. I can do this." I raised my left hand and conjured a light. "And they can't stop me. Gods can make mistakes without falling."

"You don't know a thing," she said. "You're nothing more than a pathetic human messing with forces far beyond her station. This battle will end, and you will die."

The area around us warped as she transformed. Wings unfurled behind her back, spanning the width of the room, while her body turned from human to fallen angel—huge, devastating, and cloaked in deadly power.

I raised my hands, summoning divine and celestial fire. It was like holding a candle in front of an inferno. But I stared her out, willing her power to rush over to me. It didn't... but a surge of energy gripped my right hand. *The demons outside. I can reach them. And...*

I could absorb strength from the portal, too.

Earth was my realm, the source of my power. Light and dark shimmered between my hands, forming a blade of light and darkness both.

"What—?" She glared. "You shouldn't be able to do that."

"You don't know what hell I walked through to get these powers," I said. "You don't know who I am—and what this world is capable of being. And I will *not* stand by and let my realm die."

The ceiling above cracked under the power pulsating from my blade. She hissed, her wings pulling in, and it hit me that she'd been holding back, keeping her power contained in this room. I hadn't.

"STOP THAT."

Her voice boomed and my body left the ground, slammed into the wall. A wall that was cracking, light seeping in from outside. Not from this realm or even the portal, but from all three worlds at once. She hissed and stepped back, her gaze turned away. Babylon flickered to Pandemonium and then to Earth, and she roared in fury, turning to human size. Her aura shrank as light from our sky skimmed across her.

Her weakness... she couldn't look at the sunlight.

"Seriously?" I raised an eyebrow. I held the blade but didn't use it. "That's your—wait. The vampires. You wanted their powers. But Inspector Angler could absorb them... you wanted to become *him.*"

That was why she'd worked with him. And with Lythocrax.

"I almost did." Her lip curled. "But I can't take on another's power when I transform. Not yet." She stared at me. "Kill me, and let me be reborn as what I truly am."

"Oh, no." I lowered the blade. "You really think the

Divinities will gift you with a body which can walk in the sunlight? They don't give a shit. Besides, you can regenerate without their help, right?"

"No," she said. "We can regenerate, but we're reborn as we were before. Only Divinities can truly raise someone as a new being, when the world is reset and reborn as what it may truly be. Except for him."

"The end of days," I said. "That's what this is all about? Lythocrax is using you, Abyss. He, and the Divinities, won't give you what you want."

"They will," she said. "They might reign in their heavens and cast me down, but I remember them, and they will face retribution."

"If you're trying to make me feel sorry for you, it won't work." The blade vanished from my hands. "You killed and hurt a lot of people, and permanently damaged my home. I won't give you what you want, Abyss. If you want someone to come and finish you off, you're welcome to it. It's not like there's any shortage of demon realms to take over."

She shook her head, her face pinching. "Even if I did—it's too late. Lythocrax's puppet has gained too much of the gods' powers."

"It's his own fault," I said, though my heart sank. I'd hoped that closing the portal would shut off Inspector Angler's power, like it would the false Emarial.

She gave me a grim smile. "Now you know how it feels to be set against the will of the gods."

"It's not the gods, it's a sad, lonely arch-demon who knows I can finish him off if I put my mind to it."

Power continued to spiral through me, while the demon-glass tower cracked, bits of the wall fragmenting. She made no move to stop it. The portal shrank as the tower fell, even as my body trembled under the onslaught of power. I wasn't supposed to take in so much. Light blurred my vision, a familiar light. Death...

Wait.

I took a step back, scanning the portal for Inspector Angler. He could absorb the portal's magic, too, and if it was half as overwhelming to him as it was to me... *I know how to kill him.*

I pushed my magic outwards, aiming at him. I might not be able to see him from here, but I knew he'd be standing right in the middle of the portal, feeding on its power. But not all of it. Too much power and he'd burn out, even with the arch-demon raising him from death every time he fell.

I pushed all my power, all the raging magic in my demon mark into him.

He couldn't stop it. The mark would absorb it all, whether he liked it or not. Power spiralled outwards, threads of lightning and fireballs rising to the sky. The portal shrank further, and the blurred shape of Pandemonium's palace and Haven City's streets disappeared, turning to Babylon's wasteland. The former inspector staggered towards me with murder in his eyes, but he'd taken in too much. Far too much.

His body ignited. A scream shook the heavens, and the portal shrank around him, swallowing him up. One crack, and all was silent.

The wasteland was all that remained. The other realms, cut off. *Earth.* I only hoped I hadn't been too late to stop the demons from destroying the city. Emarial and Nikolas had disappeared, too, forced back from the explosion as the tower had cracked and the portal had shrunk around it.

But part of it remained. I sensed it, glowing at the foot of the tower.

"Come on," I told the arch-demon. "If you want a realm to rule over, get in that portal. Pandemonium seems your kind of place. I'll let you have it. It makes no difference to me."

"You have no authority to order me around." She stood back beneath a heap of debris, as though she expected Earth's sun to reappear and scorch her.

"Tough," I said. "Don't think you can overturn the will of the gods, Abyss. It's hopeless. They're not coming to help you."

"*You* did it," she snarled.

I shrugged. "Just come with me and see. You never know. It's that or get torn apart by the fallen." I hadn't seen them on the battlefield, but they'd be free now. If Zadok or the shadow arch-demon had a problem with that, they'd have to take it up with me.

"Fallen," she hissed. "Abominations."

"Aren't we all?"

I approached the portal. It'd shrunk to pentagram-sized, small enough for me to close. But first, I waited until Abyss was right behind me, her warlock disguise surprisingly fragile-looking. The instant we reappeared on Pandemonium, she backed into the shadows, hissing in fury. Even the high walls of the palace didn't keep out the sun. The demonglass reflected beams across the palace ruins, but the tunnels remained as dark as ever.

"See?" I indicated the tunnels. "There's a whole world down there. Go right ahead and claim it."

She tilted her head. "You're not going to kill me."

"We both know I don't get to pick when you finally die, and I have places to be," I told her. "The gods won't get their great performance from me. They've lost."

"This realm," she said. "I've seen worse. The sun can be taken care of." She indicated the high walls.

"Good," I said. "If you need to speak to me… find the demon called Dienes. He's learnt a lesson or two about loyalty. But I swear to you, if you come after Earth again, I'll break every bone in your body."

"That seems a fair deal," she said.

"One last thing," I added. "Fiona. Azurial's bound to her. His soul is, anyway. I want his soul ripped away from hers and banished to hell."

"The Divinities alone have the power to do that," she said. "A soul cannot be removed."

Dammit. I'd left Fiona on the battlefield, with no guarantee she'd even make it out alive. But there was no way this arch-demon could help me.

I backed towards the portal, panic kicking in. Jumping through, I landed on Babylon—then Earth. Unlike the other two realms, it had no demonglass, so the portal had burned to nothing more than the outline of a pentagram beside the guild's ruins. A *celestial* pentagram.

Oh shit. Farrell. He'd believed he was following *someone's* orders. I'd bet my celestial blade he'd done it. *He deserved what he got.*

Even without the portal's presence, the war raged on. Bodies of warlocks, celestials, vampires, humans, littered the street. Instinctively, I tapped into my demon mark for guidance, searching for Azurial's presence. Nothing answered.

Worry brewed in my chest. I'd seen Nikolas fighting Emarial—the false demigod—and I'd seen the vampire king kill Zadok. Maybe permanently. But there was no sign of any of them. I followed the sounds of battle, my feet pounding against the tarmac.

Around the corner from the guild, vampires warred with warlocks. Power rushed into my mark, so suddenly I skidded to a halt. *What...?*

They'd advanced to Grade Three. The virus had upgraded, and was now the same level as demigod magic—demon magic. The same magic my mark fed on.

I raised a hand and absorbed the vampire's magic, redirecting it into the air.

"Stop!" I yelled at the warlocks. "Stop—I can take the vampires' power from them. I can stop this!"

Finally.

Power surged through me, and the vampires dropped back as they realised what I'd done. I'd drained the demonic influence—Abyss's influence—right out of them. Whatever remained—free will or not—compelled them to stop fighting. Some of them. Others continued, driven into a frenzy by the smell of blood in the air—but their eyes had lost that flat blackness of the demon's spell.

Fiona.

I didn't want to kill my best friend. There *must* be another way.

"Stop!" I yelled again. The warlocks gradually began to realise their enemies weren't fighting back any longer. Javos stopped, abruptly, and yelled at them to halt. *Thanks for that.*

At his side, I saw Rachel, covered in blood but alive. But no sign of the others.

Except...

Apart from the fighters, Clover stood glowing with angelic light. In her arms was Fiona.

I ran to her, heedless of the others, and skidded to a halt in front of her.

"Clover," I said. "What happened to her?"

"I temporarily shut down the demigod's influence," she said. "My magic—isn't what it was."

"You're not... human." I'd known... somehow, on some level, but seeing her etched in light made the distinction unmistakable. But she didn't look like the illusion of the angel I'd seen.

"I was reborn into this body," she explained. "And I did

the best with what I had, but I'm not—I'm no true angel. In celestial terms, I'd be Grade Three or lower."

"You have angelic power," I said. "Can you—can you use it to help Fiona? She has Azurial's soul bound to hers, and he wants me dead. The celestials, too."

Maybe this was how he'd planned to infiltrate our realm after all.

"I'll see what I can do. I can't take away someone's magic, but it's possible for me to neutralise it." Her face was set. "This would shorten my own lifespan, but I've lingered here long enough. I believe… I don't remember my life before this one, but I feel that I knew… I knew that this realm would soon be targeted, and I came here in order to prevent exactly this."

"Wait—what?" I gaped at her. "Since when could angels be reborn as humans?"

"Since when could Divinities bring humans back from death?" she answered. "We make the most of the powers we have, whether we chose them or not. And I choose this."

Fiona gasped. Fire poured from her hands, and a scream rang in my head. The magic rushed into my demon mark immediately, and I gritted my teeth, staggering backwards. Azurial's magic dissipated, and there was another flash of light.

Golden light enveloped Fiona's body, and her aura… changed. Light replaced the dark, whiteness smothered the burning orange of Azurial's presence, and her eyes flew open.

"Am I in heaven?" she asked.

I smothered a laugh. "Nope. You're not dead." I looked questioningly at Clover. "Where—where did he go?"

"The Divinities alone know where," she said matter-of-factly. "Fiona, you're freed from the demon, but you're likely to have side effects. You wear his mark, though he lives no longer."

"It's okay," she said. "I always wanted to be a badass like Devi. Can I breathe fire?"

"If you can, let's hope you can keep it under control this time," I said. "Also, half of what I did was sheer luck."

"You saved three worlds from Armageddon," she said. "I mean—I assume that's what happened."

"More or less." I turned to Clover. "You must have really wanted to come and save Earth to sit through decades of working that close to the inspector."

"Why do you think I retired early?"

Fiona laughed. "You really are an angel, aren't you? I actually got to meet one."

"Yeah." I smiled at her. "You did. And we won. It's over."

A shadow passed over Clover's face. "It's not going to stay this way," she said quietly. "On the surface it looks the same, but the cracks between realms are weakening. Babylon… used to be the buffer, between Earth and the nether realms. That realm is where I died, and was reborn. The celestials made a deal with the angels to protect any other realms from falling. So the Divinities left, their offspring were trapped, and their world fell into ruin. But yours survived."

"And you came back."

"I came back to fight with my comrades against the netherworld again. The Divinities aren't what they used to be. I fear for what it means for the future… now that the link with the nether realms is no longer secure. That realm might be benign in comparison to some of the terrible dangers that lurk on the other side."

"Some of us will always defend it," I said. "What about the Grade Four celestials? I assume at least some of them survived. And there are others, globally."

"True," she said, "but it *is* the guild who's drawn the demons' attention—the Divinities' attention."

"Occupational hazard of being demon killers, to be honest," I said. "Let them do what they like. Even the inspector, if he made it out. I'd like to see them boss an arch-demon around."

We didn't outnumber the demons. But I'd shown there were ways to beat them. Even the Divinities. They might gift us power, but that didn't make them our owners.

"So what does that make Devi?" asked Fiona. "I mean— you know, I think we all know she's not going back to the guild. Or to anyone who'll boss her around."

"No way," I said.

Clover looked at me. "You're a whole new breed—a celestial demon, whose soul is her own."

"The mark is still Lythocrax's."

"Yes," she said. "And your other mark is the Divinities'. That is the price we pay for what we are, and what we do. But you've more than proved you can handle the gods as necessary."

"I should bloody well hope so." I looked around. "This is… I never wanted the world to end up like this. I know it's not my divine mission anymore—they don't really care—but it feels like I failed in that. Is that a ridiculous thought?"

"Not at all," she said. "The Divinities alone decide."

"They did this," I said quietly. "Didn't they? We only stalled them."

She nodded. "And Babylon still has a part to play. Your warlock is there. Let's find him."

I looked at Fiona. "Want to come?"

"Honestly… I think I've seen enough."

"I'll take care of her," Rachel said, bounding up to us. "Nikolas is alive, by the way. Last I saw he was taking Emarial to pieces."

"Good," I said. "We need to get into Babylon."

Clover passed me a handful of demonglass fragments.

"I assumed you already used your own stores," she commented. "I'll see you later, Fiona."

Fiona's awed expression told me DivinityWatch would be getting one hell of a story from her later. But for now, I threw down the demonglass and stepped into Babylon.

The battle had ended here. The tower's ruin cut a path through the wasteland, pieces of shattered demonglass spilling into the river.

And two brothers, standing amongst the other warlocks, identical shadow-like wings splayed against the dark sky.

I stared at them. "You haven't killed one another."

"Yet," Zadok put in. He was covered in blood. Demon blood mostly, though I was certain I'd seen the false inspector snap his neck. That was demigods for you.

"I won't rule it out," Nikolas said, in a similar condition. "He's the one who let the arch-demon into his tower."

"When did it happen?" I asked.

Zadok gave a half-mad laugh. "Does it matter? Do I have to spell out the threats she made?"

"What, to set you on fire?" I asked casually.

He flinched. "You never cease to be an ungrateful, petulant human. If I hadn't distracted that mockery of a vampire, you'd have died before you could get to the arch-demon."

"Maybe I would, maybe not. You still caved to an arch-demon and nearly got my world destroyed in the process."

"I can only offer my apologies," he ground out, like the words pained him. "It was never my intention to be taken prisoner in my own home." His gaze drifted to the tower, his jaw clenching.

"You're not coming to Earth," Nikolas said flatly.

"How did you—"

"You're predictable," he said. "And you'll destroy everything you touch. You know that."

Zadok bared his teeth. "Want to know why? She left me—you both left me to die in that castle. The other warlocks wanted me dead from my first breath, and when I'd clawed my way out of the dirt and gained their respect, I would rather die than submit to you again. Do you think they respected me as his son, the way they did you? They despised me, they beat me, and they would happily have slaughtered me."

"Then your punishment shall be to stand in the dirt with them again," said Nikolas. "I let you have the tower because it kept you out of the way, but with the fallen now free from their prison, I think they'd have considerably more difficulty gaining the warlocks' respect than you did, and rather more than I did. I wasn't handed the position. I earned it. And I can think of worse fates than taking care of the beings you imprisoned."

Zadok looked at him in disbelief. "You're putting me in charge of babysitting the fallen?"

"So it *was* you who locked them underground," I said. "Not Nikolas."

"*Both* of us," he growled.

"Correct, but you might have freed them at any time," Nikolas said. "As I assume from the times they escaped and attacked me." He looked at me. "None of us has ever been able to speak with them before. Perhaps I will face punishment from my father for freeing them, but I'm willing to take the risk. You try living amongst the other warlocks, Zadok. It won't kill you."

"They want to," he said. "Some of them—"

"Grow a pair," I snapped. "You try living underground for years. I'd say it's more than enough payment for the lies you've told and the times you attacked us."

Zadok stood rigid with anger. Then he took off, wings beating against the sky.

"He has nowhere to go but the castle." Nikolas drew his arms around me. "I knew you'd find a way to win. Is she alive?"

"Yep," I said. "I convinced her to leave Earth alone. Sorry I left you here."

"You needed to help your friend," he said. "I saw her—the angel."

"Not exactly," I said. "Clover... she's something else entirely. But she did help. Fiona might end up with demon magic. I don't know. And as for me, I'm... different."

"You're divine," he said, kissing me on the mouth. He tasted of ashes, and brimstone, but I didn't care. I held onto him like the world was ending after all.

"I meant it," he murmured. "Come with me to Babylon or stay on Earth. It's your choice. Where you go, I do, too."

He drew back. Behind him, stars had begun to appear in the sky again. One thing could be said for the demon dimensions—they didn't hold back on the special effects.

The celestials would rebuild. They'd need a new headquarters, since that was the second one they'd lost in less than a decade. But I wouldn't be joining them.

"Earth," I said. "And here. The demon realms have grown on me."

He grinned. "I knew they would."

ABOUT THE AUTHOR

Emma is the New York Times and USA Today Bestselling author of the Changeling Chronicles urban fantasy series.

Emma spent her childhood creating imaginary worlds to compensate for a disappointingly average reality, so it was probably inevitable that she ended up writing fantasy novels. When she's not immersed in her own fictional universes, Emma can be found with her head in a book or wandering around the world in search of adventure.

Find out more about Emma's books at
www.emmaladams.com.